THE REBEL'S GUIDE TO PRIDE

ALSO BY MATTHEW HUBBARD

The Last Boyfriends Rules for Revenge

THE REBEL'S GUIDE TO PRIDE

MATTHEW HUBBARD

DELACORTE PRESS

Text copyright © 2025 by Matthew Hubbard
Jacket art copyright © 2025 by Jess Vosseteig

Visit us on the Web! GetUnderlined.com

Educators and librarians, for a variety of teaching tools, visit us at RHTeachersLibrarians.com

Library of Congress Cataloging-in-Publication Data is available upon request.
ISBN 978-0-593-70721-0 (hardcover) — ISBN 978-0-593-70723-4 (ebook)

The text of this book is set in 11-point Kievit Serif.

Editor: Alison Romig
Cover Designer: Casey Moses
Interior Designer: Ken Crossland
Production Editor: Colleen Fellingham
Managing Editor: Tamar Schwartz
Production Manager: CJ Han

Printed in the United States of America
10 9 8 7 6 5 4 3 2 1
First Edition

Random House Children's Books supports the First Amendment and celebrates the right to read.

The authorized representative in the EU for product safety and compliance is Penguin Random House Ireland, Morrison Chambers, 32 Nassau Street, Dublin D02 YH68, Ireland. https://eu-contact.penguin.ie.

For the queer rebels they force us to become.
And for the scared kid I used to be
and the pride he finally found.

All I want to be is very young always and very irresponsible and to feel that my life is my own to live and be happy and die in my own way to please myself.

—**ZELDA FITZGERALD,** ALABAMA SOCIALITE, FIRST AMERICAN FLAPPER OF THE ROARING TWENTIES, REBEL

CHAPTER 1

Sometimes you have to face your fears, whether you want to or not.

And I was absolutely terrified of heights. The metal edge of the billboard's catwalk scraped my knees as I tried to muster the courage to stand. Climbing the rusty ladder up two stories to the roof of Jones Hardware hadn't been easy, especially with a can of paint in tow. *I've made it this far,* I encouraged myself, taking a steady breath of warm night air. *Just don't look—*

The concrete sidewalk of the town square waited below, and my eyes snapped shut. A gust of wind tousled my long, grown-out hair as I gripped the edge. If my father were here, he would ask me one simple question. It was the same question he'd asked when I came to him afraid of the boogeyman or when I was nervous while learning to ride a bicycle. "Anthony Zeke Chapman," he'd drone, "what have I told you about fear?"

Don't let anyone see it.

That was what I'd heard my entire life, him telling me

to hide my weaknesses so I could be the best version of myself. The version *he'd* molded me into. For the longest time, I'd thought that was who I wanted to be too. The *best* reputation, the *best* grades, the *best* type of gay—silent, so the world wouldn't put a target on my back.

"Piss off," I said to all the memories of James Anthony Chapman, the JACass.

I forced myself to open my eyes and stand. My hands were shaking as I checked the time on my phone. Its lit screen flashed three a.m., and I shoved it back into the pocket of my vintage leather jacket. Summer break officially began three hours ago. My nosedive of a junior year was over, my life free from the shitshow it had become since last December. If I were still talking to my father, he'd say that he had tried to warn me about coming out . . .

Gripping my backpack straps with white knuckles, I turned to see how high I'd climbed. A halo hovered over the town square thanks to the orange-hued streetlamps. But it was the darkness lapping at the edge of their receding glow that captured my attention. That was exactly how it felt living in Beggs, Alabama. Growing up here had taught me that everyone expected you to blend in, with that same perfunctory shine. And if you couldn't—or if you refused to—fit it into their definition of "good," you weren't welcome.

"Learned that the hard way," I whispered under my breath, the words lost with no one around to hear them.

Somewhere deep inside was the old version of me, who still answered to Anthony, my first name, inherited from my father. I wondered what Anthony would be doing right now. If he was still on the varsity baseball team, the Wildcats, or if he was partying out in the cow pastures and pretending to flirt with cheerleaders or if he was in bed without a worry instead of roaming the streets. But it didn't really matter, because this new version of me, who went by my middle name, Zeke, was here, just out of reach of the town's deceiving glow, and he was no longer welcome.

And that made me angry.

I'd given up on sleep hours earlier, the news Mom dropped at dinner still too loud in my head: the divorce was final after five months of back-and-forth between their lawyers. I'd snuck out of the apartment and jumped on my dirt bike. Drove to the Fort Wood neighborhood, where we once lived. Climbed through my old bedroom window to get the shoebox I'd secretly kept in the bench seat beneath the sill. I had left it behind when we moved out because I'd thought I wouldn't need it anymore. Thought the secrets I'd been forced to keep didn't belong in our new life, where I wasn't *his* son anymore. But leaving it there with him didn't feel right either.

It weighed heavily in my backpack as I turned to look up at the billboard. The smiling father-and-son duo was a ten-foot reminder of the past, a promise that Chapman Law was a *family* business. That version of me was as much a stranger now as the father beside him. Other than my blond hair and his brown, we were so much alike. Same blue eyes and fake smile and dress clothes. We weren't the same, though. Not anymore.

That Anthony Chapman was supposed to graduate as valedictorian next year. He'd go on to study at University of Alabama, where he'd get accepted into the School of Law. Eventually, he would pass the bar exam and join the firm. Then he'd be just another JACass . . .

"Fuck that," I swore, rage outranking my fear of heights.

I bent down to grab the paint can and brush. They'd been sitting on our old back porch from when he'd had the house repainted. The cheerful sky blue felt symbolic of his fresh start, but now it was time for my own.

My body froze as an engine sounded, and I peered over the edge. A cop car slowly crept around below me. Panicked heartbeats sent me crouching against the catwalk, hoping the officer wouldn't see me. A minute passed excruciatingly slowly, without any flashing lights or yells for me to "stop right there!" I risked a glance over the catwalk's edge and saw that I was alone again.

"Figures," I breathed out.

Beggs was too sleepy-eyed of a town to notice. Everyone believed what they were told instead of actually paying attention. They worked on their cattle farms and plowed their fields with tractors and carried on none the wiser. They couldn't see through the picture-perfect lie my father sold them. And it was time to finally expose him for who he really was after the hell he had put us through.

...

Laughter bubbled out of my throat when I stepped off the ladder. The last flutters of fear made it come out in a stutter. "Ah-ha-hah." I wiped the grit from my palms on the ripped, old jeans my father loathed, and I looked up with a grin.

So worth it.

A giant penis in sky blue stretched across the ten-foot picture of my father. I'd made it as graphic as possible, complete with two very large testicles. The perfect metaphor. I let out another laugh and grabbed my phone to take a souvenir picture. My handiwork wouldn't stay there long after he saw it in the morning. At least he'd know exactly what I thought of him.

"Suck on that," I muttered, focusing the camera.

Right as the flash went off, muffled voices sounded just inside the hardware store. Then the metal side door sprang open with a loud screech. I jumped as fluorescent light washed over me, then stumbled back on my ass by the dumpster.

"Bro, you can't drive home," someone was saying.

That smooth, deep voice was a ghost from the dugout. I knew it belonged to the tall guy whose figure was complemented by the baseball uniform in ways I'd fantasized about. Damian Jones shuffled outside, and I froze so he wouldn't see me. He had his arm around a stumbling Billy Peak, the new pitcher since I'd quit the team.

"You're still lit, man," Damian added, struggling to keep Billy upright.

"Am not," Billy slurred in contradiction. His pale face was pinched, his legs wobbling as he tried to keep up with Damian's strides. "Give me my keys—"

Damian cut him off. "You just spent the last hour barfing in the cornfield." He leaned Billy up against the building and locked the side door. "Bro, you owe me big time for cleaning your ass up in my dad's bathroom."

"I gotchu next time, ugh—" Billy dry heaved, and Damian groaned.

They'd obviously been at Josh Boone's barn blowout to celebrate the start of summer. I'd gone the last two years, dragging my best friend, Sawyer, along even though she hated my old jock friends. Those so-called friends had deliberately excluded me tonight. Not that I wanted to go. But the fact that his party had happened without me made me miss who I used to be. I could've been there tonight, pretending to be the guy everyone loved instead of dealing with so much shit.

"C'mon, I'll drop you off at your house," Damian began, steadying Billy, "but I swear if you spew in my truck . . ." He fell silent as he squinted in my direction. "Anth—er, I mean, Zeke?"

Billy twisted around, nearly falling, and slurred, "Tha hell you doin' here?" Another heave. "C'mere so I can kick your ass, Fastball."

The old nickname sent a jolt of anger through me. I sprang back to my feet. "Fuck you, Peak," I bit out. He didn't get to call me that, not after he'd accidentally outed me last fall.

"You wish—"

"Bro, you're drunk." Damian put a hand on Billy's chest as Billy lunged at me. "Don't start shit."

As much as it pained me to admit, my father had been at least partially right about coming out. It made me a target. If I hadn't left my phone unlocked, if Billy hadn't tried to prank me and seen the private browser tab I'd forgotten to close, if he hadn't called me a slur—maybe then I wouldn't have *had* to come out and endure all the hell that followed. But in that moment, it'd felt like he was daring me to deny it, and I refused to be manipulated by someone else.

"Yeah, Peak," I said, squaring my shoulders. "I thought you learned your lesson."

"Zeke, don't," Damian warned as Billy struggled to find words.

Billy had made sure the guys on the team wouldn't be chill with me in the locker room by spreading a rumor: "Anthony Chapman is only on the team to suck down our 'brotein.'" I had tried to play it off, but it was clear I wasn't welcome when my gear was trashed. That was the final push I'd needed to quit before the holiday break . . . right after I rubbed poison ivy all over Billy's jockstrap.

"Thought you learned yours, Fastball," Billy finally managed with a sneer, trying to shove Damian back. "Or should I call you Brotein now?"

His haphazard smirk rattled me. That stupid rumor had only been the beginning, with more spreading after the new year. Eventually, I used them to my advantage. The rumors became step one in getting back at my father. His obsession with me having the *best* reputation was the reason I was determined to have the *worst*. I'd taken my golden-boy status and tarnished it. No more class president who won by a landslide or perfect student who gave more than 100 percent or all-star who took the Wildcats to the state playoffs two years running.

My popularity had been a double-edged sword, but now it was time to live up to who I'd become. "You wanna go?" I asked, dropping my backpack to the ground. "Or are you still too busy scratching your rashy balls?"

"Not again," Damian groaned in exasperation. He rubbed a hand over his face, eyes pleading with me not to start something. Then the corners of his mouth grimaced against the rich brown of his cheeks. At one time we'd been good friends, but now he looked at me like I was trouble. That's all he and everyone else did: stared and made assumptions about my life.

I turned around and almost let it go. Almost grabbed my

bag and ignored the both of them. Almost started toward home so I could sleep before Sawyer and I went swimming. *Almost.* Until Billy called out the same slur he'd thrown around countless times in the locker room. Once, I might've been scared of him and of being called *that,* but not anymore.

"Dare you to say that again," I said slowly, spinning on my heels.

"I said you're a—"

My fist knocked the word out of his mouth. Pain radiated from my knuckles up through my elbow, but I felt too damn good to care. And for a moment, I relished his shocked expression. Then I remembered why his nickname was "Lightning." His punch came out of nowhere. I was suddenly flat on my back with my eye throbbing, staring at the penis-graffitied billboard. A chuckle rattled through me imagining my father's reaction, hoping he'd feel the same way I did just now. Put in his place.

CHAPTER 2

"**W**hat's the plan for this summer?"

No reply as sounds of destruction rang out. I squinted at Sawyer Grayson, my right eye obnoxiously swollen behind the Wayfarer sunglasses I'd scored thrifting. She sat cross-legged in a dinosaur-print bathing suit while she played on her phone. Her blue-tipped black hair swept across her sunburned shoulders as she leaned closer to the screen. She bit her bottom lip, and more explosions sounded from the X-Men gaming app.

"Almost, almooost, c'mon!" she yelled in concentration. That was the thing about her—she was always focused. From starting the first Queer-Straight Alliance at school to having her top colleges already picked out, she set her sights on a goal and rarely missed. Sometimes she also set goals for me, and then she'd push me to reach them with just as much determination.

"Stop playing that game," I demanded, waving a hand in front of her face, "and give *me* attention."

"Stooop, dickhead," she huffed without looking at me. "I'm trying to level Storm up."

The X-Men was how she and I became besties in middle school. We'd been enemies long before then, thanks to her bullying me during dodgeball at recess. Her jealousy over the fact I was always the teacher's favorite had spiked when we were in seventh grade. We were at Estrella Books and both reached for the last copy of an X-Men graphic novel. Neither of us wanted to let it go, and hands would've been thrown if our moms hadn't made us share it. Somehow, while we sat on the tiny chairs in the children's section, I realized she wasn't *so* bad.

That was the start of Sawyer-and-Zeke's list of traditions.

Since then, reading the comics together had become a staple of our relationship. Over time, we added fall concerts, video game marathons for winter, and hiking adventures in the spring. However, summer came with its own traditions: binge sessions of our favorite *Doctor Who* episodes, my sneaky birthday celebration, the library's movie night, the Ferris wheel on Founder's Day, but, most importantly, celebrating our first day of freedom at Beggs Blue Hole in the nature preserve.

I let out a resigned sigh and lay back on my jacket while Sawyer played her game. She'd given me hell for turning into a "bad boy" trope when I'd started wearing leather, but it was extra protection on my dirt bike, not to mention it was a size too small and enhanced my biceps. Its woodsy scent was soothing as I tilted my aching face toward the sun and tried to relax. The weight of finals, an anchor that had finally sunk my GPA, had lifted. The JACass couldn't pressure me anymore, and I wouldn't let him take my freedom before senior year. Before he'd inevitably fight me on his future dream.

"Finally!" Sawyer's shout rang out, startling me. She gave me a triumphant smile, only for it to downturn a second later. "What's wrong, Z?" she asked.

The honey of her eyes turned sticky with pity as she waited for me to be honest. That was another thing about her. She could always see through my bullshit. As if I were wearing a Halloween mask of the new version of me, and she wanted me to reveal who I really was underneath.

"I'm dying of boredom, that's what," I deflected, focusing on the sunlight glinting off her wire-frame glasses.

"You're sooo melodramatic."

My mind raced in search of the right words to tell her the divorce was finally settled. There weren't supposed to be any secrets between us, another staple of Sawyer-and-Zeke. But I couldn't bring myself to tell her *everything* yet. That was the problem about communication—you had to actually talk. And I didn't know the words to use, didn't know how to begin explaining.

How my coming out publicly last December caused my parents' divorce.

How my dad had tried to manipulate me into staying closeted for "safety."

How it was Mom's final push after years of tolerating his controlling behavior.

"Yeah, well . . ." I trailed off. Even if I'd known how to tell her, Sawyer would've pushed me to do something about it. To confront my father and get over it. Only I wasn't ready to do that. For years, he and I had always been a team, those grinning faces on the billboard, who had each other's back. Then I came out despite his disapproval and discovered he only cared about himself. About what people would think of him and his perfect image.

"Well what?" she prodded, still waiting for honesty.

"What you meant to say is 'fun,'" I said instead while she dipped her toes into the water. "But I'll also accept 'zealous' or 'exuberant.'"

"And to think you only scraped by in AP English, despite me making you flash cards."

I forced a laugh as we stared out at the blue hole, the chuckle lodging in my throat. She thought I'd been too stressed about the divorce and insisted on tutoring me. I let her believe she was helping, even though I'd come close to failing all my classes on purpose. It was step two in getting back at my father, and it fueled more rumors that dismantled my reputation.

Zeke's such a gay disaster and *Zeke's too worried about the D to study* and *Zeke's a burnout.* At least this was a version of me *I'd* chosen. I let my hair grow long, skipped class, drove the green dirt bike Mom and I built instead of the new truck he'd gifted me, whatever I could do to be someone other than the *best* Anthony Chapman.

Now they all looked at me like I was trouble.

I could feel the eyes of Beggs High School watching on the other side of the blue hole like the non-player characters they were. No doubt all the NPC assholes we went to school with had heard about Billy punching the shit out of me. Slowly, I lifted my hand toward them with a middle-finger salute. "Keep staring, and I'll give you something to look at!" I yelled.

"You're such a simp for attention," Sawyer teased, kicking water at me. "It's like you want another black eye."

"I'm not a simp—"

"You literally painted a giant dick on your dad's face." She held her hands apart in a length measurement for emphasis and laughed appreciatively. "Don't get me wrong, it's hilarious . . . but judging by how many times your mom has called, I'm betting your dad knows you did it."

"Good."

"Zeke, seriously . . . What's up?"

I groaned, still not wanting to talk about my father, and turned to her. The blistering sun had kissed her freckled cheeks, and *that* was what I wanted. To spend the next two months with sunburns as we repeated today over and over again.

"We need to add to our traditions," I pointed out, changing the subject. "And I'm most def in favor of spending every moment right here."

"About that . . ." she started hesitantly. "I got a job at The Cove—"

"But it's the last summer before senior year!" I cut her off, my voice pitching with a whine. "You're definitely getting accepted to the University of the South, and then you'll have to move next summer . . ."

"I *know*," she stressed, "but my dad begged me." Her family owned The Cove, and it was the fanciest restaurant in Beggs, where everyone went for an Occasion. Anniversaries, prom, business meetings, trying to sway your estranged gay son into living with you so you can shove him back in the closet. "It's not like I wanna be a host for stuck-up assholes."

"I'm so gonna die of boredom!" This time I was purposefully melodramatic, to hide the pang in my chest. Not having Sawyer around, not being able to escape the thoughts that kept me up all night, would make this a positively shitty summer.

That focused expression was back as she leaned over and scooped up a handful of water. Then she cocked an eyebrow before flinging it, soaking my old mathlete tournament shirt. "Can you do us both a favor and calm the hell down?" she asked. "We'll still do our summer traditions."

My reply was to flop back on my towel in mock distress.

"You can come hang with me at the front desk and eat free food, or you could get a server job there"—I contorted my face in horror, and she narrowed her eyes—"or if you are that desperately bored, you could hang out with us in places other than the QSA meetings you sometimes attend."

By *us,* she meant her and her longtime crush, Kennedy Copeland. Sawyer had spent years scrolling Kennedy's Cosplay-Cheerleader TikTok account dedicated to Black characters—not to mention every day of eleventh grade freaking out after Kennedy joined the QSA. They wouldn't be so bad to hang out with if Kennedy's bestie, Cohen Fisher, didn't go everywhere with her.

Cohen and I had once been . . . something. But we were nowhere near friendly now, not after he burned me freshman year. His last text message from back then was seared in my mind: *I never want to talk to you again.* And I refused to willingly subject myself to more of his jerk attitude than necessary. Just being in the Queer-Straight Alliance together was pushing it.

"You know that antagonistic fucker and I can barely be in the same room. I'm this close"—I held my thumb and pointer finger up—"to knocking that condescending sneer off his face."

"Please," she began with a leveled gaze, "do not get into

another fight before Saturday's over. It's the first *ever* Pride in Beggs—your first since *finally* coming out to everyone—and we have to keep our shit together until then." She brought her hand up to her chest, another tradition we'd started in honor of our mutual admiration of boobs. "I titty promise that I'll be the one throwin' punches if y'all act up."

I couldn't blame her. She'd spent most of junior year begging Mayor Buchanan to have the celebration, and the QSA had gotten enough signatures on their petition before I'd joined. Despite the mayor's lack of support, Pride would officially happen on Saturday, all because of her.

"I titty promise to be the best gay ever," I swore, pledging my allegiance, and flashed a reassuring smile to hide all the traces of doubt.

There was only one step left in getting back at my father. I had to be his definition of the *worst* type of gay, which meant being out and proud. I'd been trying ever since December, but I still didn't know how. I'd spent too long being silent, reserved, *discreet*. Being the JACass's idea of the *best*. Being someone who was confused by where they fit in with the LGBTQIA+ community. Not knowing how to be this best worst version of myself made me feel like a failure, and that was something else I didn't know how to tell Sawyer yet.

• • •

There's a run-down building right off Beggs Town Square. I only ever knew it to be the old Walt's Diner that closed when I was a kid. My mom, however, saw what it *could* be. She used her life savings to buy it on the same day she left my father.

In three months' time, she'd opened Roaring Mechanics. Its vibrant emerald-green logo shined like a beacon of hope.

Automotive repair was in her genes, and owning her own shop like her father's had been a lifelong dream. My father had never allowed it, though. *What would people think if my wife did manual labor, Katherine?* He never understood why she wanted to tinker on engines. That's why she secretly taught me how, just like my grandfather had shown her. Working on the family SUV had become our thing over the years. But I never thought living above the mechanic shop would also become our thing.

That week between last Christmas and New Year's Day had been a blur, but I can still remember how she'd kept promising to make it right as we moved in. With each box we unloaded, I'd replayed the series of events: I came out, my father told my baseball coach it was a joke, the argument over dinner that led to Mom slamming down her fork and declaring, "Enough!" Each moment had led to us starting over, but the second-floor apartment was a considerable downgrade from the plush life we'd had before.

My new room was tiny in comparison to the one I'd grown up in. There was just enough space for a bed, nightstand, and dresser. I told myself it was temporary, a quick escape until she found us a house. Yet nearly six months later, we were still here, still living among boxes and clutter as she tried to save up enough money. At least the lone window in my room opened to a fire escape. I was able to climb down and ride my dirt bike when the walls felt like they were closing in.

And sneak back up without alerting Mom of my comings and goings.

I used it to avoid her after the blue hole. She'd given up on calling me while we were there, and the silence was much worse. I knew she'd have a lot to say when I finally left my room. Until then, I was doing everything I could to put it off.

My backpack was on the bed, the contents of the shoebox I'd swiped from the old bedroom dumped out. Over the years, I'd been using it to hide everything that earned my father's disapproval. The first spark plug I'd changed in the family SUV. Club forms for the QSA I'd been too afraid to fill out. A rainbow flag Sawyer brought back from last year's Birmingham Pride, even though we'd argued over me not going. Every volume of the X-Men graphic novels, because he didn't consider them "real" books. An old edition of *The Montgomery Southern Gazette* newspaper. And a picture of Mom holding me as a baby.

I picked up the frame, a finger tracing along the glass. Mom was standing outside of my grandfather's mechanic shop in Montgomery. Both of us were looking at the camera, my toothless grin wide as I held on to a doll. That might've been the first and last time I'd been truly free, without the JACass domineering my life.

After setting the picture on the dresser, I turned my attention to the newspaper. It was from June 2023 with the headline "THOUSANDS MARCH ON WASHINGTON, DC, FOR PRIDE." But it was the photo accompanying the article that had stuck with me. An unnamed man was caught mid-scream as he waved a sign protesting anti-LGBTQIA+ bills. The way he stood tall in his black leather jacket identical to mine, ripped jeans, the same maroon Converse sneakers I spent a month searching for—he was who I always wanted to be.

Unapologetically queer.

I carefully tacked it on the wall by my nightstand and then unfolded the rainbow flag. It was huge, with bright colors that lit up the bare white walls of the room. That was how my life felt now after the divorce—a fresh canvas I could color in. I glanced at the space above my headboard and knew it would look perfect there.

As I hung it up, I heard the distinct sound of a chair scraping across the floor. My breath stilled as footsteps padded down the hallway. Mom had left the small dinette she used as a home office, each creaking step coming closer to my room.

Here we go, I thought as the doorknob twisted. Her presence brought the smell of flowery perfume like the gardenias she'd planted in our old front yard. Slowly, I pushed in the last thumbtack on the flag without looking at her. Silence exuded from where she stood at the threshold while I waited for her to lay into me.

"Zeke," Mom finally said, but her tone didn't denote any anger. Instead, it sounded like it always did when she called me the middle name she'd chosen. Like she said it with a smile because she named me after Zelda Fitzgerald, her favorite woman in history.

"Sorry I didn't answer your calls," I said with caution, finally turning toward her. "Sawyer and I were swimming and—"

"Dear god." Mom cut me off with a sharp intake of breath. "What happened, hun?"

She hurried toward me and tilted my chin down to get a better look at my eye. Heartbeats throbbed in my face as she studied the bruise. Lines etched on her brow, and I knew *that* look. It was the same overthinking one I saw in the mirror— along with the same heart-shaped face and unruly blond waves.

However, it was the green of her eyes that set us apart, never letting me forget I was my father's son.

"Did you get in *another* fight?" she asked through an exasperated sigh.

"What's your definition of a fight?" I countered. "Because I threw a punch, and then he threw one. That's all."

"That's two too many." She pursed her lips, standing on her tiptoes to inspect the damage. "At least you don't need stitches again."

"It was totally my bad. I misjudged Billy's strength. Next time—"

"There better not be a next time, Zeke. You're gonna get hurt if you don't stop picking fights." She shook her head slowly, collecting her thoughts. "Does this have something to do with what happened to your dad's billboard?"

"No . . . Well, kinda. More like really bad timing."

"He called to give me an earful."

"Oh?" My curiosity was piqued. "*Please* tell me he's as upset as I'm hoping."

"Upset would be an understatement," she admitted and sat down on the edge of my bed. My triumphant grin was short-lived as she exhaled slowly, fixing me with a pleading stare. "You can't keep causing trouble, Zeke. And don't even get me started on your grades. He had a lot of thoughts about how it was *my* fault they slipped this last semester."

I ducked my head, biting at my lip. We'd had the same conversation right after midterms. My father blamed Mom, and she blamed him for pressuring me. "They're not so bad, Mom."

"Not bad?" She laughed loudly like it was the funniest joke. "You bombed so hard that you nearly failed eleventh grade."

"I think the operative word is 'nearly.'"

No longer amused, she leveled her gaze. I started to argue but stopped myself. There was no use, because she was onto my self-destructive mission. "Sorry," I said and took a seat beside her.

She reached across the quilt and grasped my hand. "Hun," she began, squeezing it gently, "I know it's been hell, but you can't let what happened affect your future, okay?"

I nodded even though I didn't buy her concern. No matter how many times she apologized, she'd still allowed my father to micromanage my life for years. Now I didn't know what I wanted anymore. Didn't know who I was without his rules looming over my head. Sometimes, I caught myself wishing I could go back to before. To when I never had to think about where Anthony stopped and Zeke began.

"You need to try," she added. "Stay out of trouble this summer and start senior year fresh." I shrugged again; school was the last thing on my mind. "Maybe you'd stay out of trouble if you had a summer job."

"A *what*?" I blanched. "Everything's fine, I promise—"

"You've been making a lot of those but not keeping them." The firm line of her mouth told me she'd made up her mind. "It's either work or be grounded like your father suggested."

"I'll take the first option," I said quickly, unwilling to give him the satisfaction.

"Thought you'd see it my way," she said, and bumped my shoulder. "Good thing I already got you a job."

"Doing what exactly?"

"You'll be my mechanic assistant this summer," she explained. "It'll be like old times when we worked on the SUV together."

I nodded as the words sank in but knew it would never be like before. Neither one of us was the same person we used to be. The divorce was the first time she'd stood up for herself, for me. My father had manipulated her into thinking she needed him. However, that didn't excuse the fact she'd allowed him to keep both of us under his thumb. She still felt like a stranger I didn't know how to trust.

"When do I start?" I asked, accepting my fate.

"Tomorrow—"

"I'm supposed to help the QSA plan for Pride," I interrupted. "We're meeting before Sawyer has to work . . ."

She considered me for a moment and let her gaze drift to the rainbow flag I'd just hung up. "Fine." She obliged, her narrowed eyes softening. We both knew it hadn't been easy for me, and she was trying to be more supportive. "You'll start Friday."

I groaned inwardly and tried to summon the strength to get through this plot twist. Summer freedom was already fading, and it was only the first day. It would be a long two months stuck in this small-ass town with nothing to do.

CHAPTER 3

Sawyer and I were on the oversized sofa in her basement, or "the bachelorette pad" as she called it. The home theater setup included a television so big it wouldn't fit in my new bedroom and too many speakers to count. It was perfect for hours of gaming and blocking out the rest of the world. Even more so for our Whovian summer tradition.

"This scene makes me feral," I said as the episode's title sequence finished.

The annual rewatch of our top *Doctor Who* episodes had arrived at my number one favorite. The start of series five held a special place in my heart. The Doctor had just crashed his time traveling ship, the TARDIS, and emerged in his new form, the actor Matt Smith taking the helm as the eleventh version of the character. He was so wet, so glistening, so disheveled that it had given me many emotions when I'd first watched it.

"No doubt this moment was my sexual awakening," I added as he climbed out of the TARDIS.

"Amy Pond in her police costume was mine," Sawyer said dreamily. She was referencing Karen Gillan, who played the Doctor's new companion. "The red hair and short skirt were all the proof I needed."

We'd started watching this show the summer after seventh grade when the internet had gone out because of a heat storm. Unable to stream, her mother had dug out old Blu-ray seasons of the show, and we were immediately obsessed. After we'd watched this specific episode, we looked at each other in awe. Both of us had *known* we weren't straight and shared this new discovery—that's why it was so important to me.

Things had been simpler that summer. We'd made it a habit to patrol the streets, like the Doctor searches the universe to help people in need, to protect our neighborhood against threats. Of course, we'd argued over who was the Time Lord, but I refused to be just a companion. That sense of control still stuck with me too, and rewatching episodes was comforting. It felt like we were back to being kids who could tell each other everything. So much had changed since, but maybe . . .

"I went out patrolling last night," I said with forced casualness, casting a glance over at her. "Like we used to do."

"God, I haven't thought about that since eighth grade," she said with a laugh, her phone chiming with a notification. "You'd been worried about what would change when you finally told your parents you were gay . . ." She fell silent, her thumb stilling as she checked the new message. Her eyes went wide with realization as she looked up at me. "They finalized their divorce, didn't they?"

I nodded, unable to speak. Unable to feel anything other than the same vulnerability I had back then.

"I'm sorry," she said, dropping her phone to grab my hand. "I know it's been hard on you, and the divorce news dropped out of nowhere."

"Out of nowhere," I repeated half-heartedly.

Only it wasn't, not in hindsight. After she'd helped me find the courage to tell my parents, Mom hugged me while my father had only urged me to keep it quiet. I never told Sawyer how he scared the hell out of me with hate crime statistics. He'd warned me that nobody in Beggs would welcome me, that they would think less of our family.

His self-serving efforts had stopped me from coming out with Sawyer like I'd planned to do when we started high school. She knew he was strict, but not the extent of his dominance. All this time she'd thought I was the one afraid of what other people would think. Getting back at my father after all these years was the real reason I'd suddenly joined the QSA. Sawyer had been over the moon when I told her I was finally ready to be a part of her club, but what I'd really wanted was to show him I wasn't the son he'd brainwashed.

"Now you can move on with your life," she added softly.

"I'm trying."

I risked a glance at her as the episode played in the background, and she was watching me. Still waiting for me to pull my mask off. I couldn't tell her my reasons, couldn't begin to describe how I felt like a big fraud for having an ulterior motive for helping with Pride and the QSA. Guilt coiled in my stomach like a snake.

"So . . . uh . . . where's your girlfriend?" I asked, avoiding her stare. "Thought she would be here by now."

A beat passed as she shifted gears to catch up, but I knew

she wouldn't ever let it drop. "Kennedy is not my girlfriend," she said, voice pitching as she grabbed her phone, and I was grateful she took the bait. "I haven't worked up the courage to ask her yet."

"*Why* are you nervous?"

All I got in reply was a one-shoulder shrug, bright pink blooming across her cheeks as she checked her new message. The crush on Kennedy had only strengthened since Kennedy had joined the QSA. It'd turned into a slow burn of yearning in the hallways, dragging me to pep rallies to watch her cheer, mastermind-level outings where we'd accidentally bump into her . . . and unfortunately Cohen.

"It's been a year, Saw." The oversized sofa pulled me into its cushions as I paused the next episode. "You make out with her like every damn day. And other *stuff*. What are you waiting for?"

"You tell me," she said with a sigh, gesturing toward me. "You have all those guys you've 'other-stuffed' but none of them are your boyfriend."

"I'm just comfortable with my sexuality now," I said over the roar of doubt, wishing it were true. "Plus guys love—"

"I bet they do." She cut me off with an exaggerated eye roll. "But whenever they want something more, you do the Z-step."

"First off, I can 'other-stuff' whoever I want," I said, and stuck my tongue out at her. "And secondly, what does that even mean?"

"Yes, you can," she began, holding her hands up in surrender, "and I'm not saying you can't . . . but you do have a habit of dancing around their feelings before you bail."

"Damn . . ." I trailed off, not denying it. Not explaining my reasons. "Wait, why are you bullying me right now?"

"Don't you *dare*," she said haughtily. "I'm *not* a bully . . . anymore."

I gave her a pointed look, pushing a strand of hair off my face. Her stint as my tormenter was still a sore subject. She'd get defensive and forget why she was reading me in the first place. Her temper at being called out was fleeting, though. She deflated as her eyes went distant in thought.

"It's just that . . . I think Kennedy might be a Zasshole too."

"Excuse you, I'm not an asshole about it," I pointed out. "I make sure they always have fun— Wait, do people call me *that?*"

She shrugged and twirled her hair, the blue tips spinning with her thoughts. That focused look was back, and I knew her mind was moving faster than the TARDIS. I wanted to tell her Kennedy wasn't like me. That all the guys I'd dated since January never knew the real me, just Zeke, who caused trouble. It was easier to bail before disappointing them.

"Don't go there," I told her, leaning over to nudge her shoulder. "No doubt Kennedy likes you."

"I hope so." Another sigh, another glance at her phone. "Sometimes I get the feeling she isn't comfortable being out. Not with all the crap happening in town."

"Totally get that."

I hadn't been aware of how hard it was to be out, not until the Pride Day debacle. The mayor had renounced his support after he'd caught hell for permitting the QSA to use the town square. But he couldn't stop us from doing it, not with Sawyer's petition. She'd gone through all the legal requirements, and I hoped my father saw us celebrating—saw me being the best worst type of gay person, or trying to be at least.

"Besides, the way she looks at you is pure thirst," I added. "So stop flipping out."

"Kinda the way you still look at Cohen?" she teased, pulling a me and changing the subject.

"It's more like I want to set him on fire," I corrected, throwing a pillow at her. It bounced off her glasses as she laughed. "And we agreed never to mention Extremely Shit-tacular Freshman Fall."

"You're the one who joined mathletes even though you *hate* math, because you wanted to flirt with him." She laughed, throwing it back at me.

"It wasn't a big deal," I grumbled. "At least I won us the tournament."

"I recall you were devastated, even lamenting about—"

"We're sooo not discussing this. It's over. Done." She eyed me over the rim of her glasses, but I refused to encourage her whole Zeke-and-Cohen bit. She thought it was hilarious that I once liked him. "He's the asshole-iest asshole there ever was. The end."

But it was more than that.

I'd fallen for Cohen on the first day of high school. We had known each other since we were kids, but he had changed over the summer. His disheveled look reminded me of the Eleventh Doctor when I saw him in the hallway: pale skin splotchy from rushing to class, dark curls adorably messy, his boldness with the rainbow pin on his bookbag—all of it made my brain glitch. I had wanted to be like him, to be near him so badly I joined the team.

A car engine sounded outside, and I inhaled deeply. The breath pushed through my lungs as I mentally prepared myself to see him. We might be forced to deal with each other again because of the QSA, but I made sure he knew I hated every second of it. There were no more longing glances or bumping hands or hopes to be his boyfriend. Only an immeasurable distance between who we'd been and who we'd both become.

"They're here," Sawyer announced, immediately smoothing down her hair. Checking her breath and double-checking her deodorant. "How do I look?"

I choked down the nostalgia and gave her the once-over. The dressy blouse she'd changed into for her host shift was pristine, her skirt short and flirty, and her heavy white Docs lent a cool touch. "Fabulous as always," I assured her. "With an edge of desperation."

"Not funny." A knock sounded, and her voice pitched as she called, "Come in!"

"And you said I was the thirsty one," I mocked as the basement's outside door opened.

With the deadliest of glares, she threw herself on the cushions. Then she stretched back in a relaxed position. "Hi," she said, all cool and collected despite how keyed up over her maybe-girlfriend she was.

Kennedy stepped inside, shouldering her tote bag with *BHS Cheer* embroidered across it. The TV's glow made the hazel of her eyes shine as she searched for Sawyer. Then the corners of her pink-lipsticked pout lifted into an easy smile. It was clear to see why my best friend was crushing hard. Kennedy was effortlessly cool, even in the Beggs High School cheer practice uniform.

"Hi," Sawyer repeated, transfixed.

"Hey," Kennedy said, and tucked a black twist braid behind an ear.

They stared at each other for what felt like an excruciatingly long time. At first glance, no one would think they meshed. Kennedy was the definition of preppy-and-popular, Sawyer a quirky nerd of a badass. But it was these moments when they fell into each's orbit that made it obvious they were perfect for one another.

"Ehem . . . Do you two need a room?" I joked to break the silence, and the throw pillow smacked me in the face again.

Kennedy's smile grew wide as she sat down on the sofa, dimpling her dark-brown cheeks until she took in my bruised face and blanched. "The hell happened to you?"

"Billy Peak . . ."

My voice went quiet when Cohen appeared in the doorway. It was like we'd switched places, with my hair long now and his chocolate curls cut short in a perpetual state of bedhead. He wasn't the same boy I'd blurted my truth to over linear equations—the one who'd been both my first kiss and first heartbreak. He'd gotten taller, thicker—with a peach emoji in his chinos. That once-adorable grin was replaced with a scowl whenever he looked at me. That look, paired with his polo-and-prep personality, only reminded me too much of who I used to be.

"Would say sorry that asshole gave you a black eye, but you probably deserved it," he said by way of greeting, his voice grouchy. Condescension was written all over his infuriatingly cute face.

"You can do better than that weak-ass hot take," I replied,

and gave him the middle finger. Billy had bullied him for being fat, but here he was standing up for the jock out of spite.

"You two," Sawyer began, motioning between us, "need to keep. Your. Shit. Together. For Pride Day."

"It's the Zasshole you have to worry about," Cohen said, taking a seat far away from me. "He's too dumb to know how important this is."

Dumb. That's what he thinks of me now. Like everyone else, he only sees what he wants to see. My hands balled into fists as a smug grin spread on his face. "Cohen," I said through gritted teeth. "I really want to give you a black eye right now, see how you like it. But I won't because I promised Sawyer."

He scoffed like I was a joke, rolling his eyes. "I'd like to see you try—"

"Oh my god," Kennedy interrupted. "That must be a new record. Only thirty seconds before you're threatening each other."

"He started it," I protested.

"Yes, he did." Sawyer narrowed her eyes at Cohen before looking at me. "But you're gonna end it, right? Because you know how much this means, and I'm your best friend—"

"His *only* friend," Cohen inserted.

"—who worked really hard to make this happen," she finished, ignoring his remark.

She expectantly waited for me to oblige. That was how she operated, always calling the shots. Sometimes it was easier to go along with it instead of butting heads. Let her take the lead since she was the gay guru, and I was just . . . here.

"Fine," I said, slowly unclenching my fists. "I'll keep my shit together."

"Since when have you kept it—"

Kennedy cut him off. "Let's just make it through Saturday, Cohen. Then you two can pound each other."

"Ew," I spat out quickly.

"That doesn't mean what you think it does," he told her, trying his best to ignore my glare. "Can we just get this meeting over with already?"

"Finally something we can all agree on." Sawyer took a deep breath, then exhaled roughly as she grabbed her tablet. "We have a tight schedule for Saturday, and we"—she pointed at Cohen and me again—"*have* to make sure it goes as planned. Mayor Buchanan is just waiting for us to give him a reason to cancel this whole thing, so nothing can go wrong."

Buchanan hadn't even wanted to celebrate Pride Month in the first place. After the QSA got enough community signatures, we'd been allowed three hours instead of a full month. I'd been helping them cram as much gay as possible into each one, thrilled to know my father would hate every minute of it.

"I'm opening the drag show at noon," Sawyer read from the agenda she'd created. After years of writing X-Men fanfic, she was performing as the tap-dancing Captain Jaymes Catz character she'd created. "Kennedy's helping me with my drag king gear, so that means you two—"

"Will be helping the vendors get set up," I finished.

"I'll handle it," Cohen corrected, giving me side-eye. "Your only job is to not be late."

I opened my mouth to insult him, but Sawyer held up

a finger in warning. My comment died on my tongue as she continued. "After the show, the community tents will open up. We'll each take turns working the QSA table until it's time for the parade to start."

The parade would be the ultimate fuck-you to my father. The route would go right by his law office, and I knew he'd come out to watch. That's what he'd done when I rode in the Homecoming procession last year. He'd soon see me up on the QSA float holding a pride banner with Cohen. I couldn't wait to smile and wave at him. Show him I'm speaking up, proud to be out—pretending like I wasn't the biggest fraud for doing all this for the wrong reasons.

"We're gonna have *so* much fun in the parade, Coco," I said to him with a wink, shoving down the doubt that threatened to shake me.

At the sound of his old nickname, crimson erupted across Cohen's cheeks. I'd called him that during the quiet moments we'd shared in between study sessions. In those moments we'd listen to Bleachers albums while sharing headphones and talk about our lives. But when he'd asked me to be his boyfriend, I'd been too ashamed to tell him my father wouldn't approve, too afraid to wear a bold rainbow pin and hold his hand. So, I blew him off with some lame excuse about being friends, even though it hurt. I'd felt bad until he immediately moved on to the mathletes captain.

That was how our rivalry started.

"We can be each other's wingmen if there are any hot guys in the crowd," I pushed, fanning the flames. *If I can't fight him, then . . .* "Maybe Geometry Derick will be there!"

"You've turned into such a himbo," he said indignantly, the

blush giving way to annoyance. "Pride is about being heard, not finding someone to smash."

"Excuse you, but I take offense to that." I jabbed a finger at him. "And I know what Pride is."

"But do you really?" he asked, shaking his head. "You joined the QSA after *we* did most of the hard work. Are you even paying attention to what's happening in Beggs? What's happening with state laws and the Supreme Court?"

"Whoa, way to go from zero to a hundred. Of fuckin' course I'm aware of that," I said, an edge to my voice. I'd been right there with them as we met with the mayor and watched the hateful fallout from the petition. I kept trying to be good enough, like him, but it felt like I was constantly playing catch-up. "I'm not dumb."

"Maybe if you actually cared—"

"Enough!" Sawyer yelled in exasperation. She blinked slowly, took her glasses off, and cleaned them with the edge of her skirt. "Neither of you are allowed to talk until we go over this."

Cohen let it drop but kept staring at me. For a moment it felt like he was *actually* seeing me. That he knew the real me, the Anthony Zeke Chapman underneath this hard-ass disguise, the one he had once fallen for. But then he shook his head and wrote me off, just like everyone else. It only added insult to injury that he was still as beautiful as he'd been when he treated me like I mattered. I wanted to tell him this was all an act. Instead, I forced myself to keep quiet and grabbed my phone from the sofa arm. Forced myself to scroll Instagram and double-tap pictures of comic book artwork. Forced myself *not* to care.

CHAPTER 4

The grand opening of Roaring Mechanics had been celebrated with a makeshift speakeasy. Mom had gone all out with a fake store in the lobby and a secret phrase to enter the garage. It had been a celebration that only invited guests knew about. The 1920s theme complemented how she'd decorated the shop, with art deco floors and a portrait of Zelda Fitzgerald on the back wall.

From my spot under a minivan, I could see that painting. The iconic woman had been part of our family since I was a kid. Mom used to tell me stories about Zelda's childhood before bed, when we'd been in the old garage, anytime it'd been just her and me together. I knew that Zelda had met her husband the summer she turned eighteen. Two years later, in 1920, he was her escape from Montgomery, Alabama, and her strict father so she could finally live—

"We have a last-minute oil change coming in."

Mom's voice drifted under the minivan, and I snapped my

attention back to the engine above me. My hands ached as I gripped the wrench and tightened the plug. It had been a non-stop day of emptying inky goop from engines into drain pans and refilling them with fresh oil. I took a deep breath, inhaling the smell of grease, and rolled out from under the car on the small dolly mechanics used.

"Great," I said through a yawn, and sat up, stretching my neck.

"Mmhmm," Mom hummed as she adjusted the green shop hat over her blond waves. Her eyes softened as she looked down at me. "I know this must be jarring for you, and you never had to work before . . . but I'm really glad to have you down here."

What she meant was that she needed the extra help but couldn't afford to hire someone. Money was tight now, and the support payments from my father were barely helping us make ends meet. But she wanted to prove she could take care of me, of us.

"I mean, this *is* punishment for flunking my junior year," I mumbled.

"Almost flunking," she corrected with a wry grin.

I shot her an unamused grimace, my face going slack as she took a seat across from me. We sat in silence for a moment as sounds from the lobby TV reverberated off the tiled floor. I checked my phone so I could count down the hours until the QSA set up for tomorrow. It wasn't that I didn't want to be near Mom, but she kept trying to talk to me like we were back in the garage at our old house.

"Hey, Zeke," she continued, forcing the conversation, "I know how hard it's been . . . Are you doing okay?"

"I'm fine," I replied quickly, not wanting to rehash the past for the third time today. She was trying to prove she was here for me now with the incessant questions. But it never got us anywhere. The topic brought up too many emotions. And it always ended with me feeling guilty for the fact that, deep down, I resented her for letting my father walk all over us.

Her gaze held too much pity, and I quickly averted mine. My eyes went back to the portrait of Zelda and the smile she wore as if she knew exactly what I was going through. It was easy to imagine living a life like hers. One day I *would* get away from the JACass and all his plans. But I still didn't know who I was without them.

"You know, you remind me even more of her now," Mom commented.

I glanced over, and she nodded toward the back wall. "What do you mean?" I asked.

"Zelda never let anyone stop her from doing what she wanted," she said. "She never tried to be perfect, she was a rebel. A free spirit who partied in speakeasies and kept everyone on their toes. Just like you've been doing since . . ."

I chewed my lip, my hands fidgeting as I looked up at Zelda. Maybe I could be like her. Maybe I could live my life and not give a shit about what other people thought was *best* for me. It was like when I held a wrench in my hand, wielding it under a vehicle's hood. How it felt to know I could easily take apart any engine and put it back together. Complete control—that's all I really wanted.

"How about Pride Day tomorrow?" Mom continued, pulling me out of my thoughts. "Everything okay with that?"

"Guess so?" I said, this time with my voice rising. What Cohen had said still shook me. *Are you even paying attention?*

"You guess?"

I rolled my shoulders back like Coach had taught us to when we were tense with stress. There had been no nerves when we'd planned Pride, but I'd gone out riding again last night. Unable to sleep. Unable to get Cohen's voice out of my head for miles and miles.

"Nothing I can't handle," I said in a determined voice, more to myself.

"If I haven't said it already," she started, "I'm glad you're getting involved."

Another attempt to prove she was here for me. She'd been going above and beyond since we moved out, to ensure I was supported. As much as I appreciated her efforts, it felt like it was a little too late.

I sighed roughly and shrugged. "I don't really do much—"

"It doesn't matter," she corrected. "You're speaking up by being part of it. That's what's important now. You never know who's listening, so be proud."

Pride is about being heard. But to me Pride felt like a fight. A war between who I should be and who I was.

"Just promise you'll be careful tomorrow—" I started to interrupt her, but she shook her head. "You're never careful. What you're doing is more important than getting into stupid fights."

"Fair." I reached up, tenderly touching the bruised skin around my eye. "Fighting's bad, I know."

"One more thing," she added, standing as a car pulled up to the garage door. The last-minute appointment was the only thing between me and getting out of here. "Promise you won't—"

"I won't get in a fight, I swear."

She pointed a finger at me, grit under her nails like mine. "—that you won't take the bait if someone tries to provoke you," she finished.

"Got it."

I rolled my eyes, but what she'd said echoed inside me. *You never know who's listening, so be proud.* That advice was more supportive than what my father had said when he'd found out about Pride Day. He'd told me to be quiet and not draw attention to myself. He'd warned that people would protest. It'd made me feel like the space my friends had fought to take up didn't matter, that it was easier to stop trying than to risk causing a scene.

. . .

The Beggs Town Square was nothing more than a bit of hoity-toity landscaping. It housed a raised pavilion and a monument in the square's center commemorating the town founder. Fancy pea gravel lined the sidewalks as they twisted and turned with small-town charm, leading toward the statue. My parents had taken me to see its installation when I was a kid, Mom and me playing hide-and-seek in the bushes along the paths.

I could still remember darting out of the hydrangeas beside that marbled likeness of Mr. David Beggs and his faithful donkey. Could still remember how this kid had been snapping pictures of it with a retro camera from the '90s. He'd grinned and told me how the founder single-handedly built this town, and I stared up at it with wide eyes. That was the moment I knew that one day I wanted to do something important too.

It was also the moment I'd first met Cohen Fisher.

But he didn't remember how he'd smiled at me or how we'd played around the square that day. We'd grown apart only to come back together freshman year, only to grow even farther apart after our falling out. So far that he no longer felt like the person I once knew. Even though he could still often be found with a vintage camera, he was a stranger who made me feel like I would never be good enough.

He was a few steps ahead of me as we passed the statue in a rush. The evening was dragging on while we worked to hang up the last of the QSA membership flyers. Every time he would hold one up for me to tape, he'd let out an irritated sigh if I took too long. Yet he never complained. I didn't know what was worse, his quietness or the threat that at any moment he could turn into a sharp-tongued smartass.

The streetlamps flickered to life in the settling dusk as I trailed after him. The beams were a spotlight on Sawyer's hatchback. Its molten shade of orange glinted as two shadows kissed in the front seats. After we'd turned the pavilion into a makeshift stage, Sawyer and Kennedy decided to take a break. And by "break," they'd obviously meant an hour-long make-out sesh while I was stuck with Cohen.

"Can you *hurry*?" he called, finally breaking his silence.

He was at the next lamppost, and I could see his eye roll from here. "Can you not walk so fast?" I replied, making sure I took my time catching up to him.

"I have somewhere to be after this," he said.

"A hot date?" I teased with a sneer. He only shook his head instead of sparring with me. "What?"

"Nothing." He grabbed the tape out of my hand and hung up the poster himself. "I promised I wouldn't let you get to me."

"What does that mean?" I asked, rushing as he hurried to the next post.

"You know exactly what it means." The expression on his face, how it went slack, deflated my grin. "You're trying to get under my skin because that's what you do, and I'd much rather get this over with."

I wanted to argue with him, but I was too tired after working all day. "Fine," I said in a huff, dropping the pretense. "If you need to be somewhere, then go. I can finish this by myself."

He shook his head severely as we continued walking. "This is too important to risk you screwing it up."

"What the hell?" I grabbed his arm and stopped him in his tracks. "I'm here helping, so why are you—"

"I'm just giving my opinion, Zeke."

"If you're gonna ride my ass, at least buy me dinner. Damn."

A flicker of disgust, of something similar to annoyance, flashed across his face. Then he jerked his arm out of my grasp and held up the flyers. "Do you even know *why* we're hanging these up?"

"Because the QSA is leading Pride Day," I said. "I can read—"

"It's not just that." He rubbed at his messy bedhead, a humorless laugh echoing into the dusk. "Why are you even in this club?"

"Let me see," I said, counting on my fingers. "I'm gay. It's the only queer club at school. And my *best friend*, Sawyer, started it."

He ignored my emphasis, conflict knitting his brows as he studied me. "God, you're such a bad gay."

"Excuse me?" My voice broke despite myself.

The guilt struck, sinking its fangs into my stomach. He was right, and I knew it. Knew that my involvement with the QSA was for selfish reasons, that my ulterior motive was shitty, that I didn't know how to be gay without hearing my father's voice telling me to stop flaunting it. I was a failure at being their version of the best and being my father's version of the worst.

"I, uh, I'm pretty sure you can't say that," I managed.

"It's the truth, Zeke. You're so worried about yourself that you don't notice what's really happening in town." He pointed at the flyer, reading the last line. "'Beggs High School *needs* you to join the QSA.'"

"So what?" I asked, snatching it from him. "We already have four members. Maybe we'll get a few more."

"Hopefully we will." He stared at me as his glower dimmed to despair. "The principal changed the rule for clubs. If we don't get at least twenty people signed up, the QSA will be disbanded when school starts back up in the fall."

"Nobody told me about that!" I exclaimed in frustration, rereading the flyer. "Nothing on here says that."

"We've talked about it in meetings." The edge dropped from his voice as he spoke. "But you don't come to all the meetings, and when you are there . . . you're not really present."

"That's because . . ." Because I didn't know how to be someone who belonged in the QSA. And I didn't know how to tell him the truth or explain myself. "Cohen . . . I mean, it's because . . ."

"It's okay, Zeke." He took the flyer from me, then walked

onward. "Let's just get through tomorrow. Maybe we'll get some sign-ups, and then you can resign from the club since it doesn't seem like you really want to be here anyway."

"It's not okay . . ." I called after him, my voice a whisper.

I suddenly felt like I was up at bat, a human-shaped jumble of nerves. I leaned against the lamppost and tried taking a few calm breaths, another tip from Coach. But there were too many curveballs as I attempted to swing the doubt out of my head. *Pride is about being heard.* Strike one. *You never know who's listening.* Strike two. *You're a bad gay.* Strike three.

There was no winning when it came to Pride. My eyes burned, and the stars in the sky blurred. No matter how hard I kept trying, I didn't have anything to feel proud of.

CHAPTER 5

I couldn't get Cohen out of my head. His biting remarks had followed me home. Lurked in the corners of my tiny bedroom. Haunted my dreams while the sheets twisted around me. Breathed down my neck and woken me a little after three a.m. I'd slipped out onto the fire escape and ridden around town until moonlight gave way to sunshine.

And then I kept riding until it was time for Pride Day.

My dirt bike rolled to a stop back at Beggs Town Square, and I hesitantly put down the kickstand and dismounted. Everything Cohen had said about the QSA amplified the JACass's warnings. But there were only rainbow flags waving, laughter and excitement drifting with the breeze as I scoped out the square.

Parade floats were lined up at the ready, and community tents were popping up in two rows along the landscaped grass. On one end, Sawyer and Kennedy set up speakers in the pavilion while Cohen snapped photos of the sponsors. They were sweaty, their "Beggs High School QSA" tie-dye shirts wet from summer heat. Had they given me one? I tried to remember, feeling suddenly out of place. I'd sleepily thrown on a vintage *Doctor Who* shirt from the 2000s and a pair of grease-stained jeans hours ago. But now I felt stupid. After shimmying out of my jacket, I tied it around my waist as the truth sank in. As Cohen's admonition from last night rang true.

Before the guilt could strike again, I set off on a mission. *I'll prove to them I'm not a bad gay.* I searched for something to do other than "not be late." The van for Estrella Books was parked next to the curb, and someone was struggling with boxes. My sneakers crunched on pea gravel as I marched over with determination.

"Need some help?" I asked, reaching out to steady the wobbling stack.

A woman peeked around the corner, and relief eased the tense lines of her brow. A lock of long salt-and-pepper hair fluttered as she blew out a sigh. "I wouldn't say no," she admitted, a kind smile dimpling her olive cheeks. "If you don't mind."

"That's what I'm here for." I took the boxes from her and cut my eyes across the square. "I'm Zeke with the Beggs High QSA."

"Carmen Bedolla." She held out her hand, then let out a laugh, its trill light and airy, as she realized my hands were full. "What you're doing today is nothing short of beautiful."

"Yeah . . ." That's all I could say as I followed her toward the tents. The bright rainbow colors and laughter, the community coming together despite the mayor—all of it was supposed to make me feel proud. But it made me feel like an even bigger fraud.

"Thank you for what you're doing," she added as we reached the bookstore's tent. "I'm so grateful you asked my shop to be part of Pride."

"It, uh … it wasn't really me," I admitted weakly, unable to fight my growing imposter syndrome. "My friend Sawyer and the rest of the QSA did most of it. I'm just here, I guess."

"You showed up today," she pointed out as I set the boxes on the table. "Not everyone is brave enough to show up." Her smile never faltered, and it felt like she was seeing me. That she somehow knew the hidden parts I'd kept in that shoebox.

"Thank you, ma'am," I said, my voice rising.

"And thank you for helping, Zeke," she replied as my phone buzzed in my pocket. "We need more people like you to raise their voice, especially with that hateful propaganda the mayor is pushing. Someone needs to make him listen."

Her unwavering eye contact made me nervous. Unsure of what to say, I fidgeted with my phone and checked my notifications. A message from the QSA group chat flashed across the screen. "Guess I better help set up," I finally said with a polite smile.

She wished me a happy Pride, and I wanted to thank her again. Tell her how much I needed her kindness. My voice got stuck in my throat, though. Too many emotions were lumped together. All I could do was give her a small wave goodbye, keeping my head down as I read the new texts.

QS-SLAY!

APRIL 4, 2025

KENNEDY

> we can use the pavilion for
> the drag stage

TODAY AT 11:23 AM

SAWYER

okay everyone get in place we're about to start

COCO

Is the Zasshole even here yet?

COCO

Oops. Wrong thread.

My brow furrowed, wrinkling even more when I realized what he meant. Then I reread the last message before today. That had been two months ago, and they'd evidently started a new group chat without me. *How did I not notice?* I questioned, stomping my way to the sidewalk. The divorce proceedings had been hectic at home, Mom's worry spilling over into mine. So much had been going on, and maybe I had been too distracted to pay attention to our QSA meetings. But that wasn't an excuse for them to leave me out. They didn't know all the sordid details. They had only decided to exclude me because . . .

I'm not a good gay like Sawyer or Cohen or Kennedy. That guilt was back, but I pushed it down. Pushed myself to keep walking so I could prove to them—to myself—that I wasn't who my father had made me.

My stomps grew more determined, and I kicked at the ground in annoyance. A brightly colored scrap of paper skittered to the side in my pissed-off strides. I slowed to a stop, the line "Beggs High School needs you to join the QSA" barely visible. It was one of the flyers Cohen and I had hung up. Its edges were crumpled from being trampled, the corners torn like it'd been ripped down.

There was another a few feet away.

And another.

They were gone from every single lamppost in the square. Posters hung in their place, and I stepped to the closest one to read the violently red ink. "Support Mayor Buchanan's Family First ordinance and keep our children safe," I read, voice stumbling as I saw the last line. "Proudly supported by City Attorney J. A. Chapman, Esq., of Chapman Law."

There was no doubt this was a result of the backlash brewing in town since the petition. The fact that my father supported it sent an icky rage through me. *Have the others seen this?* Hands shaking, I tore it down. Then I was moving, jogging to the next one. Part of me felt like I should run home, hide the posters in my shoebox, and accept what was happening in town like I was raised to do.

But I wasn't Anthony Chapman anymore.

I tossed each crumpled ball to the ground, not caring who saw. One after another as I traced the same path from last night. The white paper ripped from the posts as my breath grew ragged—

My rampage skidded to a halt. The roar inside me quieted, my shoes sinking in the pea gravel. Blood rushed to my ears as I gazed across the town square at *him*. The slicked-back brown hair, the polo tucked into ironed khakis, the same fake-ass smile from the billboard.

James Anthony Chapman. The JACass. My father.

A spark pushed me through the crowd toward him. My tongue pressed to the roof of my mouth as pressure swelled in my chest. I wanted to tear into him. But I stopped abruptly when I saw the short man beside him. White hair cropped and neat, matching beard. A grin as obnoxious as the pristine linen suit he wore.

Mayor Buchanan.

My father leaned over, whispering into the mayor's ear, and then they turned toward the pavilion. The mayor waved to the crowd while he climbed the steps, like this was planned. A wave of voices crashed against me as I tried to make sense of what was happening. Something wasn't right. Sawyer was getting ready in the changing tent, and Captain Jaymes Catz was supposed to welcome everyone to Pride Day.

Buchanan grabbed the microphone, his grin growing wider, and I shoved my way to the front. A piercing gaze pinned me in place before I could cause a scene. My father shook his head and held a hand up for me to be quiet. The gesture made my mind trip over all the memories of when he'd done it before as the mayor's Southern twang rang out.

"Hellooooo, ladies and gentlemen," he greeted the crowd, his voice reverberating through the speakers. "It's gonna be a good day today, and I wanted to take a moment to address you fine folks of Beggs with a special announcement."

He paused as if waiting for applause, but there was another wave of disgruntled tension. I glanced around as everyone nervously mumbled under their breath. Then I caught sight of Sawyer pushing toward me, beard halfway glued on. Kennedy and Cohen were on her heels in a frenzy.

"What. The. Hell?" she asked, out of breath, coming to a stop.

"Why didn't you tell us your dad would be here with the mayor?" Cohen demanded with an accusatory tone.

"Like I knew this was gonna happen," I said with too much force. "If *you'd* bothered to actually pay attention, you'd know I don't talk to him anymore."

Cohen opened his mouth, but his voice was lost in the static of the microphone. "I'm proud to officially announce my Family First ordinance today," Buchanan continued with open arms. "In order to protect the values of Beggs, I'm rolling out new city legislation to prioritize our children. The first step is banning public displays that flaunt unnatural sexualities and adult cabaret performances. As such, I'm here to tell you Pride Day is officially canceled, as it violates this ordinance."

A beat of silence settled over the square as his words sank in. "What the *actual* fuck?" Sawyer seethed, ripping her beard completely off. I grabbed her shoulder before she could rush the stage.

My father gave me another sharp look, but this time it didn't stop me. I inhaled deeply and bellowed, "You can't do that! We got signatures!"

The JACass's face flushed scarlet, and I jutted my jaw in defiance as the mayor continued. "The folks of Beggs have spoken up," he declared, ignoring my outburst, "and it's my job to listen. I've revoked the permit for today's festivities. Please remove your materials from city property within the next hour or be fined."

A cacophony of boos erupted around us, but the mayor just smiled and exited the pavilion. My father didn't spare me a second glance as he followed. Didn't even attempt to explain himself.

"What're we gonna do?" Kennedy asked, a quiver in her voice.

"I guess we have to break stuff down and clean," Cohen muttered. He ran a hand through his messy hair, shoulders slumping in defeat. "The last thing we need right now is to get in trouble."

Trouble rattled in my brain as Sawyer blinked furiously. "This is total bullshit," she said, her words vibrating with rage. "He's only doing this because of the backlash from the town. Because he wants the small-minded votes at the Founder's Day election. So he can stay in office and keep . . . keep . . ."

She fell silent as too many voices called out to her for advice. The vendors asked Kennedy what they needed to do, asked Cohen where to move the parade floats. Nobody paid me any attention as all three of them searched for the words to say. Because they had organized today on their own, worked hard to make it possible. And all I had to show for it was guilt. Maybe if I had helped more, or maybe if I still talked to my father, I would've known what was happening. Maybe I could have warned them.

"I guess this means Pride is over," Sawyer finally said.

She sounded helpless, and her eyes watered behind her glasses. It only intensified my anger. My head spun with more curveballs. *Are you even paying attention? We need more people like you to raise their voice.* But Mom's voice sounded like the bat cracking with a hit—*You never know who's listening, so be proud.*

"Be proud," I said aloud, chasing away any uncertainty.

I didn't want to accept this, didn't want to keep being a fraud. What I needed was to be free of this town and my father. Face the fears he'd engrained in me. Be like Zelda Fitzgerald, a rebel who never let anyone stop her from doing what she wanted and lived her own life and partied in speakeasies . . .

Wait.

Something snagged in the back of my mind, and memories flashed: the portrait at Roaring Mechanics; my mom throwing a speakeasy party for the grand opening; her pride over her accomplishment; my father, who'd stopped her dream for years; how he'd held a hand up to stop me. That JACass and the mayor and this shitty town were all doing the same exact thing, and . . .

A speakeasy, I thought, glancing to where my father had stood on the pavilion with the mayor. *What if . . . What if Pride was a secret celebration too?*

The idea of defying the ordinance felt more and more right with each excited thump of my heart. I turned to Sawyer, tears spilling down her cheeks. She had worked hard to make today happen. So had Kennedy and Cohen and the bookstore lady and everyone else who had signed that petition. I needed to show them I was here too. I'd joined the QSA to prove I was the best worst type of gay person, and this was finally my chance to speak up.

"No," I said, raising my voice. "We're gonna celebrate Pride anyway."

CHAPTER 6

"**H**ey, Zeke."

I gripped the rainbow piñata as someone said my name, bracing for the inevitable. Everyone kept asking questions I couldn't answer. They all looked to me as though I was a leader like Sawyer, but they were wrong. I was just . . . me. I didn't immediately have a response when someone asked where we'd host the secret Pride celebration. It had been that lady—Carmen Bedolla—who stepped up and offered the basement of Estrella Books. When? Kennedy had suggested nine p.m. without missing a beat, claiming it would give us enough time to get set up. And now . . .

I glanced down from my perch on the ladder. A woman stared up at me, adjusting a Bama Slammers hockey hat over her fiery curls. "How are we supposed to make a dance floor?" she asked. "There isn't a lot of space down here."

"I, uh," I tried, floundering. The downstairs of the bookstore was a narrow room with bricked arches. Inventory shelves lined the walls, while worktables were scattered along the center. *What the hell was I thinking?* I groaned inwardly, eyeing the back exit. *I should just dip out—*

"Nora, have those guys from Ryland Farms move the tables to one end," Sawyer jumped in. Her brain had immediately shifted to focus mode when we arrived, while mine couldn't keep up. "That'll create space in the center."

I watched the woman go, picking at the rainbow papier-mâché. Nervous energy filled me like it had when Sawyer and I had argued in the children's section upstairs all those years ago. There'd been this air of intimidation about her when we'd read the X-Men graphic novel together. *She'd* decided when to turn the page, whether I was done reading or not. Now she was taking charge yet again.

"Once you get this hung up," Sawyer instructed, "we need to bring down the sound system from Kennedy's truck."

"Right," I said, my voice clipped. I cautiously climbed another rung. *It's not that high.*

A beat passed as I wobbled on the ladder, and then she asked, "Are you okay, Z?"

"Why wouldn't I be?" A deep breath. "It's just six feet off the ground. That's, like, the same height as me."

"Not the ladder," she said. "I meant, are you okay after . . . you know . . . your dad and the mayor?"

I inhaled, gathering myself as I glanced down. She stood tall, and not only because of her chunky-heeled Docs. I could see her favorite shirt with the SAPPHIC WARRIOR graphic peeking out from the bib of her shortalls. She was the epitome of Pride, and I felt like a fraud standing next to her.

"Like *why* was he even there?" she pressed.

"The mayor?" I forced a grin, but she narrowed her eyes. This was neither the time nor place to discuss my father. If I told her everything, she'd go into her bully-with-kindness mode and push me to fix it. And I didn't need any more doubt weighing me down. "I haven't spoken to him since April, so I dunno."

"Does he know how problematic—"

"Why do we need a piñata again?" I cut her off, clearing my throat.

Slowly, her concern twisted into a smile. "Because we're gonna pretend it's Mayor Dickbrain's face," she relented, allowing me to change the subject. But there was a bullish glint in her eye that said we weren't done discussing it. "And I filled it with glitter to make tonight extra gay."

"Yeah. Totally. I should've suggested that," I said, tying the rainbow's string around a ceiling joist. But I didn't know where to begin suggesting anything. I wasn't like her, and all I *did* know fit in a shoebox.

"Zeke?" someone called as I climbed down, and my face heated with more embarrassment.

"Drape those flags over the lamps," Sawyer ordered before I had a chance to respond. "Here, I'll show you what I mean."

She darted off while I stood there like a dipshit. Before December, I'd known what to do. Stand on the pitcher's mound and make the bleachers erupt in cheers as I struck out the competition. Pretend to be straight and make everyone love me like my father had wanted. Keep my mouth shut and convince them I fit in. But now? I didn't know how to be me like I'd thought.

Trying to prove myself wasn't so easy.

I need a break, I decided, turning on my heels. Anything to get away from not being able to answer another question. My sneakers squeaked on the concrete floor as I walked quickly to the stairs. It was nearing nine p.m., but it was obvious Sawyer had things under control.

I pushed open the door for the main level, and I slinked out before it closed behind me. "Seriously, what the hell was I thinking?" I mumbled into the darkness of the bookstore, leaning back against the wall. No reply came other than the buzz of the neon sign by the entrance. HOLA Y BIENVENIDO it read, but I was feeling very unwelcome right now.

A shadowy figure suddenly stood from behind the register, and I startled upright. The glow from the computer screen shined across his face as he eyed me. "S-sorry," I managed, squirming under his hooded stare. "Didn't know someone was up here."

"It's all good," he replied in a velvety voice. He scanned the unlit store, running a hand through his messy dark hair. "I just finished closing up."

"I can, uh, just go back down . . ." I trailed off and turned to leave.

"Hey, you're Zeke, right?" he asked, rounding the counter.

"I'm he," I replied, turning back. The deep cadence of how he'd said my name tripped me up. "I mean, I'm Zeke."

A smirk tugged the corner of his lips as he swaggered toward me. Slowly, he came into focus in the dim lighting. The guy was tall, slender, with a tight T-shirt for Estrella Books stretched across his chest. I gulped and stepped back as he checked me out, his gaze raking over my body.

"Shouldn't you be downstairs?" he asked.

"Uh . . ." I could feel sweat beading on my forehead, and I tried to play it off. "Just needed a break from . . . you know . . ."

"Don't be nervous about tonight."

My mind raced to ask how he knew what I'd been stewing over. But I managed "I'm not."

The smirk turned into a dazzling grin. "Good, because what you're doing is brave. I wish someone would have done this over in West Point. But my hometown is as homophobic as this one. No one cares about Pride. Not like you do."

"Like me," I repeated, my cool facade threatening to crack.

"Looks like you're not afraid of a fight either." He pointed at my black eye. "Such a rebel."

"Hardly."

"For real, there wouldn't be a Pride if it wasn't for you."

"I guess," I said, more to myself. Sawyer was willing to let everything be canceled, but *I'd* done something. That had to make me less of a fraud, right?

"I'm Mason, by the way."

"I'm Zeke . . ." I blinked slowly, feeling dumber. "But you already knew that."

He laughed, an even deeper roar that made my pulse quicken. "C'mon," he said with a wink and reached for the door handle. "We'll dance those nerves away."

I let out a breath, exhaling the tension in my chest. This was no different from spending three hours in the town square. *I can handle this,* I reassured myself, following his lead.

. . .

The small basement of Estrella Books was packed. The community members who'd set up earlier were here, along with a few others I'd never seen before. They mingled as music blasted from the cheer squad's borrowed sound system. A rainbow-hued glow from pride flags draped over lamps served sophisticated nightclub vibes. Sawyer and Kennedy were dancing, Kennedy's floral sundress twirling, while Cohen was stationed by the back exit door as a lookout for the alley.

It felt like a real speakeasy.

I had been expecting something like we'd planned, with a drag show or maybe even a parade. Neither of those options was possible in the small space, but it was somehow better. Less public than the town square and stress-free after the hell that'd happened earlier. A safe space where none of that mattered.

The room was growing warm and stuffy as we danced. I didn't mind it, though, pushing sweaty hair off my face. No one could judge me down here. Not even myself. The pressure was lessening with every new song. Every spin Mason and I did on the makeshift dance floor. Every time his hands found a way to rub and squeeze and linger on my body like he couldn't get enough of me.

His warm palm stilled on my biceps, squeezing gently. He leaned in close to whisper, "Be right back." The sudden nearness of his mouth made me tingle as he excused himself.

I watched him take the stairs up to the bathroom. A smirk curled my lips as I envisioned where tonight might lead. It grew wider when I saw Sawyer motioning for me, nodding at the door before slipping outside. The next song started up while I excitedly worked my way across the room. I couldn't wait to tell her about Mason.

The music faded away as I followed her into the alley, the door clanging shut behind me. I inhaled the fresh night air and grinned. "You're never gonna guess . . ." My voice fell when I saw Cohen pacing back and forth, chewing at his thumb. "What's wrong?"

"A cop showed up," he said shakily.

"Don't worry, I handled it," Sawyer added. "Told him we were having a party for Ms. Bedolla, which technically isn't a lie."

"Hold up," I said, not following. "*What* happened?"

"It was because of the noise," Cohen explained. His anxious stride came to a stop in front of me, and he wrung his hands. "We tried to get your attention, but you were in your own world as usual."

"Sorry, I was dancing with this Mason guy," I offered. "Do you know—"

"I'm well aware of who fucking Mason Bedolla is, Zeke," he spat out.

"Wait . . . were you trying to get with him tonight?" I asked, taken aback by the thought of Cohen being sexual. Being anything other than annoying.

"Hell no, he's the absolute worst—never mind, it's not important," he nearly shouted, his words tense. "I'm freaked because we could have gotten caught, and you're too busy being *you* to care."

"Cohen," Sawyer said, holding her hands up to calm him. "It's not Zeke's fault."

"It'll be fine," I told him. "The cops are useless. I trashed my dad's billboard without them seeing."

"So you're the reason they installed security cameras after they cleaned it up?" He threw his hands up, muttering "Unbelievable."

"Relax, Coco," I urged. "Come back inside and dance—"

"I can't *relax*, Zeke." He stressed the word with sarcasm. "Do you know what would happen if we got caught? Because I actually read the small print on those Family First posters. No Pride events. Period. We could get fined or, worse, arrested."

"They're not going to arrest us," Sawyer pointed out.

"We'll at least be forced to do community service or something," he went on. "Then it would be on record when we apply to college. And there go my chances for scholarships."

"Hey," Sawyer began in a gentle tone, "we'll be fine."

"*He* will be," Cohen said to her, shaking his head. "His father will pull strings, since Chapman Law represents the town, but he *never* cared about Pride until now—"

"Stop saying that," I interrupted. "I've always fucking cared"—I motioned toward the alley door—"and we're having Pride like the QSA wanted. At least I'm trying."

"*We're* trying," Sawyer corrected, side-eyeing me. "We finally did something for the queer community in Beggs."

I wanted to ask if he knew how proud I felt tonight, but I was sick of explaining myself. "You've made it clear how hard y'all have worked," I said instead, "and I understand how dangerous the consequences are. But it's one night, okay? I'll stay here and monitor the door if you want."

"I don't know . . ." He trailed off, gulping as the thumps of music suddenly died. "Do you think the cop came back?"

Sawyer shook her head in confusion, and she opened the door to check. "It's just Ms. Bedolla," she assured him. "She asked if she could say a few words"—she checked her phone— "and it's almost time for it to end."

"Let's just go back in and have fun, okay?" I almost patted Cohen on the shoulder to calm his nerves. Then I remembered how much of an asshole he'd been and stopped myself. "This was my idea, and I'll take the blame if something happens. Swear."

A moment passed before he reluctantly nodded, mumbling under his breath. Then Sawyer led the way back inside as soft finger taps echoed through the speakers. The door shut behind me with a clang, and I took in the crowd. Everyone had formed a circle around the center of the basement, where Carmen stood. The overhead lights had been turned on, the fluorescence dancing off her rainbow-sequined shirt. She lifted the sound system's microphone to speak.

"I just want to thank y'all for coming out to celebrate Pride," she announced with a broad smile. Someone whooped, and she nodded toward the guy in the front. "That's my grandson Mason, everyone, and he's part of the reason why I'm up here . . . because it's a disgrace what Mayor Buchanan is doing to our town. The LGBTQIA-plus community shouldn't have to carry the weight of this intolerance alone. That's why I've decided to run against the mayor in the Founder's Day election next month, and I want y'all to know first because your fight is my fight."

Applause erupted, and I felt myself smiling despite the argument in the alley. Cohen might've thrown those accusations at me, but I was proud of the speakeasy. Proud that Mayor Buchanan's ordinance—along with Chapman Law's support— wouldn't succeed in silencing us without a fight.

"But first," she continued, scanning the crowd, "someone showed up to help me this morning, and I want to thank him properly, if he can come to the microphone." My eyes went wide when she locked her gaze on mine. "Zeke, I could tell you felt out of place, like you don't belong, and I want you to know that you do. Your bravery is the reason why we're here tonight."

My hands went clammy, and I started to back away. But Sawyer elbowed my side and pushed me toward the center. She said something unintelligible that was drowned out by the thunderous beats of my heart.

It took only a few strides to meet Carmen where she stood, yet it felt like I'd raced around the baseball diamond to get there. "Um, hi," I said with a breathless gulp. Everyone was staring at me, and I could feel sweat rolling down my back. "Th-thanks for letting us use your bookstore."

"No thanks necessary," she said with a small laugh. "This morning, I said we needed people to speak up and make the mayor listen. Then you spoke up. Thank you for that and for letting us be proud together."

"I don't know about—"

She held up a hand, politely stopping my objections. "You showed up and did the right thing. That's what matters."

"No," I tried to say. But someone screamed my name, and my voice was too quiet. Mason whooped again, and Carmen held the microphone up to me. "Is there anything you'd like to say?"

"Um . . ."

My mouth went dry as nerves rioted in my stomach. *Everyone will know I'm a . . .* They were smiling at me? It was as though they were seeing me, Zeke. The one who created this. Not Anthony Chapman.

"Thank you?" My voice pitched higher, and I cleared my throat. "For coming out this morning and showing up tonight."

"Zeke!" Sawyer yelled, and I braced myself for her to call me out. To tell everyone I hadn't put in any work. However, she only smiled reassuringly. I thought of how she was always so focused on what she wanted. How she'd made a long list of our traditions, from X-Men comics to *Doctor Who*. How much I wanted to be like her and feel like someone who belonged here.

"I know," I started, pointing at where she stood with Kennedy and Cohen, "that the Beggs High School QSA has fought to make today happen."

But this wasn't what the club had originally planned. They'd wanted a whole month, but the mayor thought we only deserved three hours. Then he backtracked and took away the scraps he'd given us. Everything Cohen had accused me of, not caring and not paying attention—all of it swirled in my head. Tonight had shown me what it felt like to breathe outside the shoebox I'd put myself in.

"I think Ms. Bedolla is right . . . this is *our* fight. The QSA pushed for a Pride *Month*, but the mayor wouldn't give us that, didn't even give us a day." My heart thrummed steadily with the possibility of taking back what we deserved. "Fu— I mean, screw him and those who helped him enact his hateful agenda. We'll celebrate Pride how we wanted to . . . all month long."

A rush of voices asked "Where?" and "How?" and "When?" as I turned toward Sawyer, Kennedy, and Cohen. They wore matching expressions that were part awe and part confusion. It made me feel like I was finally earning my spot in the QSA, being *good*, like the rest of them. That I belonged, like Carmen said.

"Follow me on Insta, 'at Zeke Chapman,'" I said over the crowd's murmurs. "I'll post details."

Then, silently to myself: *Once I figure out what the hell I'm doing.*

CHAPTER 7

The tree outside Mason's bedroom creaked as I nervously climbed down. My sneaker hesitantly stepped on the next branch, and I exhaled in relief when it held my weight. For a moment. A loud snap split through the early-morning silence. The ground rushed up to meet me, leaves slapping my face as the world blurred. I hit the flower bed with a heavy thump and tried to catch my breath.

I lay there stunned, looking up at the window I'd just snuck out of. A few beats passed as I waited for his handsome face to appear—for that same coy smile he'd given me last night, a lure that would have me climbing right back up to him again. However, it remained darkened despite my clumsy escape.

A dull ache radiated from my thigh as I gathered my bearings. Standing up, I felt a tear in my jeans and looked down at the cracked garden gnome that'd broken my fall. Last night had been a blur in the best possible way. After we cleaned up, Mason had given me directions to his house in West Point along with a promise of what we'd do. It was so spicy that I nearly beat him home.

There was still no sign of movement, and I grabbed my dirt bike from where I'd leaned it beside the tree. *Fucking gnome*, I griped, steering my ride out of the backyard with a slight limp. At least that had been the only mishap. Well, actually . . . I hadn't meant to fall asleep, but I'd thankfully woken up before him. It was obvious we were both dancing around each other's feelings last night. And it only made sense to bail before he kicked me out, even if Sawyer called this move "the Z-step."

Once I was in the clear, I checked my phone for the time. The screen read 5:53 a.m., and below that was a long list of texts and new-follower alerts from Instagram. I could only guess these were all the people waiting for details about next weekend. Which would require way more thought than I could muster now, especially after only a few hours of sleep.

If I even know what I'm doing.

Shoving my phone back into my pocket, I kick-started the engine and took off down the street. Guilt twisted in my stomach as I felt the creeping weight of the notifications. Before it could fully strike, I reminded myself of what happened last night. We'd accomplished Pride Day despite the curveball Mayor Buchanan threw at us. What my father had thrown at me when I came out.

My hands gripped the handlebars in frustration as I approached a four-way intersection. Ever since I figured out who I was, my father had been scaring me into submission. If he'd had his way, the speakeasy wouldn't have happened. I wouldn't have said anything at the square. I wouldn't have even come out. But with the promise of more speakeasies, it felt like I was finally facing that fear.

Slowing to a stop, I checked both ways and noticed familiar red writing in a salon's window. Chapman Law stared out at me from the Family First poster. Memories of yesterday morning flooded my mind, and it only pissed me off more.

I steered my dirt bike over to the curb and threw down the kickstand. The engine shut off, the sudden silence ringing in my ears. I swung my leg over and marched toward the poster without second-guessing myself. The message in red ink got louder with each step. So loud I couldn't hear anything else as I reached up and it tore off the glass.

Breathing heavy, I ripped it to shreds and threw them to the ground. Then I saw another one on the boutique next door. And on the store next to it.

Anger fueled me down the sidewalk, shredding poster after poster. Each tear sounded like a cheer, applause, the whoops Mason had yelled last night. Shredding the mayor's strategy to win reelection felt like the ultimate fuck-you to this town and its hate. To my father and the confines I'd been forced to exist in. Because this was my fight too, just like Carmen had declared.

. . .

"Zeke, where have you been?"

My heart hammered against my chest as I jumped, banging my head on the window frame. One leg was still on the fire escape, the other on my bedroom floor. *Damn it!* Wincing, I turned to see Mom standing in my bedroom doorway.

"I, uh . . ." She crossed her arms as I searched for a fast excuse. There was no way in hell I could tell her the truth. It would only lead to yet another sex talk. Before seven a.m. After two injuries involving sneaking through windows. "I went out . . . for a walk?"

"All night?" she replied, her lips pursing. She knew she'd caught me in a lie. "Because you never came home, and I tried calling."

"You did?" She nodded, and I grimaced. "Sorry, I didn't see a missed call in my notifications." *Because they've been blasting since last night.*

"Correct me if I'm wrong," she began as I slipped inside, "but isn't your curfew eleven p.m.?"

"Is it?" I asked with an apologetic grin. "I thought with it being summer and—"

"Don't you dare try to sweet-talk your way out of this like your father," she said with a half-hearted scoff. "You're not nearly as good at it as he is."

I knew she was joking, but my chest deflated as I sat down on the edge of my bed. "Sorry," I mumbled, feeling the ick of being compared to him.

"Where were you?" Before I could answer, she added, "You weren't fighting again, were you?" She scoured my face for signs of a scuffle.

"No, I was with Sawyer," I admitted, which technically wasn't a lie. "We were working late with a QSA . . . meeting . . . and I accidentally fell asleep." Another technical truth.

Seeming to buy it, she leaned against the doorframe. "He keeps calling me," she said as she massaged her temples. "Because you keep sending him straight to voicemail."

"Ugh," I groaned, falling back across the bedspread. "One, nobody talks on the phone anymore. And even if I did . . . I blocked his number."

"Zeke."

"Mom."

"He's still your father."

"I'm not his son," I said, rolling over to look at her. "I want nothing to do with him."

"Unfortunately, he's in your life—"

"Until I turn eighteen next month." She gave me a look that could have meant one of two things: I understand but cannot approve of your brave fight against that asshole, or it's funny you're about to be of age but still act like a child. I shrugged it off and looked back up at the ceiling. "What did he want anyway?"

"He said he saw you at Pride Day yesterday."

"I saw him there too," I grumbled, remembering how he'd turned his back to me. "Being a total dickwad."

"He's worried about you." Her words came out strained, and I knew she was fighting to be civil. "Especially after yesterday. Are you okay?"

"My head hurts," I said. "And my leg. But that's totally unrelated."

"I meant with Pride Day being canceled."

"Oh. That." If the speakeasy hadn't happened, would I be okay? Probably not, but I was definitely livid either way. "It was shitty how he was there to help cancel it. He's big mad I joined the QSA and helped with Pride Day after him telling me not to."

"He's concerned about you, that's all. Take it from me, he

doesn't do a good job of showing that he cares." She frowned, breathing out heavily. "Look, I hate being put in the middle like this. He wants to talk to you. With your grades and college to think about—"

"That's too bad." I cut her off, and she shook her head sadly. "What?"

"Hun, you have to talk to him. He's your father, and he has the right to be worried about you."

"What about my rights?" I questioned. "This whole Family First bullshit he's supporting?"

"I saw that on one of those posters," she said, sadness filling her eyes. "Someone hung one on the shop window downstairs." The still-simmering rage had me up off the bed. Ready to march down there and tear it down like all the others. She held a hand up to stop me. "Don't worry, I've already trashed it."

"Oh . . ."

I hesitated as she stepped farther into the room. She walked toward me and gave me a hug, my chin resting on her head. "Zeke, I'm sorry about what's happening. I'm sorry I didn't stand up for you better when you came out to us. I'm sorry it took me three years to finally do it."

The trembles of her voice reverberated in my chest. "It's whatever, Mom," I offered, but she shushed me.

"It's not *whatever*." Her tone was decisive as she pulled back to look at me. As though she'd rehearsed this countless times. "I thought I was nothing without your father, too scared of him leaving me to see how scared you were, and I won't let that happen anymore. You're my son, and I'll do everything I can to fight for you. Because I'm proud of you."

"You are?" My voice came out in a whisper, and I was fearful she'd take it back.

She nodded as she wiped at her eyes. "Everything you've done with the QSA, even if they canceled your Pride Day celebration. You're invested in something again, like who you used to be."

"I'm nothing like *him*."

"You're still the boy who helped me in the garage." She sighed softly, like she was remembering all those times it was just us. "You cared so deeply about fixing things and working with your hands to put everything back together. That's what I'm talking about. That's who I remember, not the young man your father tried to mold you into."

I thought of the spark plug I'd put on the dresser next to the picture of us. It was proof that I was her son too. That part of me had been hidden away with all the others. It was hard to remember with how my father's loud opinions drowned everything else out. I'd resented her for letting him push us around, but she and I were more like strangers now. It felt like I was getting to know her all over again. I could remember how she was as loud and rebellious as Zelda Fitzgerald, capable of fixing things too. And she was trying to fix the past even though it was complicated. That had to count for something.

"Even though you've grown so much since then," she continued, "you're still just a kid, okay? You might think you're tough, but bad things can happen if you aren't careful, especially if you're using a rusty old fire escape to sneak in."

"I'm always careful, Mom," I promised, despite the ache from falling that morning.

"That might be the funniest joke you've told," she deadpanned, pointing a finger at me. "No more sneaking around."

"Thanks, I try," I said with a laugh to dodge her latter statement. Because the Pride speakeasies would require copious amounts of sneakery. There was a chance she'd understand why I wanted to do them. I couldn't risk it, though.

"With that settled, how about I make us some pancakes?" My stomach immediately rumbled at the thought of food. "I'll take that as a yes," she surmised, pushing me toward the door. "Go wash up and— Hang on." Her eyes lingered on where I'd landed on that gnome. "Why are your jeans ripped?"

"No clue," I blurted quickly, backing into the hallway.

Last night had been fun. So had this morning with Mason. But I didn't want to explain *any* of the last twelve hours to her. It finally felt like I was taking charge of my life, especially if it was pissing my father off. *Even more reason to start planning for next weekend.* I grabbed my phone from my pocket and fired off a quick text to the group chat.

QS-SLAY!

ZEKE:

Meet tomorrow? We have to plan for Saturday ➤

CHAPTER 8

My name is Bronwen with the library, and
we'd like to offer our third floor for Pride.

The Instagram message had burned in my mind since yesterday. It was an answer to a question I hadn't thought to ask. An
answer that had my mind sprinting ahead to next Saturday as I
steered my dirt bike along the streets in search of a plan.

"We'll only do it if there's some privacy," Sawyer said decid-
edly, passing my phone to Kennedy.

With a deep breath, I glanced up at her from my spot on the
bachelorette pad floor. I had to bite my tongue instead of saying she didn't get to make that call. "Actually," I began evenly,
"I checked it out last night. There aren't any windows up there,
and the back entrance is hidden from view. It wouldn't be sus."

I stuffed a handful of yogurt-covered raisins into my mouth
and chewed aggressively. They were my favorite, and Sawyer's

mom knew to keep the pantry stocked for me. Between chomps, my neck prickled as Cohen stared me down with narrowed eyes. It was like the last time we were down here—him looking straight through me. He absently pulled at the collar of his polo, revealing a peek of chest hair that hadn't been there three years ago.

"Like what you see, Coco?" I teased, even though he could've asked me the same.

Rather than disregarding me, as he was prone to do, he cleared his throat as his ears reddened. "You're disgusting," he muttered, shifting his gaze to the raisins. "I didn't think anyone *actually* ate those."

I shoved more in my mouth and offered him the open bag with a wink. "Want some?"

"Hard pass," he said instead of picking a fight.

Something was off with him. That trademark glower was gone, and in its place was too much thoughtfulness. I knew that look, had worn that look often since December. If he hadn't made us enemies, maybe I'd ask if he was okay. Maybe I'd be more worried about him instead of relieved he wasn't giving me the third degree.

"I think we should do it," Kennedy said, snapping my attention away from Cohen. She pulled her hair into a loose ponytail, her yellow nails bright against her dark twist braids. "What do you think, Co?"

He glanced at me again and sighed. "The third floor is a wide-open auditorium with a stage," he said without enthusiasm. "It would technically work."

Sawyer tilted her head to the side in confusion. "How do you know that?" she asked.

"I read for the children's story-time hour last spring," he explained, and then he cut his eyes toward me again. "Let me stop you before you give me hell. Yes, I volunteered there. Yes, I'm trying to round out my college apps for the fall. Yes, I did like it."

I should have snapped back at him, anything to knock him out of his weird mood. But the dread of going back to Beggs High to start senior year felt like a kick in the balls. *Not today*, I told myself, refusing to think about the future. What mattered was now, what we were doing for Pride Month. That much I could control.

"Then it's decided," Sawyer said, taking charge as usual. "We'll have it at the library."

"What she said," I muttered, grabbing my phone. "I'll, um, let them know."

"But it's monitored by the security patrol," Cohen added with a warning tone. My fingers stilled on the touchscreen, and I could tell by the waver in his voice that he was still shook. "Someone will most def notice everyone coming in."

"Fair," Kennedy agreed.

"Z," Sawyer began, "didn't your mom have a plan for that with her grand opening?"

"Uh . . ."

I thought back to March and how Mom had set up the lobby like a store called Zelda's Music Emporium. She'd stocked the shelves with her old CD collection and assigned me as the guard since I was too young to attend. When guests arrived in their Roaring Twenties fits, they had to ask if we had any albums from this old girl group called the Spice Girls. Only then were they allowed to enter.

"She had a fake music store with a password."

"We need a cover story like that," Sawyer said thoughtfully with focus mode etched on her face.

"But it's a library," Kennedy pointed out.

I chewed on my lip as I tried to think, and I watched Sawyer do the same. My gaze fell down to her faded blue shirt with the NEHS acronym peeling off. She'd had it since we were inducted into the National English Honor Society. I'd since gotten kicked out, all because of Shakespeare's *Twelfth Night*. Failing that test had been the start of my streak of bad grades, but I did remember enough of it. How the main character had disguised herself to get her way . . .

"What if," I started, a plan forming, "we tell people to dress up as their favorite book character? No one would suspect it was a Pride event then."

"That's . . . that's really smart," Cohen said, a note of shock in his tone.

"I know." I grinned with satisfaction, knowing I'd proved him wrong, and turned to Sawyer. "Then you could go as Captain Jaymes Catz *and* do your drag routine since you didn't get to."

"Say less," she said with an excited clap of her hands. "We'll need to welcome everyone and then have the other drag performers I'd lined up for Pride Day and . . . has anyone seen my tablet? I need to take this down."

Kennedy dug in her tote bag to retrieve a pen and notebook. "Here, just use this," she said, handing them to Sawyer. "And write down that we should see if any of the QSA community supporters want to set up a table. The third floor is big enough."

"Then we can do our original plan," Sawyer said as she scribbled. "I could start the drag show. Does that work?"

A beat passed before I realized she'd directed her question at me. I nodded in agreement, stunned that she was deferring to me now. "We could even borrow the decorations from the shop's grand opening," I suggested, "and since we already have a stage . . . maybe someone could talk to the crowd again, like Carmen did?"

Sawyer smiled reassuringly. "I think that's a wonderful idea, Zeke." I shrugged it off, but she held her hand to her chest. "I'm proud of you, titty promise. You're really stepping up."

"Thanks," I said, a blush heating my cheeks.

From my periphery, I could see Cohen staring at me again. I refused to give in and look. To see just how much he disagreed with her. Instead, I put my hands behind my head and stared up at the popcorn ceiling. My eyes roamed the ridges as I forced down any traces of doubt.

. . .

Two hours later, we'd finally sorted all the details for Saturday. The library was on board with what we had planned, and all that was left to do was make a post about it . . . without making a post about it. Kennedy had said to be inconspicuous, and Cohen returned to form with a smartass remark. *It means to not attract attention,* he'd said. *Put your Insta on private like mine.* I'd reminded him that we purposefully unfollowed each other years ago, and he hadn't spoken since.

I glanced over at the corner of the sofa while I scrolled on my phone. He was doing the same, the glower back in place like it had never left. The tension was excruciating, growing stronger by the second. I checked the time and realized that Sawyer and Kennedy had gone to get the pizza delivery more than thirty minutes ago.

Ugh, I groaned inwardly as my stomach rumbled. Unable

to keep scrolling, to keep pretending like Cohen wasn't sitting there stewing, I cleared my throat. It was too loud in the too-quiet basement, and he startled. "They've been gone waaay too long," I said awkwardly. "I bet they're totally making out again."

"Just now figuring that out?" he asked. The sarcasm was half-hearted at best. "They'll be at it for another fifteen minutes, at least, before they realize they left us down here."

"Right, right . . ."

He made a noncommittal grunt as his fingers typed on his phone. I watched his brow unfurl. For a moment I could see the Cohen I remembered. The same guy beneath the asshole personality who'd made my brain glitch.

"Who do you think you'll be for the speakeasy?" I asked, unable to handle the dead air between us.

"Dunno."

Strike one, I thought, closing my eyes. "Well, I might go as Zelda Fitzgerald." I'd given it some thought ever since we'd come up with the idea, and the painting of her in Mom's shop kept coming to mind. "My mom has a dress and wig from the grand opening I could use."

"She's not a character, Zeke," he pointed out, shooting me an annoyed glance. "She was an actual person."

Strike two. I inhaled, exhaled through the unrelenting urge to punch the condescension off his face. "Correction," I tried again calmly. "She played the character people wanted her to . . . a goddess of chaos, the first American flapper. It was really because of the time frame and her upbringing, but I think it was all for show . . . What?"

His mouth was agape. "Nothing," he muttered, red splotches spreading across his cheeks. "Just forgot you used to be smart."

"Strike three," I bit out, turning to face him on the sofa. "What the *hell* is your problem?"

He blinked rapidly, and I could practically see his thoughts racing. Ripples of that guy I used to know, who he turned into, someone else entirely new who was too serious all of a sudden. "Zeke," he said through a breath. "Don't start with me."

"You started it, Coco," I seethed. "Despite what you said, I'm actually trying to be a *good gay* and you keep trashing me. What gives?"

"Sorry," he muttered. His warm brown eyes studied me for a moment before he swallowed roughly. "I shouldn't have put you down like that, and I apologize."

"Seriously, stop." I gestured wildly at him, the newfound civility cringe-inducing. "You're being weird as hell right now."

He started to say something, a rebuttal on the tip of his tongue. Then he stopped himself and shook his head. "I can't go Saturday," he finally said, glancing down at his lap.

"That's okay. You can help with the next—"

"No." He cut me off. "I don't think it's a good idea."

The audacity. After everything he'd called me out on, every hard truth he'd thrown at me? How I didn't do enough for the QSA, how I don't pay attention to the laws trying to erase us, how Pride was about something *more*—and he didn't think my idea was good enough?

"Why?" I asked, my voice biting. "I know you were freaked because of the cop, and I understand. If we do get caught, you can blame everything on me. Everyone else does."

He was giving me a stare down again, all the versions of him flickering as he considered what I said. I'd thought he saw the real me before, but now I knew it was the opposite. I was seeing the real him. And he was nervous and scared.

"I appreciate you saying that, really," he began, his words pillowed in softness, "but I can't risk my future. Not like this. I already told Kennedy, but . . . I'm volunteering with Carmen's campaign. Plus, I'm working at The Cove and—"

"You asked me if I was paying attention," I blurted. He was too concerned about his perfect college applications. Too much like how I used to be. "But are *you*? What we're doing is important."

"I didn't say it *wasn't*." He sighed heavily. "I think we can change more minds on the inside, and helping the campaign will do that. Pride is about more than throwing parties, Zeke. You would know that if you did more with the QSA when we needed you, not now when it's convenient."

If he'd said that earlier, I might've decked him right on the spot. There was no winning with him. I knew he was anxious. I couldn't fault him for that when I was as well. It didn't stop the sting of his words, though.

"Nothing about this is convenient, Cohen," I pointed out.

"Look"—he tugged at his collar again, and his shoulders slumped—"I'm glad you finally felt comfortable to come out and get involved for *whatever* reason, but I'm worried, okay? What if you get caught and the speakeasies hurt our cause? That'd only give Mayor Buchanan ammunition to use against us."

I opened my mouth to argue, but I knew what he said wasn't a lie. That didn't make his digs hurt less.

CHAPTER 9

If you did more...

I leaned back in my chair and took a deep breath. Inhaling the grease-saturated air in the Roaring Mechanics lobby, exhaling until my lungs burned.

My eyes grew heavy, the AC an escape from the hot garage. I slumped down farther in the chair with a groan. The entirety of my body was sore from unloading a shipment of tires earlier. The extra muscle I'd put on from baseball was gone, and now I felt weak in more ways than one.

I blinked slowly up at the *Montgomery Evening News* playing on the mounted TV. The drone of the reporter's voice mixed with the soft music playing from Sawyer's phone. She'd taken charge of the decorations Mom said we could use for the "QSA event," throwing out all my suggestions so far. I'd just finished untangling the string lights she decided we needed, but there were so many boxes left to go through. And sleep was catching up with me.

My eyelids fluttered, and Cohen's voice ricocheted—

"I'm obsessed with Chappell Roan's new album," Sawyer said suddenly. I startled upright and rubbed at my face. "Like fully prepared to make it my entire personality for the foreseeable future."

"Can't wait for her fall tour," I said with a yawn, shaking my head to wake up.

"About that . . ." Sawyer trailed off as I reached for another box, biting her lip in thought. She'd been doing that for the last few hours, as though she wanted to say something but didn't know how.

"What about it?" I asked.

"On a scale of only-slightly-pissed to butthurt," she started, pink spreading across her cheeks as she unpacked a beaded curtain, "how bad would you feel if I went to the concert without you?"

"Hella," I said pointedly. Concerts were part of our list of traditions, a platonic bestie date. "We're *supposed* to see our favorites together. Reneé Rapp, Charli xcx, Omar Apollo . . ." I then remembered just how much those tickets had cost. Mom was barely making ends meet, and I couldn't ask for more allowance like I had in the past. "But I'll let it slide *if* you have a good reason, I guess."

"I do." Sawyer held up a glittering mirror ball. Green shimmers danced in the overhead lighting, shining across her shy smile. "Kennedy loves her too . . . and if she says yes to being my girlfriend this weekend, then, you know . . ."

I nodded, my sleep-deprived brain slow on the uptake. Then my hands stilled while unpacking an inflatable archway. "Wait. Wait, wait, wait." I blinked a few times as her words sank in. "You're *finally* asking her to be official?"

"Yep," she said, popping the *P*. Her coyness twisted into an excited grin. "Last night, she said she was ready to stop hiding. And all I could picture was walking down the hallway at school, her hand in mine, not giving a damn what anyone says."

That was all Cohen had wanted, for me to be bold with him. "That's great, Saw!" I exclaimed with too much pep, to hide the twinge of regret.

"It feels high-key dumb to be nervous about it now, especially after all I'm doing with the QSA's Pride events."

"I'm the one—"

"And if she says no," she carried on, "promise you'll go to the concert with me? And scream until our voices are hoarse? And let me buy as much merch as I want?"

I nodded in agreement rather than correcting her on who, in fact, started these QSA Pride events. She'd only get defensive, and arguing about it would only make me feel worse. The QSA, the petition for Pride, having my back all these years— she deserved the recognition too.

"But she'll say yes," I assured her, nudging her knee. "Just promise me that you two won't be that cutesy couple who do everything together and leave me fending for myself."

"Please," she scoffed, but there was the hint of a laugh in her voice. "Who knows, maybe you'll upgrade one of your boys into an *actual* boyfriend, and we can all hang out."

"You've been writing way too much fanfic," I deadpanned, "and are obviously delusional."

"What about that guy you were dancing with last weekend?" The music cut off, a new-message notification sounding. "Mason Bedolla, right?"

I felt heat coil in my stomach and a ghost ache from that damned gnome. "He was fun . . . but I doubt I'll see him again."

"If you'd stop dicking around and let someone get to know you"—she glanced up while her thumbs tapped on her phone screen—"it might be something you want."

"We're absolutely not gonna talk about this."

I rolled my eyes, and she stuck her tongue out at me. *Do I want that, though?* The last time I got close to someone it'd backfired so shit-tacularly that I got burned. Besides, I had more important things to worry about now.

"But *I'll* make sure this weekend is epic for you," I added, digging my phone from my jeans pocket. "Insta has been popping off about it."

"How many people do you think will be there?" she asked.

Opening Instagram, I checked my latest post. The four slides were pictures of a pride flag, the square's pavilion clock reading nine p.m., the public library, and a Halloween meme. I'd captioned it with "already thinking about this year's costume 😊 maybe my favorite character? ••"

"Fifty so far," I announced. She had been worried it was too subtle at first, but I posted it anyway. And I was right to do so. Comment after comment of pride flag emojis racked up. Most of them were businesses in town, some people I hadn't met. "I think we could get way more..."

A banner notification across the top of the screen distracted me. The Beggs Rec Center had just sent me a DM. Sawyer said something about too many people being risky, and I absently mumbled a "Yeah" as I clicked to read it.

BEGGSRECCENTER:
Hi Zeke, the mayor has threatened to pull
funding for our kids' program because it's

LGBTQIA+ inclusive. Your "underground"
Pride month has inspired us to continue
it regardless. I'd like to invite you to come
check it out tomorrow in hopes you'll
volunteer. Let me know if you can make it!
—Jess

Relief eased the tension in my chest. At least someone
thought I wasn't hurting the QSA's cause. A grin tugged at
the corners of my mouth, that spark Cohen had dampened re-
igniting. *Yes, I can definitely make it!* I typed. But the self-doubt
that'd been hassling me all day stopped my thumb from tapping send. Was I even qualified to go?

"Hey, Saw," I began, in hopes she'd encourage me, "what do
you think about—"

A loud thwack sounded as she kicked at a roll of green carpet. "What a flaccid dickhead," she yelled, waving her hands
angrily at the TV. I followed her gaze to where the news report
was covering the Alabama governor's homophobic campaign
messaging. "Can you believe this education reform bullshit?"

She looked at me expectantly, and I froze before glancing back at the *Montgomery Evening News*. "Yeah, um, total
bullshit," I agreed, even though I didn't understand.

"He can call it what he wants, but he's trying to erase all
traces of queer history in the classroom," Sawyer went on.
"And the corrupt Supreme Court of Dipshits won't do anything about it."

The name of the proposed education bill filled the screen.
It was a mishmash of numbers and letters. I'd never really paid
attention to the news before we moved out of the old house.

The hate couldn't reach me inside my shoebox. But now? How was I supposed to know every single bad thing happening in the world?

"I can't deal with this," Sawyer said, turning away from the TV. "Sorry, what were you about to ask?"

"Oh, um."

I fidgeted with my phone, unsure if I should tell her I wanted to volunteer. What if she wrote me off because I didn't fully comprehend the magnitude of what was happening? What if Cohen was right?

"Do you think the speakeasies could hurt the QSA's cause?" I asked quietly.

She pushed her wire-frame glasses up on her nose and shook her head. "Don't let what Cohen said get to you, okay? I get why he's worried, but we deserve to have fun too. And you were having fun, right?"

"Fun," I echoed, remembering what it had felt like in the bookstore's basement. How I'd been free to be myself and dance with Mason. How it didn't matter if I was the best worst type of gay or not. "You're right, we deserve to have fun."

"And for all anyone else knows," she added with a reassuring grin, "we're just having a party."

Pride is about more than throwing parties, Zeke.

Cohen's dig shot through me. Doubt threatened to creep in as I eyed the abundance of decorations surrounding us. We *were* throwing a party, but it was more than that. It'd inspired the Beggs Rec Center to stand up against the mayor too. That had to mean *something*. And I had to prove to myself that I could do more.

I unlocked my phone and tapped send on the reply.

CHAPTER 10

The shimmery moss shade of the dress made the blue of my eyes shine. Its neckline scooped low, and the little chest hair I had poked out. Pearlescent beading covered the bodice and fringed at the hemline—the incredibly short hemline.

Everyone's gonna see my junk.

I watched the mirror on my bedroom door and jumped around. Shimmied side to side. Shook my ass with a clacking of beads. Nothing of prominence slipped out, and it'd work for the speakeasy. Even if the degree of leg it showed was revealing. So much so that my mind wandered to Mason and whether he'd be there to witness how much thigh I was displaying. I hadn't stopped thinking about him since Sawyer grilled me about never getting too close to anyone.

I studied my reflection. Mom had called it a flapper dress. If someone had told me back in December that I'd be fearlessly wearing one, I wouldn't have believed them. Here I was, though, donning it proudly in my new bedroom.

Technically it wasn't *new*, I guess.

There had to be a time limit on how long I could keep calling it that. It still felt like we'd just moved in, like Mom had just promised this was only temporary. Now, after six months in this alternate universe, I was still unsure where pieces of my old life fit in it.

I eyed the room behind me, the button-up and khakis draped over my bed. I'd pulled them out of a box marked JACASS CLOTHES to wear to the rec center, but they looked wrong in the space. The person I'd once been didn't belong in this new life. It was like working in the mechanic shop, how sometimes broken parts had to be replaced to keep an engine running. How I could switch out bad memories for new ones.

I'm still Zeke, I reminded myself, staring at the pile of clothes I'd changed out of. A thrifted T-shirt with a faded four-leaf clover, worn-in jeans, Converse sneakers—it all made me who I was now. Less restricted, freer. *Dressing up for the rec center won't change that.*

My phone lit up from the jeans pocket, and I turned from the mirror to check the notification. The dress definitely showed my ass when I bent over; I'd have to remember that if Mason did show up. The screen flashed with new-message reminders. Sawyer had double-texted me ten minutes ago.

TODAY AT 4:53 PM

SAWYER

QSA meeting tonight?

Kennedy's coming over and we need to
finish details for the speakeasy

I started to type a response, telling her what I had planned
tonight. But I backspaced and deleted it. It was something I
had decided to do on my own, and I couldn't risk her talking
me out of it. Or worse, tagging along and taking charge.

ZEKE

busy tonight but maybe tomorrow?

SAWYER
okay . . . ?

I knew she was waiting for an explanation, but there wasn't
enough time to invent a cover story. I still had to shower and
change. Leaving her on read, I tossed the phone back onto the
pile of clothes and—

"Hey, hun," Mom's voice abruptly called out.

Her footsteps sounded down the hallway, and I gulped.
My attention snapped back to the mirror, back to the dress
I'd snuck from her closet. Panic set in as I rushed to grab my
clothes to change.

"How do you feel about spaghetti for dinner?" she asked,
her voice too close, and then the bedroom doorknob rattled.

"It's for a costume party," I nearly shouted as she stepped
into the room.

"What?" she asked, slow to register what I was wearing.

Then she shot me an amused expression. "Well, that's just not fair."

"Huh?"

"It looks better on you than it did on me." She laughed and shook her head, blond waves tumbling. "It's supposed to be loose, but you really fill it out."

"Sorry, I should've asked first. I, uh, wanted to dress up as Zelda Fitzgerald," I explained nervously. "For a, um, QSA thing on Saturday."

"Here, let me help you."

She stepped toward me as I stood stock-still. Then she was zipping up the dress's back, the metal clicking loud in between my heartbeats. The bodice grew snug at my waist and even more snug across my chest. I exhaled through the tightness and looked in the mirror again, at her smiling face behind me.

"I have some jewelry you can wear with it," she began, running her hand through my hair, "but I don't think you'll need the wig since you've let yours grow long. Just the headband should work."

"Th-thanks," I stammered, watching her watch me.

Her eyes were crinkly with a smile. And I knew that look. It was the same one she'd given me after I changed my first spark plug in the family SUV. Maybe we hadn't come so far from who we used to be. Maybe I could replace the bad memories we had with better ones too.

"So spaghetti?" she asked.

"That sounds great to me," I replied, turning to face her. "I'm going to volunteer at the rec center, but I'll be home by seven."

"Volunteer?"

"For their LGBTQIA-plus kids' program. The mayor's trying to cut their funding, and I want to help."

She took a second to study me, her eyes drifting up to the rainbow flag above my bed. "I love that you're still trying to fix things." Her hand was soft as she patted my cheek.

"I'm . . . I'm trying."

My face heated as she held my gaze, and then she stepped back. "While you're gone, I think I might head over to the bookstore and get the Women of Beggs Book Club pick. Some of my old girlfriends reached out about it." She winked and motioned for me to turn around. "Might have to pull a Zeke and keep my phone on silent so I can read. It has been ringing all day."

I felt myself smiling, both happy and sad, as she unzipped the dress. Happy that she was doing something for herself, sad that I couldn't remember if she ever had before opening the mechanic shop. Maybe I was starting to understand her better, that she was figuring herself out—how she was just a person, like me.

She excused herself so I could change, footfalls fading toward the living room. I grabbed my phone from my discarded clothes to check the time. The screen flashed 5:23 p.m. along with another text from Sawyer that I couldn't deal with. I needed to leave soon to make it on time.

I slipped the dress off in a hurry and yanked on the khakis. Then I buttoned up the shirt, shoved my feet into the maroon sneakers, and shuffled out of my room. As I made my way down the hallway, a whimsical bell echoed through the apartment. The old landline used for shop business was ringing from the makeshift office.

"Could you get that for me?" Mom called. "Tell them I'm not here!"

I yelled back that I had it and veered into the dinette. The bell sounded again with a third ring as I grabbed the clunky handle. "Hello," I answered quickly. "Roaring Mechanics is closed for the day, and Katherine Chapman isn't here."

"Anthony?"

I nearly dropped the phone at the sound of my first name, my father's voice. It was smooth, cheerful yet serious, and full of artificial sweetness. "What do you want?" I asked, my tone dropping low so Mom wouldn't hear.

"I've been trying to get ahold of your mother since you won't answer my calls," he said. "Son, we need to talk."

"There's nothing to talk about," I said, gripping the phone tightly.

"There is *plenty.*" He took a breath, waiting for a reply I wasn't going to give him. "For starters, you destroyed my billboard, which was expensive to replace. Not to mention your grades are embarrassing, and then this nonsense with the QSA—"

"Why?" I cut him off. "Why are you sponsoring this Family First bullshit?"

"Anthony," he began with a heavy sigh, "don't be immature. The mayor's plan won't affect you if you'll just keep your head down and stay out of it. You have to understand it's just business, nothing personal—"

"And you have to understand that you can't tell me what to do anymore," I said, then slammed the receiver down.

. . .

I walked it off, my feet slapping the sidewalk. The nerve of him to think I still cared what he thought. To think he could gaslight me after the hell he'd put me through. My strides lengthened as I hurried to the rec center with determination. What I'd done for Pride Month had inspired them to refute the mayor's agenda. And, in turn, my father for supporting him.

It's just business, he'd said. *Nothing personal.*

It sure as hell felt personal as the June sun bore down on me. Mayor Buchanan, even the state governor, had made everything feel like it was targeted specifically at my existence. Like I was trapped underneath a magnifying glass of laws and hate and ignorance that scorched me. I didn't know what to do about it or how I could even help. But I did know I couldn't go back to being a silent bystander.

My pace slowed as I reached the stairs leading up to the rec center's entrance. It wasn't that far from Roaring Mechanics, but I felt like I'd just run a marathon. My shirt was damp, with circles of sweat under my pits, my hair sticking to my neck. I took the steps slowly as I wiped my face with the back of my hand, tried to smooth the wrinkles from the button-up, anything to make it look like I had my shit together.

The glass entrance chimed as the panels slid open, and I stepped inside. A blast of AC hit me in the face, a reprieve from the humidity. *Fourth floor.* I reminded myself of the details they'd sent, and headed toward the elevator. *Room 13.*

Before the metal doors closed, someone stepped inside without giving me a second glance. There was no mistaking Cohen's wide shoulders and perpetually messy hair, the way his chinos fit pleasingly snug. I opened my mouth to antagonize him, still pissy over what he'd said, but his smile stopped me. It dimpled his cheeks as he typed on his phone.

For a second I admired how attractive he could be when he

wasn't making my life a nightmare. Then reality came crashing back as he looked up, shock making him stand up straighter. "What're *you* doing here?" he asked bluntly.

The overhead light flickered as the cab climbed upward. It washed over us, shining into his soft brown eyes. I tried to think of something clever, but it was like freshman year all over again—my brain glitching as he stared at me.

"Volunteering," I blurted. "For the kids' program."

He gaped at me with disbelief as if he was waiting for the punch line. "*You're* here to volunteer?"

"They, uh, they messaged me about it. On Insta, I mean. Because of the mayor."

I thought he'd be happy I was doing more, that he might say he now knew I was paying attention. He didn't, though. "Are you fucking kidding me?" he griped. His face twisted with disdain as the doors opened to the fourth floor. "No, you can't."

"Excuse me?" He rushed out without a reply, and I followed after him. His messenger bag flopped side to side as he marched down the hallway. "Cohen, what the hell?" I called.

He came to a halt and spun to face me. "I'm talking to Jess. There's no way you can volunteer here, Zeke."

"Yes I can—"

"No, you can't," he said again. There was a severe tilt to his chin as he stared up at me. "I've been a mentor for two years here, and this is too important for you to screw up."

"I know it is," I asserted quickly, grabbing his arm to stop him.

"The threat to cut funding is real," he said in a hiss, "and Jess has already dealt with too much grief for being trans. You'll only ruin everything with your Zasshole attitude."

"No, I won't—"

"But you will." His eyes narrowed, and he pulled away from me. "These kids need a role model, someone they can talk to and rely on like Jess, especially with all the bullshit happening."

"I know—"

"You don't—"

"Will you let me talk?" I asked in exasperation, and he threw his hands up. "I *know* this is serious, and I want to help . . . I want . . . to be the type of person who could've been there for me." My admission was a timid whisper, and it sent my heart fluttering.

He opened his mouth, closed it, struggled for words. "We're here to mentor them," he finally said, grasping the strap of his bag. "Help with schoolwork and answer questions because their teachers aren't allowed to discuss LGBTQIA-plus topics in the classroom. They need someone on their side. You can't . . ." He looked down at his canvas sneakers. "You can't do to them what you did to me."

"What?"

"Pretend to care and then just shut yourself off."

Though I was taller than him, he was staring down at me. As if I were shrinking, my excitement deflating. His gaze sent heat blazing across my cheeks. The same scorned embarrassment I'd felt when he quickly moved on to Geometry Derick. He still saw what he wanted to see when he looked at me. Between the phone call with my father and now this, my temper was blazing like the heat outside.

"Cohen," I began, fighting to keep my voice low, "you don't get to make me feel like shit because *you don't know me*. You don't know what my father is like, or why I was so afraid—" I cut myself off, blinking furiously. *Shit.* I hadn't intended to spill my guts.

"W-what do you mean?" he stammered. "Afraid of what?"

"It doesn't matter because I'm *here* now to make up for all the times I couldn't be." I took a deep breath and squared my shoulders. Leaned in toward him, closer, until I could count each of his long eyelashes. "You told me to do more, but you won't even let me try. So take your pretentious attitude and shove it up your ass. I don't care if you hate me, not anymore."

A flush spread up his neck, and he murmured, "I don't hate you."

"Could have fooled me." I brushed passed him and continued down the hallway.

"Wait," he called. "Your dad . . . Is that why you ended things? Zeke, don't walk away. Can we just talk—"

"Why do you even care?" I tossed back.

My eyes were welling up, but I refused to acknowledge it. He'd keep discounting me no matter how much I tried to be like him and Sawyer and Kennedy. *Not anymore*, I swore, opening the door to Room 13.

The first thing I noticed was the giant pride flag hanging from the ceiling, the next thing was laughter coming from the tables. The program had already started, with groups spread out around the room. A buzz of excitement was in the air— a giant exhale as the kids worked with their mentors. They held their heads high instead of keeping their faces down. Instead of holding their breath inside a shoebox like I had. Instead of being afraid, despite the threat in Beggs.

That was when I knew my father was wrong. The mayor's ordinance affected more than just me and the QSA. More than I could have ever understood until now.

CHAPTER 11

"**W**here were you last night?"

Sawyer's fingers clacked on the keyboard as she checked reservations. I was seated on the floor behind the elaborate host desk at The Cove, and the Friday dinner rush was set to arrive at any moment. She'd begged me to come hang but had been lobbing questions at me since I got here. "You had a 'D appointment' with Mason instead of helping me plan for tomorrow, didn't you?" she continued, eyeing me over her glasses.

"Nooo," I said through a mouthful of breadstick I'd swiped from the kitchen.

I had tried to clear my head on the walk home from the rec center. Tried to forget how Cohen had called my name as I left. The way he'd said it had made me walk faster. I didn't have it in me to deal with his hot-and-cold attitude, not after making up my mind to help mentor.

"Besides, I haven't even talked to Mason since we fell

asleep . . ." I trailed off, thinking about the unopened Instagram message I'd received late last night.

The DM had popped up moments after I approved a follow request from the private profile bedmas_22, and the preview was just a simple "hey." Given the username, I knew it had to be Mason Bedolla. I'd gotten messages like that before, knew the fun places they'd lead. But every time I went to open it, I stopped myself. Because what was the use? Mason was only interested in the person he thought I was that night . . . or his parents wanted to know why their gnome was destroyed.

I took another bite of breadstick, chewing as I thought. Then I realized it was quiet. Too quiet. I looked up at Sawyer, and her mouth was agape. "What?" I asked.

"You withheld just how *much* fun you had with him that night, and now you're just gonna drop that tidbit without any context?" she asked, swiveling in her chair to face me. "Like by sleep do you mean . . . ?" She made a crude gesture with her fingers that wasn't anatomically possible.

"Give each other a secret handshake?" I joked, and she gave me an annoyed kick with her Doc. "Okay, fine. We might've engaged in . . . extracurricular activities. And I might've slept over. It's a long story that ends with a garden gnome breaking my fall and—"

"You stayed?" She cut me off.

"Not intentionally," I said, rubbing my shin.

"So *are* you gonna let him get to know you?"

"I dunno . . ."

"Then you're gonna Z-step him?"

"I. Don't. Know," I enunciated, throwing the breadstick at her in annoyance. "It was *one* time. I think it's best if I avoid him . . . Why are you giving me angry eyebrows right now?"

"Because you're doing it again," she began with a level gaze. "The whole avoidance thing. You did it to Jonathan with the tattoo, Bailey the skateboarder, Zach from West Point baseball, and the list goes on."

"C'mon, Saw, give me a break."

"Even though Cohen despises Mason for whatever reason—"

"Who doesn't Coco hate?" I scoffed.

"Mason was *actually* nice unlike all those other jerks," she concluded.

"Damn, this is like dodgeball all over again, only this time it's . . ." I motioned offhandedly. "Dodging a dick that you're trying to throw at me."

"You know that's *not* funny, Zeke," she said heatedly, jabbing a finger at me. But bringing up the past didn't make her forget why she was shading me. "You avoid talking about your parents' divorce and telling me why you've been distant lately"—I gave in and started to explain where I'd been last night, but she didn't let me speak—"and you bailed on QSA without an excuse. Kennedy and I had to plan the best we could."

"God, you're making me feel like a—"

"Zasshole?"

"Ha."

I could tell her about the rec center's mentor program, tell her how I wanted to do something more. Judging by her attitude, she'd only lay into me like Cohen had. After the vitriol he'd spewed, plus JACass's phone call, it'd only feel like a third strike.

"I talked to my father last night," I offered instead. *See, I'm not avoiding it.*

Her mood downshifted from keyed up to full-on concerned. "You did?" she asked as worry etched on her forehead. I nodded, already regretting that I brought it up. "What did he want?"

I shrugged, tension clenching my stomach. Both my appetite and nerve were lost. I couldn't tell her everything he'd said, not without her pushing me to unpack things I'd rather keep in the past. *Okay, so maybe I am avoiding it.*

"While some would say I'm extremely good at body language, you're gonna have to give me more than that."

"And by 'some,' do you mean Kennedy?" I didn't think it was possible, but she prodded me with only her glare. "Okay, fiiine." I gave in with a deep breath. "It was the typical bullshit about my bad decisions. And when I grilled him about sponsoring Family First, he said it was just business. Nothing personal."

"That is—" She snapped on a fake smile as the front entrance's door chimed. "Good evening, Mrs. and Mr. Sinclair. Your usual table is ready." They exchanged pleasantries before their footsteps clacked down the rustic floorboards. She turned to me and lowered her voice. "That is a seriously fucked-up thing for him to say, Z."

"Right?" I leaned my head back against the desk, exhaling roughly. "I don't know how he could say that when the state governor is intentionally targeting queer kids. That's pretty damn personal to me."

"I'm so damn proud of you," she said, her eyes softening. "Are you okay, though?"

I smiled at her, bringing my hand to my chest. "I am, titty promise," I vowed. "Not letting my father get me down anymore."

"Good, because you're sticking it to 'the man' with these

speakeasies, well not literally sticking it like . . ." She made the hand gesture again.

"You'd make a great catcher," I teased. "Because you just told me to pitch a curveball."

"If that's what you did to Mason," she started, "then you do you."

We both laughed, but the tension was still taut in my chest. "Seriously, sorry for missing last night. What do you need me to do for tomorrow?"

"I have it under control, and I know you're dealing with a lot . . . So you get a pass. This one time." She winked, twisting back and forth in her chair. "Kennedy and I mapped out where to put up the decorations, so all you have to do is show up early to help set up."

"Okay," I said, and then, trying to lighten the mood: "Speaking of, did you two map out each other's mouths again?"

"What was it you said?" She pretended to think, tapping a finger on her chin. "Oh, yeah . . . We gave each other a secret handshake."

"Definite girlfriend vibes," I said, and nodded in appreciation.

"Let's hope so." Her grin was wide, pinching her pale cheeks. "All the stars are aligning in my favor."

"How so?" I asked as the door chimed again.

"Because she's using her cosplay skills to go as Captain Jaymes Catz's girlfriend, Ava Daise, from my fanfic." She plastered on another smile to greet the guests, but it dropped as she tsked. "You're late, Cohen, and not even in uniform yet."

"Sorry, the campaign meeting at Estrella Books ran late," he explained in a rush.

Anger twisted me like it had when I'd left him standing in the hallway. I ducked under the counter as though I could will myself to disappear. His habit of making me feel like shit was triggering. Balling my fists in my leather jacket's pockets, I held my breath. Afraid he'd hear me. Afraid the tightness vibrating inside me would erupt if he did.

"Go get changed before my parents see you," she instructed, reaching for a drawer handle. "Don't forget your server apron."

She opened the cabinet underneath the desk, and I saw stars. "Shit," I hissed as it banged me in the face.

"Sorry, sorry." She pushed my tangled hair back. "How's your head?"

"Haven't had any complaints," I joked, but my laugh died when Cohen's messy cowlicks appeared over the counter.

"Zeke?" he asked, looking down at me like he always did.

My cover was blown. "Gotta go," I groaned, standing with a wince. The start of a headache was forming, and I needed to be anywhere else but here. "Saw, I'll have the decorations ready. Pick me up at seven tomorrow, okay?"

"Oookay." Her eyes darted between Cohen and me in confusion.

"Later," I called over my shoulder.

It was a straight shot to The Cove's back entrance, where I'd parked my dirt bike. The hallway kept with the rustic theme, old-timey pictures and signs flashing by. With each stomp of my sneakers, I could feel the tension winding tighter and tighter inside me. *You'll only ruin everything with your Zasshole attitude,* Cohen had warned. *Just keep your head down and stay out of it,* the JACass had ordered. Both of their voices were testing my newfound resolve.

"Wait up," Cohen called, his voice breathy as he rushed to keep up.

"No," I said, and lengthened my strides.

"Zeke." He clapped a hand on my shoulder. "Can we please just talk?"

I spun around to face him, and he nearly collided into me. "There's no need. I said everything I wanted to say." *Too much actually,* I mentally added, a blush warming my face.

"At least let me apologize for saying—"

"We all know how much of a fuck-up I am. You remind me all the damn time."

"You aren't, though." The depths of his brown eyes caught me in their stare, but I refused to glitch over him. Not right now when I was on the verge of lashing out. "I'm sorry for how I handled things in freshman year. I didn't know you were afraid . . . if you would've just talked to me then we—"

"Do you know what's worse than you being a total dick to me?" I asked, and he went silent as the front entrance chime echoed down the hallway. "You pretending like you care."

"You don't understand—"

"I don't need to."

My chest was threatening to burst, and I had to get out of here before I lost my cool. Or he saw me cry. I started to push open the door, but Sawyer's voice stopped me. "Mr. Chapman and Mayor Buchanan," she welcomed with sarcasm-laced politeness.

I glanced over Cohen's shoulder and saw my father standing at the host desk. He had a generic smile in place, and the mayor's self-righteous stare was pointed at Sawyer. My fists were shaking as they were led into the dining room. I turned on my heel, and Cohen reached to stop me again. Crimson had bloomed up from his neck as he stood there, as he licked his bottom lip, as his eyes filled with pity I didn't want. Another apology was on the tip of his tongue, and I couldn't take it.

"Don't," I warned him, shoving outside.

The summer evening enveloped me with its heat as I straddled my dirt bike. The phone call and Cohen and the mayor's Family First ordinance—that magnifying glass was back. I needed to calm down. Go for a ride so the engine's warble drowned it all out. But then I glanced back toward the restaurant and faltered.

Through the windows, I could see my father and the mayor in the far-right corner. They were at the same table where he'd tried to coax me into living with him. How could they sit there and laugh like they weren't destroying my life, the lives of every queer person in Beggs?

I had to get as far away from this place as possible.

Pulling my helmet on, I refocused on kick-starting the engine. Revving the gas obnoxiously loud. Then I went to downshift and tore out of the driveway only to stop short. Across the parking lot sat a bright-blue truck. The same one the JACass had gotten me for my sixteenth birthday. The same one with a window decal for Wildcats Baseball. The same one that carried the weight of all his expectations. And I could unlock it with the fob on my dirt bike key ring.

Don't be immature, he'd ordered, but I was feeling *very* immature right now.

CHAPTER 12

Reflected green light glistened from the mirror ball. I watched it slowly spin, staring upward as Kennedy concealed my nearly healed black eye. The last two hours were spent decorating—streamers and inflatable arches, balloons and the green carpet rolled out, curtains of twinkling lights and sprinkled confetti. We'd thrown everything Mom had used for the shop at the library's third floor. And if anyone happened to walk in, they would have thought we were having a prom instead of an illegal Pride.

"This place is legit fire," I said in appreciation.

"How many people do you think will show up?" Kennedy asked, standing back to check her work.

"Maybe double what we had last time," I answered as she picked out a tube of red lipstick from my backpack.

Between the new followers and the messages from other businesses already offering their spaces for next weekend, word had spread. There was a good chance tonight would be even bigger than last Saturday. *A good chance I might see Mason again too.* Flutters rioted in my stomach at the thought as Kennedy painted my lips. I still hadn't replied to his message. Still hadn't decided if I would Z-step him.

I glanced at Sawyer on the other side of the table. Explosions reverberated from her phone's speakers as she played the X-Men gaming app. She was already dressed in her Captain Jaymes Catz army uniform, fake beard glued down and a bald cap in place. Kennedy matched his girlfriend, Ava Daise, perfectly in the scarlet bodysuit and faux-ruby diadem adorning her twist braids. And she matched the way Ava longingly gazed at the captain too. If all went to plan, Sawyer and Kennedy would be girlfriends by the end of the night.

"Who are you supposed to be exactly?" Kennedy asked after she'd finished.

"Zelda Fitzgerald," I explained, and struck a pose. The pearlescent beads of the too-snug dress glistened in the light, paired with the jewelry from Mom. I was feeling myself. If only I'd been able to find heels that fit instead of my sneakers. "She's not a character, but she played one as the first American flapper during the nineteen twenties." A moment of silence passed as Kennedy stared at me, and I rolled my eyes. "I know you're gonna say the same thing Cohen did, that you forgot I used to be smart."

"He's in his asshat era," she said with her nose scrunched up. "I *was* gonna say your headband is askew."

"Oh," I said, reaching for my phone on the table.

"Sorry that Co is being a dick to you. To be fair, he's been dickish ever since last Saturday."

"It's been longer than that," I muttered under my breath as I launched the front-facing camera.

"Where is he at tonight anyway?" Sawyer asked without looking up from her game.

"He said something about college essays," Kennedy explained. "He's worried about applications for early admittance, so he's being *extra*."

Of fucking course he's worried about the future.

I rolled my eyes, adjusting the headband, and checked Kennedy's work. The makeup really pulled together the look. Darkened brows, bright-red lips, rose blush. I'd even shaved what little stubble I had.

"Thanks for the makeover," I said. "This is perfect."

"You're welcome," Kennedy replied, putting the lipstick in my backpack. She made a noise in her throat, a hmm, and tilted the bag toward me. "What are these?"

I smirked when I saw the truck parts I'd stashed for safekeeping. "Those are spark plugs," I explained. "They ignite the combustion of air and fuel in an engine. Without them, it won't run."

Kennedy blinked in confusion, and then Sawyer inhaled sharply. "Oh my god," she said, the game forgotten as she gawked at me. "It was you, wasn't it?"

"You'll have to be more specific," I said, my smirk now a full-on evil grin.

"What did I miss?" Kennedy asked.

"Zeke's dad had a meltdown when he and Mayor Shithead were leaving The Cove and couldn't get his truck cranked."

"You didn't," Kennedy gasped.

"Spark plugs are easy to take out if you know how to do it," I offered. "And I know how to do it, so . . ."

Sawyer burst out laughing, her fake beard wobbling as she shook her head. "They had to have it towed and called a taxi to pick them up. You should have seen him marching around, opening the hood like he knew what he was doing," she managed to say between snickers. "I watched the whole thing from the host desk, and it was so damn preposterous in the best way possible."

"How dreadfully embarrassing for him," I said with a soft chuckle.

Taking the spark plugs out had been easy with the emergency tool kit under the driver's seat. The JACass better be grateful I didn't drive it into a ditch. Because that thought had crossed my mind, but I'd decided to give him a minor inconvenience he couldn't solve instead. It was a surefire way to get under his skin.

"Do you think he'll know it was you?" Kennedy asked, her cherry lips still parted in awe.

"That's the plan."

"No offense," Sawyer wheezed, "but I hope. To god. I'm working on your birthday. So I can witness even more of his preposterousness. When you both return to the scene of the crime."

"Birthday dinner with him? I think the fuck not." I grimaced and shook my head roughly. The last time we'd all been together at The Cove was to discuss joint custody, and it'd ended with Mom in tears. "I would rather have Billy 'Lightning' Peak, the *second*-best pitcher on the Wildcats, punch me repeatedly in the dick than sit through a dinner with them fighting again."

"Melodramatic much?" she teased, laughter subsiding. "I know how much you love your penis, so definitely don't do that. Because I'd have to hear you complain for . . ." She looked to Kennedy. "How long do you think it'd take for a bruised penis to heal?"

"The hell would I know?" Kennedy retorted.

"Probably way, way too long," I pointed out.

"Fair." Too much thought etched itself on her brow. She absently ran a hand over the bald cap's ridges, a result of the traumatic event that had activated her character's X-Gene. "That just means I'll make sure your sneaky birthday tradition is extra fabulous then, and we can binge *Doctor Who* afterward."

"Sneaky birthday *what?*" Kennedy asked, adjusting her headpiece.

"We go over to West Point and pretend to be hotel guests," I explained as the third floor's door clanged open. "Sneak into the complimentary breakfast—"

"Zeke?"

I turned at the sound of my name, twisting in my seat. Bronwen, the librarian who'd messaged me on Instagram, was dressed like Elizabeth Bennet from *Pride and Prejudice*. She waved excitedly to signal that guests were arriving at the back entrance.

"Showtime," I announced, standing up from the table.

Sawyer gave Kennedy a soft smile as they followed suit. Together, we took one final look around the space we'd transformed. Tonight was finally here, and no one could stop us. We were ready to party.

. . .

I lost count at fifty.

We hadn't expected this many to show up, but they were here. It wasn't like last weekend. This wasn't a makeshift party—it was an actual celebration. Everyone had come in costume, some dancing under the mirror ball while others talked and laughed and posed for pictures. There weren't second glances over shoulders or darting eyes. We were all here, all in on the same secret, all free from fear.

I walked along the outskirts while Sawyer readied the drag show. Kennedy had lined the back wall with tables for the businesses who supported the QSA. From the owners of Ryland Farms on one end to the rangers from the nature preserve on the other, they were all promoting safe spaces. I didn't expect any of them to know who I was in my Zelda costume, but a familiar face smiled at me from underneath an orange wig.

My sneakers squeaked to a halt as Carmen Bedolla waved, her glittery planet dress iridescent. Her dark-brown eyes were bright with excitement as I headed toward the Estrella Books table. After spending hours staring into Mason's, I could see where he'd gotten them from. The way she looked at me felt like he was standing there too, judging me for not replying to his message. It made my phone weigh heavy in my hand as I waved hello.

"Well, look at you!" Carmen greeted as she gestured at my dress. "Are you supposed to be Daisy from *The Great Gatsby*?"

"Zelda Fitzgerald, actually," I corrected sheepishly, crossing my arms.

"Some say she was a source of inspiration for the character," she said with a head nod. "How appropriate given these circumstances."

"Thanks, uh . . ." I almost asked if her grandson was here but stopped myself. Because it didn't matter if he was or not. "Who are you?" I asked instead.

"Ms. Frizzle from The Magic School Bus." She held up a stuffed green lizard with a flourish. "When I was an elementary teacher, I read the series to my students, even taught Mason how to read with the Spanish translations."

"That's cool." My voice was strained, hollow even. The mention of his name sent a flood of emotions through me. "Um . . . is he coming tonight?"

Carmen shook her head with disapproval. "He's grounded," she explained as the music faded out. "Something about a broken gnome and having a boy over after curfew."

"Mmm." Heat flamed up my neck while the lights dimmed. I'd inadvertently gotten him grounded, and now he wasn't here. I wouldn't see him in a costume or dance with him or kiss him tonight. And I hadn't realized how much I wanted to until now.

Maybe I should message him back, I thought, watching the stage curtains open. *At least apologize for leaving him to deal with the mess I made.*

A spotlight landed on Sawyer. She bypassed the mic stand and made her way to the middle, her tap shoes click-clacking. Then she stopped and turned her back to the auditorium. As though someone flipped a switch, the drag king persona appeared.

Captain Jaymes Catz stood straighter and adjusted the uniform. The speakers flared to life with the intro to "As It Was" by Harry Styles, and Catz waited for his cue. He did a little jig that emphasized his shoes as the beat dropped.

"Yes, king!" I yelled, rushing closer to the stage.

He was moving with precision, lips perfectly syncing with the song. All I could think about was how nothing was the same as it had been before now. I wasn't the same person I had been the morning of Pride Day. Wasn't the same me who'd stashed secrets in that shoebox. And I didn't want to be.

Nothing—and no one—was holding me back anymore.

As the song came to an end, Catz clicked his shoes together and tapped toward the front of the stage. He grabbed the microphone from the stand, sinking into the splits. "Good evening to the guys, gals, and nonbinary pals," he welcomed as applause erupted. "Thanks for coming out for our second Pride celebration!"

Sawyer had been so secretive about her drag king persona, but she was up onstage with the biggest smile now. She'd just shared part of herself without shame or judgement. The way she stood up—full of pride—made me feel like there really was a place for me, for us, here in Beggs.

"Before we begin the rest of the drag show, I want to turn it over to the library," Catz continued while motioning toward stage left. "We couldn't have done it without them."

Bronwen stepped into the spotlight, her Elizabeth Bennet dress billowing as she crossed to Sawyer. They hugged, and Sawyer passed off the microphone. "Give Captain Jaymes Catz one more round," Bronwen said, clapping her hands. Sawyer took a final bow before retreating backstage. "I know we're here for fun, but I wanted to take a moment to make a few announcements. Firstly, please know the public library has been and will forever be a safe space as long as I'm the librarian." She paused as more applause sounded. "Secondly, it goes without saying that we're all in agreement over Mayor Buchanan's asinine ordinance. If you'd like to join the effort to oust him from office, you can volunteer with Carmen Bedolla's mayoral campaign at the sign-up table in the back."

I turned, following her line of sight to Estrella Books. Carmen waved at the crowd and held up a clipboard. As much as I wanted to believe the mayor could be stopped, I didn't think it was possible. Not with supporters like my father. I'd been watching the news and knew it would only end in—

"Zeke Chapman."

The sound of my name cut off my thoughts, and I spun back around. The beaded fringe of my dress clattered as I looked up at Bronwen. *Huh?*

"I want to thank him for coming up with this genius idea for Pride Month," she explained while I felt the pinpricks of stares. "Not only has he gone above and beyond for his high school's QSA, he has also stepped up as a volunteer. The rec center is under threat of defunding because of their LGBTQIA-plus program, and Zeke has volunteered to help them continue it despite the mayor's threats."

How does she know that?

I felt self-conscious as more people looked my way. No one else knew I'd done that, not even Sawyer. Because if they knew—now that they knew—they would only tell me that I was a disaster who had no right mentoring anyone.

"Thank you, Zeke," she said over the heartbeats thundering in my ears. "You're making Beggs a better place, and that's why we're naming you our honorary King of Pride."

I cringed at the title, bracing myself for the punch line. Except nobody laughed. Nobody yelled that I was a fuck-up or that I didn't deserve to be proud. Instead, there was more applause. These strangers knew my name, knew I had started these speakeasies. And they didn't doubt me.

All I could think about was the pride flag I'd once hidden in that shoebox, the old newspaper clipping about the Pride protest. How I'd never felt like I could be me. Ever since I came out to my father, I'd been told there wasn't a place for me in this town. That I would only ever be a target.

For the longest time, I believed him.

Then I joined the QSA for the first ever Pride celebration in town. Mayor Buchanan had told us no one wanted it, that our community wouldn't support it. But people had shown up. They'd signed Sawyer's petition and set up tents and flown rainbow flags. It only proved just how wrong the mayor was. How wrong my father was.

There was a place for me here, and I finally felt like I belonged.

CHAPTER 13

I reread my sent message through sleep-bleary eyes. It was time-stamped at 2:03 a.m. Mason was all I could think about while we'd cleaned the library. I rode around town after Sawyer dropped me off, deciding whether to DM him back. Finally, after thirty minutes typing and retyping my reply, I finally hit send and went to bed. He still hadn't read it yet, but it was only eight in the morning.

It's way too early, I told myself as my mom's footsteps echoed down the hallway. *Take several seats and calm the fuck down.*

With a groan, I threw my head back against the mattress and willed myself to go back to sleep. But I couldn't get comfortable in the bright sunlight. Every time I tossed and turned, the dress's beads dug into my sides. I'd been too exhausted to change after sneaking in through the window. We'd danced for hours last night, and it was more fun than I could've ever imagined.

I smiled at the memory and felt for my phone in the sheets. The message thread was still pulled up when I unlocked it. Still unread. Forcing myself not to overthink, I swiped out of the app and tapped the photos icon.

Bronwen had used my camera to take a picture of us right before the night ended. The captured moment was of Sawyer carrying her newly declared girlfriend, Kennedy, like a bride and me hugging both of them. All three of us were grinning, and on top of my head sat a golden crown. It'd been a gift from someone dressed as Max from the children's book *Where the Wild Things Are*. An official declaration that I was King of Pride.

Me, of all people.

There was no better place for that crown than on top of my dresser. The shiny "metal" was just cheap plastic, but it was so much more than that—a testament that I was doing something more. Something right. Something I wouldn't hide away in a shoebox.

The photo faded to black as my screen went to sleep. I let it flop against my chest and looked up at the rainbow flag above my bed. Those bright colors against the white wall looked exactly how last night had felt: bold, disruptive, and, most importantly, proud. The second speakeasy proved that I was helpful, and I was even more excited for the next one.

While we were cleaning up, a bearded ranger named Owen had offered the nature preserve for the next speakeasy. I wasn't sure if their lodge's banquet hall would be best, would have enough space, would hold even more guests than the library's third floor had. Now that I was the King of Pride, I had a new reputation to uphold.

One that didn't involve me being a fraud or a burnout or a disaster.

We need a QSA meeting, I thought, unlocking my phone to text the group chat. *Then we get a game plan together and . . .* My thoughts were interrupted by a yawn. What I needed to do was wake up. Shower and rinse off my makeup. Figure out what was next.

I put my phone to the side, but the urge to check Instagram again was too strong. Another yawn ripped through me as I tapped the icon. Then I sat up in disbelief. There was a tiny red notification signaling a new message, and I nearly sprained a finger rushing to check it.

> **BEDMAS_22**
> Really glad you messaged me back.

I tapped his profile. He'd accepted my follow request, but there weren't any pictures of him to creep on. Only fancy nature shots. *Mason's artsy,* I thought. *Never would have guessed.* Swiping back to the message thread, I typed out a reply with a smirk.

> **ZEKECHAPMAN**
> why wouldn't I? 😔

> **BEDMAS_22**
> Because of the way you left.

He wanted me to stay? I could feel myself grinning as I rolled out of bed. The cool hardwood floor felt nice on my tired feet as I crossed over to the door. *What does Sawyer know anyway?* I didn't always Z-step. Maybe I could be into him, and maybe he'd be into me if he got to know me.

The smell of freshly brewed coffee perked me up as I stepped into the hallway. "Morning, Mom!" I yelled with too much cheer, turning toward the bathroom. But she didn't answer. A deep, gravelly voice from the living room yanked me down from my high.

"Come in here, son," my father called.

I closed my eyes. Tried to force myself to wake up. Told myself there was no way the JACass could be here. This apartment was our escape from him.

"We need to talk, Anthony," he added, and I bit down hard to stop from cursing at his use of my old name.

If he wanted to talk, I'd make sure he heard me once and for all. I turned on my heels, marching down the hallway with the same determination as I had in the town square. If he thought he could come here and tell me what to do, he was severely mistaken.

"Why are *you* here?" I asked, rounding the corner. He was sitting on the edge of the sofa, drinking coffee. Though it was Sunday morning, he was dressed for business. Polo and khakis, brown hair slicked, fake-ass smile that made my skin crawl. "And where's Mom?"

"She's downstairs giving us some time . . ." He went silent as he looked up at me. His eyes narrowed with disdain as he took in the dress and the makeup I'd been too lazy to wash off last night. "*Why* on god's green earth are you wearing *that?*"

"I went to a costume party last night," I grumbled, knowing where this was headed.

"You were out in public? Like that?" he asked, and took a sip from the coffee mug I usually used. "I thought you were smarter than that, Anthony."

"Stop calling me *that*." I spat the last word out, already on the defensive. "Why are you here?"

"The strangest thing happened the other night," he began, "while I was having dinner at The Cove—"

"With Mayor Buchanan."

"With Thomas, yes," he amended as he made himself at home on the sofa. "Since you're too irresponsible to take care of your truck, I've had to drive it around. We can't have it rundown." He let out a sigh as though I were his only problem. "When we went to leave, the engine wouldn't start. You happen to know why that is?"

"No clue," I said with a shrug, fighting the urge to laugh.

"I think you do, considering the towing company said the spark plugs had been removed. Take a seat." He patted the cushion beside him. I stood up straighter and crossed my arms in refusal. "Or you can keep standing there like a petulant child."

"Thanks, I will."

"You're about to be eighteen, Anthony," he pointed out.

"It's time to grow up and think about your future, to stop running around carelessly and painting vulgarities. Your GPA tanked this last semester, and how do you think that'll look on your application to University of Alabama?" I tried to reply and tell him I didn't care, but he kept talking over me. "Not good. There's no recovering from that, so I've already spoken to your coach. He's agreed to let you come back, and I'll call up UA's athletics director to see about leveraging your baseball skills—"

"No," I said, raising my voice so he'd hear me.

"Okay, I hear you, son." He held his hands out. "No baseball. That'll just mean you need to buckle down senior year. Maybe we could get you some extra credit to at least bump you to salutatorian."

"I don't think you've ever *heard* me at all." I shook my head and tried to keep from screaming at him. "I don't care about having the best grades or getting into UA or law school."

The fake politeness drained from his face, and he narrowed his eyes at me. Those same blue eyes I had to see in the mirror, a reminder he was a part of me. "Anthony, I'm not kidding around with you over this. What would you do instead? I've raised you to follow in my footsteps, and you don't know how to do anything else. Your future is on the line."

"It's always the future with you," I snapped. "I'm finally *who* I want to be—"

"Someone who dresses in women's clothes?" he countered. "Who makes a scene with that gay club?"

"Clothes have no gender, and the *QSA*," I stressed, "has made me feel prouder of who I am."

"This isn't up for debate."

He leveled his gaze at me. Before, this would have been the end of the discussion. I would have agreed to his orders and gone up to my room and kept quiet. Not anymore. I was the goddamn King of Pride. I made my own rules now.

"You know what?" I asked rhetorically, mirroring his fake smile. "You're absolutely right. Who I am isn't up for debate, and I don't have to listen to you anymore."

His jaw clenched as though he was chewing over his words before he spoke. At one time, I'd been terrified of disappointing him. I now realized the only person I ever disappointed was myself. "I don't appreciate you talking back to me," he finally said with an eerie calm.

"And I don't appreciate how you've dictated every aspect of my life," I said, matching his tone.

"Dodging my calls, hanging up on me, tampering with the truck, even being mad at me . . . all of that I understand. We'll work through it." He gestured at the dress as he leaned forward on the sofa. "But you have to stop this nonsense. You and your club are playing a dangerous game, especially after that Pride Day fiasco. All you're doing is drawing attention to yourself—don't roll your eyes at me, son. I only want what's best for you."

"I already know what's best," I answered resolutely, wishing I could rub it in his face that more people in this town supported the QSA than he'd believe.

"No, you do *not*." He shook his head slowly. "You only *think* you do, and I'm trying to keep you safe."

"Then why are you supporting Family First?"

He exhaled, his throat working roughly as he swallowed. "I've told you already, that's business. It looks good for the law firm—"

I cut him off. "But it doesn't look good to *me*. Doesn't feel good either, to know my own father believes the queer community should just disappear."

"Son, you're not like this"—he motioned at the dress and makeup again—"and if you'd stop acting so *gay*, you'd be fine with the mayor's ordinance. Keep your head down, and it won't affect you."

"Yeah, you said that." My voice was strained, my temper skyrocketing over his derogatory use of "gay" like it was a bad thing. "Only you don't understand that it does affect me and my friends and more people in Beggs than you know."

He stood then, his height almost shocking in the cramped living room. I lifted my eyes, and he tilted his head down to meet my gaze. "You need to grow up," he said sternly. But his words no longer had an effect on me.

"I *am*," I said, not backing down. Standing at my full height. "But on my terms, not yours."

CHAPTER 14

I've raised you to follow in my footsteps.

I could hear the JACass's words over the ratcheting of the wrench. The engine's sump plug came loose, and inky blackness spilled into the oil drain pan. I lay there while it poured out and wished I could get rid of my father as easily. Despite standing up to him yesterday, I wished I'd been able to tell him about Pride Month. Explain to him exactly how many people in Beggs would be affected by Family First, how many were supporting the speakeasies. Maybe then he'd understand it wasn't just business—it was extremely personal.

My phone vibrated, jerking me from the draining sludge's trance. I scrounged in my pocket and pulled it free. A grin tugged at my lips as the screen lit up with a new DM. Mason and I had been messaging nonstop. The urge to avoid replying had been strong at first, but then I remembered he was grounded. Which meant there was no pressure to make plans or go out. We were just getting to know each other with random questions and nothing more.

> **BEDMAS_22**
> Have you picked a theme for the next speakeasy yet?

> **ZEKECHAPMAN**
> not yet maybe I'll keep it a surprise and you'll have to see for yourself

Did I hope he miraculously wasn't grounded anymore? Yes. Was I nervous he would in fact not be grounded and plan to show up? Also, yes. Dancing would lead to kissing would lead to sneaking back to his room would lead to . . .

Then that would mean something else now, at least to me. Sawyer had psyched me out over him being good for me. I wondered if I was good enough for him. If I could be.

> **BEDMAS_22**
> I can't, sorry, but I'm proud of you for what you're doing. Please be careful. Scary shit is happening.

> **ZEKECHAPMAN**
> me? Scared? Never!

> **ZEKECHAPMAN**
> and thanks I'm trying to be a good gay 😄

> **BEDMAS_22**
> You're a good person. That's what matters.

Mason hasn't stopped gassing me up. It reminded me of that first night, when he called me brave. I hadn't really known what it meant, the bravery that came along with Pride. Not until these speakeasies. My fingers itched to tell him how he made me feel, how when we'd danced I could finally breathe. But this thing between us was delicate. Instead, I snapped a quick selfie, grease stains and all, with a goofy face, as a reply.

"That has to be the longest oil change in history." Mom's voice echoed under the car.

"S-sorry," I stammered. Shoving my phone away, I rolled the dolly out from under the car. She was leaned up against the tool chest while waiting for the next appointment. A crooked smile tilted her lips as she stared down at me. "What's that look for?"

"What's his name?" she asked.

"Dunno what you're talking about," I muttered, sitting up. However, the heat creeping up my neck and across my cheeks gave me away. Judging by her arched brow, she knew I was lying. We'd never talked about actual guy stuff before, just awkward discussions on the importance of condoms. I didn't even know how to broach the subject of dating with her. "It's no one."

"Then who's distracting you from work?" She winked, and I shrugged. "Fine, if you want to keep secrets—"

"I'm not keeping any secrets!" My voice shot up an octave as I worried she somehow knew about the Pride celebrations. Her expression then filled with confusion. "And, uh, I won't let Mason distract me from work," I added before she could interrogate me.

"Good, because you're doing a hell of a job here." The

wrinkle between her brows smoothed. Then, slowly, she smirked, latching on to what I'd said. "So he has a name, huh?"

"Damn it," I swore under my breath. "Yeah . . . Mason."

"It's sweet . . ." She trailed off, watching me nervously ball my hands into fists. "How did you meet?"

"During the spea— Uh, at the bookstore, I mean."

"Estrella Books?" she asked.

"Carmen Bedolla is his grandmother."

"She's a good woman," Mom said thoughtfully. "I talked to her when I went to pick up the club's book, and I love what she wants to do for Beggs. And for your community. That's why Roaring Mechanics is endorsing her campaign against the mayor." Silence fell as I digested that news. She really *was* trying for me. When I looked back up, there were storms in her eyes. "Speaking of, your father and I will be discussing how he blindsided you yesterday."

"It's fine, I can handle it."

"You don't have to," she said as a truck pulled up outside. "I'll take care of it, but maybe you and I can have dinner and actually talk about the future"—I wrinkled my nose at the thought, and she held her hands up in a truce—"with no pressure about making a decision, I promise."

"Okay," I agreed begrudgingly, and then thought to add: "Thanks for, you know, helping me deal with this."

She only grinned and patted my shoulder on her way to the lobby. I exhaled roughly, easing down onto the dolly. The wheels creaked over the art deco tile as I scooted back under the car. Everything she said was weighing on my mind. But one thing in particular had me digging my phone out of my pocket. *She's not wrong,* I thought with a small smile, checking my messages. *I do think I like him.*

> **BEDMAS_22**
> You've talked about your mom a lot, but can I ask about your dad?

As I read and reread his message, my palms grew sweaty. I didn't know how to reply to that and answer truthfully. I could feel his head on my chest, see his dark-brown eyes looking up at me. It made me want to tell him everything . . . but I was tired of rehashing the past.

> **ZEKECHAPMAN**
> there's not a lot to tell other than I will never be like him

I stared at the screen until it dimmed and went to sleep without any new messages. The idea of becoming James Anthony Chapman terrified me, but our confrontation yesterday had only reassured me. I didn't want to follow in his footsteps or grow up to be someone who'd force their kid to hide parts of themselves.

You don't know how to do anything else. When he'd first said that I thought it was true. He'd trained me into thinking my life had to look one specific way, that I had to be perfect, to be the kind of person the world expected me to be.

He was wrong.

Mom had said it herself: I was doing a hell of a job here at

Roaring Mechanics. That was *something*. I sighed, my eyes tracing the engine parts above. Then I looked around at the tools I had spread out. Each one felt at home in my hand. Gave me control.

My gaze flickered to the back wall, where I could just barely see the Zelda painting. The smile on her lips was all-knowing. Proud to have lived the life she'd always wanted. She'd been free of her father, free to be wild, free to do whatever the hell she wanted. And now I was doing that too.

...

My fingers hesitated for a moment, then I tapped post. The Instagram photo was the one from last Saturday with me in the dress. Every time I looked at it, I could hear my father's voice. *If you'd stop acting so gay.* His words had crawled under my skin, his disdain worming its way into my brain. I nearly reverted to the shame he had a habit of making me feel. However, I couldn't stop staring at the crown on my head.

Being declared the King of Pride didn't make me feel ashamed of who I was, and that was why I'd decided to post the picture. It was a reminder not to let him come into my new home, new life, and tell me what to do. Besides, the crown actually gave me an idea about where to have the next speakeasy, and that ranger guy had already offered the nature lodge. I'd captioned the photo with "meet us where the wild things are" and tagged Beggs Nature Preserve as the location.

Notifications were starting to pop off as I stretched out on the living room sofa. From comments declaring they were ready for the rumpus to an excessive use of eyeball emojis, I watched them pour in. Then bedmas_22 liked it.

Flutters filled my stomach every time I saw his username in my DMs. I was having fun just getting to know him, not that other-stuff'ing wasn't fun. His questions made it feel like I was a mystery he was trying to solve.

Before I could check his latest message, a new text notification from Sawyer flashed across the screen. She'd sent a line of question marks that immediately killed my vibe. I assumed it was in response to my post; she'd probably typed it while wearing her focused expression. I almost second-guessed myself, but then I looked back at the photo of me with the golden crown on my head. It was all the proof I needed. I *knew* what I was doing. She was just ticked that I hadn't discussed it with her first.

Leaving her on read, I set my phone on the coffee table. I pushed the doubt out of my mind while I lay there and listened to the buzz of the oven timer. Mom was making breakfast for dinner—my favorite. She'd come upstairs after a very lengthy discussion with the JACass and started making biscuits from scratch. And I knew the choice of comfort food had to be a bad omen.

"It's ready," she called.

"Coming," I replied, rolling off the sofa.

I made my way to the tiny dinette. She'd cleared stacks of papers off to the side and set out two plates. *Oh, we're def having a real talk,* I realized, plopping down on the chair across from her.

"So . . ." I searched for something to delay the inevitable, and then I saw the book she'd left sitting at the end of the table. "How's the, uh, book club?"

"They picked a great read," she answered. "About this woman who hiked the Pacific Crest Trail to reclaim her life." Her face lit up with a smile, a spark like when she'd bought the shop. "The club is planning a weekend cabin retreat to discuss it, but I don't know if I'll go."

"You should." I gave her an encouraging nod. "And, uh, do something for yourself."

"I'll think about it," she said softly, and then took a deep breath. "As much as I appreciate you saying that, we're not here to talk about me. Hun, your father—"

"I don't like where this is heading," I groaned.

She widened her eyes, almost as if she agreed. "He had a lot to say about what he wants for your future," she said matter-of-factly.

I shoveled a forkful of biscuits and gravy into my mouth. If I hurried and ate, then we could cut this short. "Like what?" I asked, swallowing even though I'd lost my appetite.

The lines around her eyes softened, and she set her fork down. Its clink against the plate rattled through me as the silence stretched out. Finally, she said, "Zeke, he only wants the best for you."

"It's what *he* thinks is best," I pointed out. "Not what I want."

"He mentioned your reluctance to law school."

"More like my refusal," I said. Unable to eat another bite, I pushed my food around the plate as her words sank in. "I'm not following in his footsteps."

I waited for her to tell me that this wasn't a joke, that my future was on the line, that I wouldn't know how to do anything else. However, she didn't throw his words back at me. "You can do whatever you want," she said instead. "Do something for yourself."

"Wait, what?" I shook my head, unsure if I heard her correctly. We'd never really talked about college before. That was something my father had decided on without her. "I can?"

"I've spent seventeen years letting your father make all the decisions, and I'll be damned if it'll happen anymore." She nodded reassuringly. "I told him you're smart and capable of making your own choices."

"Mom . . ." The sudden urge to cry burned my throat, and I gripped the chair seat.

"He threatened not to pay for school, and that's okay. I'll find a way to pay for whatever it is you want." She leaned forward and locked eyes with me. "Maybe focus on improving your grades next year for scholarships, just to be safe."

"Yes, ma'am," I promised, nodding profusely. "I'll be perfect—"

"You don't have to be perfect." She held my gaze with unwavering warmth. "You just have to be you."

I wanted to jump up and hug her. Run around the apartment and scream. Call my father and tell him his dream was no longer my fate. But all I could do was slowly release my grip on the chair, the weight of a wrench still heavy in my palm.

CHAPTER 15

*D*octor *Who* played on the bachelorette pad's TV. The Doctor and his companion Amy had just traveled from 1890, where they'd met Vincent van Gogh. They brought the painter back to the future to see how much his life mattered. It was one of the top episodes on the Sawyer-and-Zeke list, and the ending made me cry.

Usually.

I was so annoyed at Sawyer. It was one of her favorites, yet she was too preoccupied with texting Kennedy to even pay attention. At least I was capable of ignoring my DMs. It had been my turn to ask Mason a question, and I felt bold enough to ask his idea of a perfect first date. Despite the fact that my palms were sweating after I pressed send, I'd set my phone to the side. Because that's what *we* did when the Doctor was saving the universe.

The credits began to roll, and I glanced over at her. Both the bowling shirt and baggy jeans she'd found thrifting made her look tiny. But her attitude was enormous as her thumbs continued to tap out messages like I wasn't here. She'd been giving me the cold shoulder ever since I came over. I knew she was still ticked about the Instagram post. She hadn't said much to me other than demanding an emergency QSA meeting tonight to plan the next speakeasy. I'd agreed even though I'd already made up my mind about what we were going to do.

I reached for the remote and stopped our episode queue. A hush flooded the basement as she ignored my lingering glare. *Whatever,* I groused internally while unlocking my own phone. Instagram was still open to the message thread with Mason, and my heart soared when I saw that he'd replied. Then it plummeted as I read his messages.

> **BEDMAS_22**
> Idk the perfect first date. Never really been on one.

> **BEDMAS_22**
> What's your god tier band?

He'd completely ignored my hint, instead of playing along like I'd hoped. I should have just asked him out. But no, I'd been too much of a chickenshit. I sent back that I loved Bleachers, then threw my phone down on the sofa. *First Sawyer and now him?* I huffed in annoyance and waited for her to notice me.

A full minute passed, and I couldn't take the deliberate silence anymore. My annoyance bubbled over. "So," I began loudly, "is Kennedy on her way yet?"

"She just finished summer cheer practice," Sawyer said without looking up.

"And Cohen isn't coming?" I pressed, hoping she'd thaw out.

"Nope."

She was deliberately holding a grudge against me, when really, I should've been holding one against her. Even after they'd completely left me out of planning for Pride, I'd come through and saved the day. *What else do I have to do to prove myself?*

"Any more sign-ups for the QSA?" I pressed, watching her ignore me. "I know the principal has that new rule about needing twenty members."

Finally, she lifted her face from her phone screen. Surprise melted her icy attitude. "No, we haven't . . ." She trailed off, but I knew she wanted to ask how I knew about the rule.

"Cohen told me," I explained. "In the middle of verbally trashing me."

"What is it with you two?" she asked with an eye roll. "Are you *still* bitter over Geometry Derick—"

"Why didn't you tell me about the new rule?" I cut in. She went silent, twirling a lock of her hair. The blue tips spun while she bit her bottom lip in thought. Then I remembered how Cohen had texted the wrong thread on Pride Day. "And why did y'all start a new group chat and leave me out?"

"Z," she began with a sigh, "I know you don't care. Or you didn't until now, I guess."

"What is that supposed to mean?" I sat up straighter, angling toward her as Cohen's words stirred in my memory. *You're not really present.*

She gave me a condescending shrug. "You've never shown much interest in the QSA or celebrating Pride before now."

"You . . . you really think I don't care?" I asked over the swell of guilt.

"I guess I just don't get why now you're all suddenly into Pride."

"Uh . . ." I couldn't find the words to make her understand she had it right in all the wrong ways.

"Is it because Mason's into it?"

"No, it's not—"

"Being out and proud because it fits your new personality," she started, gesturing from my long hair down to the rainbow on my T-shirt, "that's not what it's about, Zeke. The first Pride was an uprising, and if you haven't noticed, we're still being forced to fight for our rights."

My hands fisted, fingernails digging into my palms at the accusation. "Sawyer," I said through a steady breath, trying to find the words to explain everything I'd kept from her for so many years. How the JACass had ruled my life like a dictator. How I was told that I couldn't be out like her. "It has been really hard for me, okay?"

"And it hasn't been hard for me?" she retorted. "I hear the shit they say about me, see the looks they give me when I'm not acting textbook femme. Being a lesbian in this small-ass town isn't easy either."

"That's not what—"

"And Kennedy, do you think it's easy for her?"

I shook my head, too many thoughts buzzing in my mind, and glared at her. "Why are you biting my head off?"

"I'm not—"

"Are you really *that* pissed about the speakeasy?" I inserted. And before she could answer: "So what? You're gonna sit there and bulldoze me like we're back in middle school?"

Her eyes went wide, and I knew I'd struck a nerve. "I'm the QSA *president,* and you didn't even discuss it with me before making plans for the club," she said heatedly and too quickly, as though she'd rehearsed for this very moment. "In fact, you didn't discuss *anything* with me before deciding we were doing a month of speakeasies."

"Saw, c'mon." I laughed, trying to defuse the situation, and brought my hand to my chest. "It was just an Insta post. I didn't do it on purpose, titty promise. I'm sorry—"

"It was a total simp-for-attention move, and you know it." She closed her eyes and exhaled roughly. I could tell she was trying to mask how hurt she was. "Are you even taking this seriously?"

I'm trying! I yelled inwardly. "Look, I wasn't trying to offend you," I said with forced calmness. "It was because of my—"

She cut me off. "I bet you didn't even consider the safety of everyone at the nature lodge."

"*What* an astute observation," I said sarcastically, standing from the sofa before I lost my temper. She wasn't in the mood to let me explain myself. And I was on the verge of blowing up like I had with Cohen. It didn't matter if the rangers had ensured everyone's safety when they'd offered, or that I was doing all this to prove to Sawyer and the QSA that I *was* good enough. "I'm gonna dip out."

"Are you for real right now?" she shot back. "Kennedy isn't even here yet, and we have to get this plan in place, especially since you already announced it."

"Don't worry about it," I said, holding back what I really wanted to say. That I couldn't sit here and let them both shit all over me. That I was so pissed I was seeing red. That I refused to let anyone tell me what to do, how to be. "I'll figure it out since it's *my* fault."

. . .

My palms gripped the handlebars as I gave the dirt bike some gas. Warbles sounded from the engine. I turned sharply out of Sawyer's neighborhood, picking up speed. The headlight beam lit up the darkened streets of Beggs while my mind raced, my phone weighing heavy in my pocket with messages from Mason I couldn't reply to, a message in the group chat demanding I come back.

Sawyer might've been pissed, but now I was too. She didn't care enough to let me explain myself, just like Cohen. It was like dodgeball all over again. We might not be playing the game anymore, but I was still ducking her aim. Ever since she and I became friends, she always called the shots. First at recess, and now with the speakeasies.

But they were *mine*. She was trying to take them away from me. Doubt ensnared me as I drove home.

You have to stop this nonsense rattled inside my head as I looked up at the new Chapman Law billboard my father had installed. The picture of us in matching dress shirts reminded me that I'd had no authority over my life when the photo was taken. Now I got to decide what my college plans were and live with Mom and be out like I should've been all along. That's why I'd really wanted to join the QSA, to find a way to be me. I just hadn't realized what I was doing before the speakeasies.

I lowered my gaze to the town square and saw the Family First posters still on the lampposts. It was as though we'd never set up Pride Day. Not a single rainbow flag was still flying. Mayor Buchanan had done his best to soothe the anger we'd caused with the event, a debacle that had been covered up with his new ordinance.

My eyes moved toward the pavilion and the donkey statue. A literal jackass, just like my father, like the mayor and everyone else who supported him. I could feel the spark of anger deep inside my chest as I stared at it. How it'd once mesmerized me but now made me feel like I didn't belong in Beggs. That I needed to keep my head down so nothing could hurt me.

I gripped the handlebars harder in frustration. If only they knew we hadn't gone anywhere. We were still here, still celebrating Pride. My line of sight focused behind the statue on the bright lights of Jones Hardware. The front window displayed signs for a paint sale, and I glanced back at the billboard. An idea formed as I steered the dirt bike toward the parking lot. This town was in desperate need of a reminder that they couldn't erase the pride in Beggs.

It was as though I was moving on autopilot, the same as when I'd climbed up that rusty ladder weeks ago. I lowered the kickstand and marched to the hardware store. A waft of cold AC blasted me as the automatic door slid open. Blinking away the harshness of the fluorescents, I searched the aisle signs for the paint section.

"Welcome to Jones," a clerk called in a smooth baritone. "Can I help you find something?"

My momentum fizzled to a stop. The sound of Damian's voice took me back to that same night when Billy punched me. I wanted to spontaneously combust. To be anywhere other than here.

"Zeke?" Damian called, and I reluctantly turned.

He was propped up on a stool behind the register. The store's orange shirt was bright against the brown expanse of his biceps, stretching tight as he crossed his arms. I focused on the white hammer logo instead of meeting his gaze. "Didn't realize you were working here," I muttered, a ghost ache radiating from my right eye.

"Dad needed help this summer," he said carefully. Too carefully. My attention snapped up to his face. The reserved set of his mouth told me he wasn't in the mood for bullshit. "We're about to close."

"I won't be long," I offered, unable to move as he considered me. His tight expression was giving apprehension. It was the same one he wore when he was up to bat, bases loaded at the bottom of the ninth inning. "Look, man, I'm not here to start anything. I just need to get some paint and I'll be gone."

He nodded once, his jaw relaxing. "Sorry about Peak," he said with a sigh. "How's your eye?"

"Fine." The bruising had nearly faded, along with the sting of Billy's words. "It was my bad. Totally forgot they don't call him Lightning for nothing."

"For real," he breathed out. "I tried to stop him, but you were making it worse."

"Sorry," I said. "It's just that the team's response to me being gay . . . Billy has been such a dick about it. And yeah. I'm sorry, man."

We maintained eye contact for a few seconds, and then he nodded once. "I don't give two shits about you being gay, just so you know."

"Thanks, Damian. Really." I tried to smile, but I couldn't. I'd just assumed Damian was like Billy, was like the others who'd gone full-on paranoid in the locker room.

"I know it might be too late, but I'm here if you want to talk." He shrugged, offering a smile. "I never stopped being your friend. Okay, that's a lie. I might've been mad at you for like five seconds when you quit the team without telling me. I had to hear it from Peak."

"Sorry I didn't give you a heads-up," I offered.

"We're all good, bro," he said, glancing at his smartwatch.

"Right, you're about to close."

"Let's hang soon, okay?"

I nodded, turning toward the paint aisle. Just like that, we were on friendly terms again. It felt like we were back in the dugout and sitting together on the bench. As though I hadn't tried to fight Billy and put Damian in the middle of it. Too bad Sawyer and I couldn't make up so easily.

Some fights hurt worse than getting a fist in the face.

CHAPTER 16

BUCHANAN IS A JACKASS

I smugly stared at my newest Instagram post as Mom talked to a customer. The donkey statue was coated with pink paint, with those four words written in black. The caption read "Whoever did this is a true king." I'd worked quickly after leaving the hardware store, snapping a picture before anyone could see me. The only person who knew I'd bought the paint was Damian. Before I could worry about him snitching, though, he'd commented with laughing emojis. Maybe we really were all good.

Too bad Sawyer and I weren't.

She hadn't brought up the post. I'd expected her to call me a simp again, and then we could go back to being good. However, she completely disregarded any mention of speakeasies when she dropped off the decorations from last Saturday.

Which meant she was bottling up her emotions and would explode the moment I got in the way.

But I wouldn't give her a reason to. The next speakeasy had to be perfect. Bigger and better than the last one. Nothing could go wrong. Then I'd prove to her just how seriously I was taking this. I may have joined the QSA with ulterior motives, but I wasn't that same Zeke. I'd spent too many years being afraid and quiet—I was anything but that now.

If only Sawyer could see how proud I finally was.

With a sigh, I locked my phone. The dolly wobbled under my weight as I sat up to peer into the reception lobby. Mom had just finished up with the customer and was on the phone. The brake repair had been our first job of the day, and it was already lunchtime.

Things were slow. Too slow. My hands were itching to take something apart and put it back together. If nothing else came in soon, I'd resort to tinkering on my dirt bike until the rec center's program meeting tonight. The engine warble could be fine-tuned—

"We have a tire alignment coming in," Mom called, breezing back into the shop.

"Thank god," I muttered.

She laughed and dropped down onto a shop stool. "You have at least an hour to keep messaging your new boo."

"Nobody says that anymore."

Despite the secondhand embarrassment over her outdated lingo, I couldn't stop my grin. Mason had been out with his friend when I'd Van Gogh'd the donkey. He'd messaged as soon as I made the post and said he wished he could do something that brave. Then we'd stayed up late DM'ing. Everything I was discovering about him made me crush even harder. And if he was out last night, that meant he wasn't grounded anymore and maybe he'd be at the speakeasy . . .

"Have you asked your *new boo* out yet?" Mom continued with a gleam in her eye.

"Stoooop," I said, throwing a grease rag at her.

My face must've been neon red judging by the way she smiled at me. I had to make the first move since Mason wasn't picking up on any of the hints I'd dropped. "If it matters," she began, nudging my foot with hers, "he was very nice and polite when I met him."

"You *what*?" My voice pitched high; I was unsure of where she was going with this.

"Remember how the shop is endorsing his grandmother's campaign?" I nodded, still in shock. "She had some signs for me to put up, and Mason helped me load them into the SUV. We had a nice chat, and he— What do you kids call it? Passes the vibe check?"

"Oh my god." My stomach twisted at the thought of them talking. "What did you tell him?"

She held her hands up in surrender. "Calm down. I didn't say a word about you. But if you want to know what I found out . . ." I waved my hand, urging her to get to the point. "Jeez, okay. He's very sweet, smart, and knows his politics. Said that helping the campaign would prepare him to run for Congress one day."

"Oh," I said quietly as my heart plummeted.

"What's wrong?"

"Uh . . ." If he was into politics, then he'd find out how much I didn't know. "I'm kinda dumb," I admitted, not meeting her eyes.

"You're not dumb." She threw the grease rag back at me, and I ducked. "Sure, you might've done some dumb things with your grades, but that doesn't make you stupid."

"I meant about politics and . . . stuff."

Talking about it made me uncomfortable. Cohen dragged me for being a bad gay, and Sawyer was so condescending about the QSA. They made me feel worthless and . . .

"I'm trying," I added hastily. "Watching the news and trying to figure out what it all means, but it kinda goes over my head."

"That doesn't make you stupid," she said, the teasing gone from her voice. "I've seen how you *are* trying, and that's what matters. No one expects you to know everything or have the perfect solution. You tried to make our town better with the QSA's Pride Day. That's more than a lot of people do. They just sit back and accept whatever happens. Just keep paying attention, and you'll keep learning."

Her words were reassuring. "I definitely don't accept the Family First ordinance," I said forcefully.

"A lot of people don't," she said. "Just look at what happened last night in the town square with that statue. The campaign against his reelection is gaining traction. He's threatening to punish the person who vandalized it if they're caught."

"I'm glad someone called him out," I said without remorse.

The chances of me getting caught were slim, even if I'd posted the picture. No one saw me do it. Besides, the rush I felt knowing it pissed him off was worth it. Mom had just said I didn't need to have a solution. But if I'd gotten him this shaken up, I really was doing something right.

Even Mason had said I was brave.

. . .

The last time I'd seen Cohen, I stormed out of The Cove. He'd been standing at the back entrance, with crimson blooms across his fair complexion and mouth agape. That same expression twisted his handsome features as I stepped into Room 13. He was seated at a three-person table with a tween, and he glanced up at me as the door clicked shut.

He waved, but I pretended not to notice as I searched for a seat. There was only one left. At his table. Right across from him. *Damn it,* I griped, wavering by the doorway. *I could just come to the next—*

"Zeke! Thank you for coming back," a melodious voice called.

I let go of the door handle with a reserved sigh, turning around. Jess, the program leader, was by Cohen's table. She exuberantly waved me forward, and my stomach sank when I realized she wanted me to sit with him.

"Cohen has agreed to help train you in mentoring," she said as I crossed over. "He's helping Addi with homework, and they're both super excited to have you here."

That felt like hyperbole judging by the expression still on Cohen's face. His blush spread down to his neck as he moved his camera off the seat. I reluctantly pulled the chair out, and Addi grinned, looking up from the workbook. "I go by they/them pronouns," Addi introduced themself with a wave, their smile faltering. "Not that my teacher cares."

"We talked about this, Addi," Cohen said to them under his breath. His voice was too soft, too smooth in comparison to how rough he usually was with me. "The teachers at Beggs Middle School are forced—"

"I *know*, Cohen," Addi said with an exaggerated eye roll. They slunk forward and dropped their head onto the table, their afro puffs shielding their face from view. "It's sooo mean how the governor and now the mayor won't let us be us, ya know?"

I swallowed nervously. They knew more about the state laws than I did. *What am I even doing here?* At any minute, Cohen would leap up and yell at me some more. He'd out me as a fraud, and then it'd get back to everyone who came to the speakeasies. They'd all know I didn't deserve to be King of Pride.

"If you have any questions about the process, just ask my right-hand man," Jess said, nodding at Cohen. "I'll be in my office if you need me."

She made her way across the room, and I wanted her to come back instead of leaving me alone with Cohen and Addi. Wanted to confess I was too stupid for this. Instead, I swallowed my fear and cleared my throat. "Nice to meet you," I said to Addi, refusing to look at Cohen. "I'm Zeke."

"What're your pronouns?" they inquired thoughtfully.

It was the first time anyone had ever asked me that. "I prefer he/him," I said, sitting down.

Addi nodded, smiling up at me. Then the expression faded as they looked back down at the homework on the table. "You any good with English essays, Zeke?" they asked.

"I used to be," I said, doing my best to ignore Cohen. "What's your assignment?"

"My teacher next year, Ms. Jemison, she wants me to write an essay on what my home feels like so we can introduce ourselves when school starts." They cut their eyes to Cohen. "And he doesn't like what I've written. But who cares? Who even gives summer homework? Ugh."

"Addi, I didn't say that," he said, shaking his head. "I said it wasn't what the directions stated."

"You'd follow the rules even if they said 'Jump into the park's pond,'" they muttered, causing me to snort a laugh. Because he really would.

"I'm obviously no Cohen, but I could try to help," I offered. "What did you write exactly?"

"How Beggs doesn't feel like home with the laws and stuff," they said simply. "They're hard to understand, and I feel dumb even if my daddy said all I had to know is that he'd protect me. But ya know, sometimes it just sucks."

Cohen's lips parted, and he gave a little inhale like he was about to launch into a speech, but I jumped in. "It does suck," I assured them. "I feel that way too."

"You do?" both Cohen and Addi asked.

"Uh . . ." Cohen eyed me intently as he waited for my answer. "Yeah, I'm still trying to figure out what's happening out there in the world, and I feel dumb. I didn't have a dad who said he'd protect me, so you're already off to a good start."

"You're not dumb," Cohen said, but I didn't know if he was talking to me or Addi.

"No, you're not," I told them. "My mom said that we don't have to know everything. At least you're trying to understand. That's what matters."

"That's what I've been trying to tell you—them." Cohen turned to Addi, his face reddening. "You're not dumb for writing this essay, but I don't think that's what Ms. Jemison meant. She wants to know about your bedroom or if you have a pet. Things like that."

"That's boooring," they whined.

"It doesn't have to be," I offered, risking a glance at Cohen again.

"How would you write about your bedroom then, Zeke?"

I thought for a moment, my brain flashing back and forth between the apartment and the house. "I'd write about the pride flag I have hanging up in my new room," I said. "It makes me feel at home now because I couldn't hang it up in my old house."

Addi thought for a moment, their face lighting up. "I have one of those!" they said. "It's on my bedroom door, and my daddy has another on the front porch."

"Write about that then," I suggested.

They stuck their tongue out at Cohen, and stood up from the table. "I'm gonna get a soda, and when I get back, I'll get to work."

I grinned as they stomped off, but my face fell when I saw Cohen's expression. His damned brown eyes were wide as he licked his bottom lip. My defenses were already up when he said, "That was good, Zeke."

"Oh." I sat back in the chair, uncertain if I'd heard him correctly. "Are you sure? Because I can do better. I don't want to mess this up. Please tell me what to do."

"You handled that perfectly." He lowered his voice, checking over his shoulder. "And you're not gonna mess anything up. I'm sorry"—he held his hand up as I started to object to his apology—"about your dad. I know you don't wanna talk about him, but can I at least get something off my chest?"

I nodded, chewing on my lip.

"It all makes sense now, how we couldn't . . ." I didn't think it was possible for him to get even redder, but he did. "What I mean is, I'm glad we're mending things . . . and I'm sorry for giving you a hard time and being a D-I-C-K to you."

"I think these kids know how to spell, Coco," I teased half-heartedly, uncomfortable at his prolonged eye contact. The unamused tilt of his mouth said he wasn't taking the bait. "Fine, but *why* have you been such a giant, enormous, massive D-I-C-K to me?"

"Because I didn't know who you were, Zeke."

"And now you do?"

"I'm still getting to know you." He swallowed roughly, his throat bobbing. "What I do know is that you're doing great things for Beggs. I wish I could be as brave as you."

Brave?

First Mason and now Cohen had called me that. I couldn't look away as his eyes crinkled with a shy smile—it reminded me of the way he'd smiled when he asked me to join mathletes. It was like the old me and this new version of me were colliding together, overlapping. And I was suddenly worried that my brain might be glitching over Cohen Fisher again.

CHAPTER 17

I once had a foolproof plan for studying. It required two components: waking up three hours early and coffee. So much coffee. Each cup only added fuel to my cram sessions, taking me closer and closer to a perfect grade.

Preparing for the next speakeasy felt like that.

Since I'd gotten home last night, I'd been cramming. The pressure was pressuring. I had to prove I could do this. Maybe then Sawyer would think I was brave too. She'd always seen me as her shadow, someone who followed her lead. That had been okay when life was out of my control. Now I knew better.

I have to make this epic, I thought, staring down at the blinking cursor on my laptop. Light from the newly unpacked lamp spilled across the keyboard as my hands stilled. I'd typed up a list for tomorrow. The same decorations from last weekend would work, and Owen the ranger said I could use their sound system. I'd made a playlist before falling asleep, envisioning a giant party and how it'd felt to dance with Mason that first night.

But I wasn't so sure if that was enough.

With a sigh, I reached for the steaming cup of coffee on my nightstand. I'd been stuck on brainstorming ways to make it bigger. Nothing was coming to mind yet, no matter how hard I searched online for ideas. I took a gulp of bitterness and closed my laptop in defeat.

"What else?" I questioned, glancing around my room.

No reply except for the soft rustle of my curtains in the breeze. I watched sunbeams cut through the gray light for a moment before I realized it was morning. Which meant Mason might be awake.

We'd been chatting until midnight about my best friend woes, and he'd fallen asleep before replying to my last message. The urge to check my DMs had me searching the sheets for my phone. I grinned as a familiar notification lit up the screen, and I unlocked to read the thread.

12:05 AM

ZEKECHAPMAN

Sawyer wouldn't understand why I couldn't stand up to my father

ZEKECHAPMAN

I need to do this for myself and now she's big mad because I'm leading the speakeasies even if she is the QSA pres but they were my idea

12:09 AM

ZEKECHAPMAN

does that make me a bad person?

BEDMAS_22

I don't think it makes you a bad person at all. I'm sure she'd understand if you'd just talk to her?

BEDMAS_22

Also, good morning. ☀

ZEKECHAPMAN

good morning ☀

ZEKECHAPMAN

it's too complicated and she'd just try to fix everything instead of letting me figure it out myself but I'm glad we're talking 😊

He was typing a response. I could picture him in his bed, his dark hair haloing him on his pillow. The image made me smile as I took a sip of coffee and waited. The stillness of a new day was disrupted by caffeine-fueled heartbeats and the sounds of Mom getting ready in the other room. I listened as she shuffled around, watching my screen intently until a new message popped up.

BEDMAS_22

Glad we are too ☺ and I'm glad you're doing this for yourself. You can talk to me about anything, even those things about your dad. I will try to understand if you'll let me

Mason had called me brave, and I was starting to feel even more so as I reread his message. Without doubting myself, I started typing. Listing out everything the JACass had done, why I had been kept from coming out before, how I was trying to be the right kind of gay. All of it poured out of me like a dam had ruptured.

I hit send, then dropped my phone on the bed like it was on fire and stood up. The screen remained dark for a minute, then two. There was no going back now. I really hoped he'd meant what he said about being able to talk to him. That he wouldn't be disappointed by the real me and Z-step like I'd done countless times and then—

A sudden, sharp knock on my bedroom door scared me. I jumped, spilling coffee down my Wildcats Baseball shirt. For a second, I thought Mason had appeared in the hallway to tell me how much of a fuck-up I was.

"Y-yeah?" I stammered, voice thick.

"Are you awake?" Mom asked. "I need to talk to you."

"Yeah. Um. Give me a minute." I rushed to change my shirt, nearly knocking over a stack of empty moving boxes.

"Take all the time you need," she called, "and if you're doing boy stuff—"

"Ohmygodno."

My face scorched worse than my chest as I opened the door. Mom stood there in her green Roaring Mechanics shirt. One of her delicate eyebrows rose as she noted the wadded-up shirt in my hand and the laptop on my bed.

"Hun," she said. "No reason to be embarrassed. It's perfectly natural—"

"We are absolutely not doing this."

I sat back on the edge of my bed. My mental capacity was limited to one difficult conversation at a time. I couldn't handle anything else after confessing all my deepest, darkest thoughts to Mason.

"What, uh, did you want to talk about?" I asked.

She gave me a tight-lipped smile and stepped into my room. "Your father texted about your upcoming birthday."

"What about it?"

"You know how we usually take you out to eat at The Cove . . ." she started hesitantly. "He asked if he could—"

"No."

"—take you this year. He wants to talk."

Damn it, Sawyer jinxed me. "Hard pass," I said, risking a glance at my phone. Still no new messages.

"Zeke, I get it. Trust me, I really do." She huffed from the heaviness of her words. "I won't make you, but I think you should."

"Why?"

"He wants to discuss the future with you." I opened my mouth to protest, but she held up a finger to stop me. "And you can tell him what we decided. I'll go with you if you want, and we can present a united front. No matter what he says, you'll be eighteen and free to make your own choices. I'll make sure he leaves understanding that."

"Fine," I muttered. *Because I want to see the look on his face.* "Only if you come too."

"Then we'll both go."

She let out a tense exhale and leaned against the doorframe. Slowly, she took in my room. I watched her gaze travel from the pride flag above my bed to the picture of us on the dresser.

"I should've done that for you a long time ago," she said, voice quieter. "Present a united front, I mean."

Her expression flickered from sadness to the remorse I'd come to know. "Mom," I heard myself say, "we are now."

She gave me a watery smile. "I know you had a hard time coming out because of him, but I'm relieved you have the QSA now and that Sawyer is there for you." At the mention of her name, a pang rattled inside me. "Especially with how scary Family First—"

"I'm *not* afraid," I said forcefully, mainly to myself.

"It's okay if you are," she added softly. "You don't have to hide it."

But it wasn't okay. Too many people were looking at me to be their King of Pride. To be brave despite the ban and . . . I *wanted* to be that person.

"An uproar is starting," Mom continued, "because someone vandalized that statue in the town square."

"Oh?" I fought to keep my face neutral.

"It's all over the Beggs Facebook Group. They're blaming Carmen's campaign, and now the mayor is doubling down on his Family First bullshit. I swear if I could, I would divorce James Anthony Chapman all over again for sponsoring—" She took a breath in an attempt to maintain her composure, sparing me an apologetic look. She motioned to the mug on my nightstand. "Didn't expect to get this deep before coffee. Is there any left, or do I need to brew some?"

"I might've finished a pot," I said sheepishly, shoulders rising. "I needed the boost to figure out tomorrow night."

"What's happening?" she asked through a yawn.

Shit. I rushed to find an excuse. "A party. Event, I mean. For the QSA. To, um, get more club sign-ups. For the fall."

"A membership drive?"

"Yeah . . . that."

"Still that boy who wants to fix things," she said fondly, looking once more at the picture frame. Then she turned to leave. "Okay. I'll put another pot of coffee on and get the shop open. Just meet me downstairs when you finish."

"Be there in a minute," I called as she retreated into the hallway.

But I wasn't anywhere near done. I glanced back at the laptop, her footsteps in sync with the blinking cursor. Everything was spiraling in my mind. The uproar in town and the statue and the mayor and what Cohen had said at the rec center and lying to Mom about Saturday's speakeasy . . .

A membership drive, she'd called it.

An idea began taking shape. Tomorrow could be about getting more sign-ups. Then I'd single-handedly save the QSA. I reached for my phone to text the group chat. However, a new-message notification paused my excitement. Mason had finally replied. My heart thundered in my eardrums as I tapped it to read it.

Relief eased the tension in my chest. I laughed softly, a faint "hah" as air rushed from my lungs. Because this response meant that he *must* like me, despite every messy thing in my life.

BEDMAS_22

I'm sorry you had to go through all that, but that doesn't make you any less of a person. I promise you aren't a bad gay either, Zeke. Not everyone is brave enough to rebel against the mayor. Promise me you'll be careful because things are getting crazy around here. A restaurant in West Point was shut down because of a drag brunch, and I don't want anything bad to happen to you. ♥

CHAPTER 18

The summer after seventh grade, the JACass had rented the nature preserve's lodge to celebrate Chapman Law's fiftieth anniversary. He'd wanted to honor the family legacy after Grandpa Chapman passed away. It was why we'd taken that matching photo together, an unveiling of the future of the law firm. He'd paraded me around to meet clients until I escaped out onto the deck to catch my breath.

Back then, I hadn't known why I was suffocating. Only that the long rectangle of a room was closing in on me with each handshake, with each expectation-lined smile. But now, standing in the same spot I'd been in when he announced his vision for my future, I wasn't afraid like I had been before.

I pushed my shoulders back, pushed that dark memory away. Mom had let me borrow her SUV to haul the decorations, and I'd spent the last three hours transforming the banquet hall into something new. The projection screen where Chapman Law had made the announcement with our photo was now covered in a pride flag. Tables where I'd been forced to kiss ass were put away, giving space for a giant dance floor. And most importantly, there was no one with a firm grasp on my shoulder steering me around.

"This place looks great," called a familiar gruff voice.

Owen, the ranger who'd offered up the lodge, stood inside the main door. He'd been dressed as Miles Morales the last time I'd seen him, but tonight he was wearing a rainbow-colored shirt. Its bold white letters declared he was an ally for his child. It was endearing, and I wished my father was like him. So much so that it caused a lump to rise in my throat.

A nod was all I could manage as I double-checked the decorations I'd put up. By myself. Sawyer and Kennedy would be here any minute now and see what I'd spent three hours on. Streamers hung from every beam of the pitched ceiling, twirling from the AC vents, while the curtains of twinkling lights lined the walls. Complete with the green carpet leading from the entrance to the inflatable arches, the inside of the lodge was officially ready for a party. All that was left to do was organize the QSA table.

"My kid's too young to be here tonight," Owen added, crossing over to me, "but they told me to tell Zeke hello for them."

It took a moment for my brain to catch up, but then I noticed something familiar about Owen's eyes. *The rec center.* "You're Addi's father?" I asked.

He nodded, shooting me a wide grin. "Thank you for helping them with their essay," he said. "They said the pride flag makes them feel safe, and now they've convinced all our neighbors to hang one up."

"That's great," I managed. The lump was getting bigger,

harder to swallow around. The rainbow flag had never made me feel safe when I was younger. It'd been intimidating, made me want to hide.

"Addi is the reason I'm volunteering with Carmen Bedolla's campaign," Owen said, looking around the hall. "Whatever I can do to make them safe in this town."

"Thank you," I blurted. "For offering this space and, uh, being a good dad. I'm glad Addi has you."

"And thank you," he said, clapping me on the back, "for all your hard work. I'm sure your dad is proud of what you're doing."

"Yeah . . ." He didn't know the JACass, but for a second I imagined how life would've been different if he were like Owen. If I had been supported like Addi.

The door swung open behind me, slicing through my thoughts. Sawyer and Kennedy had finally arrived. I plastered on a fake smile to mask my burning eyes and readied myself for their reactions. But when I turned, the corners of my mouth fell in confusion.

Cohen? He waved awkwardly when his eyes found me. *Why is he here?*

"Be right back," I told Owen, excusing myself.

"I'll get the sound system ready," he replied.

Cohen's gaze swooped around the room as I made my way over to him. Astonishment washed over him as he took in the lodge. It was moments like these—when he was unguarded, emotions on his sleeve—that reminded me of the crush I have on him. *Had.*

"You did all this?" he asked.

"Why, is something off?" I rushed to say. "I can fix—"

"It looks great," he said quickly with his hands held up.

"Thanks . . ." His niceness made me skeptical. It was one thing at the rec center, but now? "Why are you here?"

"Sawyer and Kennedy went out on a date," he explained, his attention snapping to the supplies on the QSA table. "So . . . I wanted to help set up."

"That's nice," I said, disappointed they'd be late. "For them, I mean. When they get here . . . what?"

He worried his bottom lip and cut his eyes toward me. "About that," he began while unloading the QSA supplies. "I wanna give you a heads-up that Sawyer is pissed . . . and they're not coming tonight."

"What?" I asked, unsure if I'd heard him correctly.

"She says you're acting like you're the QSA president," he explained with a wince. "Not that I think you are! But she said you were reckless. It's obvious you pulled that stunt with the statue. And if you get caught, they'll find out about the speak-easies. Then the club will be targeted and we'll definitely be disbanded when school starts."

Targeted? First Sawyer told me I wasn't doing enough, and now I was doing too much? My chest deflated as I glanced back at the decorations I'd worked so hard on. "No one saw me paint the statue," I assured him, my gaze drifting to the sign-up sheets I'd put on the table. "And at least *I'm* trying to save the QSA."

"You don't have to explain yourself to me." He let out a soft chuckle, and . . . *Oh my god.* He was smiling at me. "I really appreciate you stepping up. That's why I'm here to help you."

"But you're against"—I waved a hand absently around the lodge—"all this."

"I get it now, why you're doing it. What it means . . ." His smile softened into something more intimate, more reminiscent of the quiet moments we'd once shared. "You're more than useful, Zeke, and I'm sorry if I made you feel less than that."

"Stop," I said, unable to bear it. "Why are you being so . . . so . . . *nice* to me?"

He inhaled deeply and avoided my eyes. "Because I'm the Zasshole, okay?" His exhale was rough, long-winded. "I've treated you like shit because . . . because I was jealous of you."

"Of me?" I couldn't keep the bewilderment out of my voice. "*Why?*"

"You're better than me at everything." His face was getting splotchy again, and I knew he was being honest. "People always like you, even Derick had a thing for you. You were great at baseball, the top of our class, everything. Now you're even better at being out and proud than I am—"

"No, I'm not," I inserted, forgetting about the table setup. "I'm not good at that. At all. My father—"

"You don't have to explain anymore." He let out a timid laugh, almost a sigh. "I'm sorry I never asked if you were okay after you came out."

My mouth opened, closed, opened again as my brain glitched. Went into static mode. Rebooted. "Thanks?" My voice quavered. Guests began to arrive, their softs oohs and aahs echoing through the banquet hall. "I probably wouldn't have told you the truth if you had, seeing as we weren't . . . friends. So, uh, don't feel bad."

"We are now, though."

Are we? He'd said it as if it were fact. No trace of his usual sarcasm.

I didn't know what to say. And I didn't know how any of this made me feel.

...

The speakers blasted Beyoncé, the bass thumping through my chest. I'd been dancing nonstop for the last hour while purposefully ignoring the QSA table. Cohen was sitting there, right in my periphery. The unlikeliest person to take my side. It should be Sawyer taking sign-ups and rooting for me. My best friend, who is supposed to understand me, who I shouldn't have to explain myself to. Yet she wasn't here, and I was relieved—and still weirded the hell out by how unsettled it made me—that Cohen had shown up instead. She'd only push me until I caved and apologized for what I did in the square.

And I wasn't sorry at all.

Painting that statue had felt good, calling out Mayor Buchanan even more so. The fact that it had pissed him off gave me satisfaction. Sawyer couldn't take that away no matter how insolent she was acting. If she'd actually shown up instead of being a rude-ass, she'd see that word was spreading about Pride. That double the amount of people had shown up tonight, including a shocking appearance from Damian Jones.

The ending notes of the song sounded, and I pushed into the crowd. Farther and farther away from the QSA table. My only job tonight was to be the King of Pride everyone expected me to be, dance instead of worrying—

"Omph," I groaned and nearly fell as someone bumped into my side.

"Sorry," the guy said, strong hands steadying me. "Hey, it's you."

I knew those hands. That voice too. "Mason?" I gasped as the next song started. A surge of giddiness made me smile. "You came!"

"Decided to stop by," he said, raising his voice over the song.

"But I thought you couldn't come?" I asked, leaning in close to his ear.

"Guess you heard about me being grounded?" His breath was hot against the side of my face as I nodded, and it reminded me of the way his skin had felt underneath my fingers. "If someone hadn't snuck out and broken that gnome, I wouldn't have been."

"Sorry." I forgot what I was about to say. His hands gripped my waist and pulled me close. "Uh . . . hi."

"Hey," he whispered back.

He pressed his body up against mine, hands roaming up my shirtfront one button at a time. We vibed for a moment as the song blasted, as my mind played a baseball game. *He really didn't Z-step me.* Swing. *Because he's here.* Swing. *Even after everything I'd told him.* Home run!

His warm palms wrapped around my biceps. "Really happy you made it tonight," I said breathily.

"Yeah," he replied.

"And I appreciate what you said to me," I added, wanting to get it off my chest. Building up my nerve to ask him out. "I was thinking—"

"Huh?" he asked as a soft melody played next.

I stopped his hands, gripping them tightly as we swayed to the tempo. He hesitated for a second before giving in to the slow dance. My heart raced as he laid his head on my shoulder. His cologne was woodsy and comforting as I inhaled, exhaled. This guy knew me because I'd let him in. If I was brave enough to do that, then I could ask him out.

"Mason," I began in a whisper, "do you wanna maybe—"

"Get out of here?" he finished, looking up with a devilish grin. "Only if you don't break any more garden gnomes."

"Not that," I said with a laugh.

"We could go to your place, then," he suggested. "And I'll even promise not to get you grounded."

"Wait." This was not going how I'd expected, and I tried to get it back on track. "I know we're doing this backward, the whole hooking up first before we got to know each other."

"I think we know each other pretty well," he said in a husky voice. Then he leaned in closer. "I know you liked it when—"

"Do you wanna go out?" I blurted, blushing profusely. "Like on a date?"

"A date." He stared like he hadn't heard me correctly. I watched the excitement slowly slip from his face. "Zeke, hey, you're a fun guy and all, but I don't date."

I stopped dancing, my feet glued in place. "You don't?" He shrugged, and I felt the ick of embarrassment. "I thought we were . . . that you and I . . ." *Have I been misreading the signs?*

"It's that I have too much going on," he explained, hands falling away. Our bodies were too close together, and I took a step back. "But we had fun that night, and we can have fun again, if you want."

I blinked several times as his words sank in. As I realized it was almost the exact thing I'd said to guys before. As it hit me that I'd misjudged him. He was officially Z-stepping me. "Fun, yeah," I said weakly, taking another step back. "I'll be back, I just . . . uh, need to be somewhere else right now."

"Come find me," he called as I turned, "and we can get out of here."

The banquet hall had felt huge hours ago, but now the walls were closing in. Had I misconstrued everything he'd said? Everything he'd made me believe about myself?

I passed by the QSA table in a near run, and the sound of my name slowed my stride. Cohen asked if I was okay. But I only caught every other word between shuddering heartbeats. I couldn't deal with more uncertainty after what'd just happened. With a sharp shake of my head, I kept moving toward the exit.

• • •

The night air was heavy, the humidity pressing down on me as I leaned back against the deck railing. All I'd intended to do was collect myself. Let the wave of emotion roll off me so I didn't start crying. Get my shit together and pretend it hadn't bothered me. Yet thirty minutes had passed, and I could see through the window that Mason was already dancing with someone else.

I knew I'd have to go back inside at some point and talk to him. Every time I tried to, though, I couldn't. The level of stupidity I felt rooted me in place. *So this is what it feels like to have your feelings danced around?*

The party was in full swing, and people were still arriving. However, I was ready for it to be over. To take Mom's SUV back home and exchange it for my dirt bike. What I needed was to ride the streets and forget everything—Mason's "let's just be friends with benefits" letdown and Cohen's mood shift and Sawyer's anger.

Voices drifted up the lodge's steps, and I gave a weak smile as more guests arrived. It was as pathetic as I felt. They passed me on their way inside, and music briefly echoed into the night. As soon as the door closed, I dropped the pretense and ran a hand through my hair. Who was I kidding? There was no way I could go back in there and pretend to be okay. I broke out in a nervous sweat at the thought, my button-up sticking to my back. But I couldn't leave either.

The music got louder again, and I looked up. Cohen was standing there with an unreadable expression. His face was tense, head downturned. *Fucking hell,* I griped as he shuffled his feet. *I can't handle whatever his deal is now.*

"Zeke?" he said, worry deepening the line between his brows. "Are you okay?"

"I'm just, uh . . ." I tried to think of an excuse, but my brain was too exhausted from the emotional somersaults. "I needed a break."

I turned my back to him, hoping he'd take the hint, and leaned my forearms on the deck railing. The forest surrounding the lodge was eerily still in the moonlight. With no breeze, the June heat was stifling and thick. A bead of sweat rolled down my temple while I waited for the door to open. For him to go back inside so I could be alone.

Instead, he leaned up against the railing beside me without

saying anything. I studied him as he looked out at the preserve. The moonlight dappled across his hair and face, over the slight bump in his nose, over his full lips. He swallowed, throat bobbing, and then caught my eye.

"You were, uh, you were dancing with Mason Bedolla."

The reminder was like a knife twisting in my side, and I let out a ragged breath. "Unfortunately," I muttered. My hands clasped and unclasped as he turned toward me.

"God, I can't stand him," he huffed with intense disdain. "Was he a dick to you?"

"No." I shrugged, feeling embarrassed. *Should I tell him?* He evidently wanted to be on friendly terms now, and Sawyer wasn't here to help me keep my shit together . . . I let out a heavy sigh. "I was a dick to myself for thinking he liked me."

He blinked slowly, tilting his head. "What do you mean?" he asked.

"We've been messaging on Instagram for a while now, and I thought we were becoming a thing."

"Wait . . . What?"

"Like asking each other questions, getting to know each other. And I could've sworn he liked me." I chewed on my lip, my eyes threatening to tear up again. "I dunno, I'm stupid."

"Zeke, oh my god." Cohen shook his head, cringing. Red erupted up his neck and spread across his face. "You thought Mason fucking Bedolla—"

"I get it." I cut him off. "Y'all obviously have history, and you hate him now."

"That's an understatement, but you're wrong—"

"I *know*, and I'm sorry for making this awkward for you." I chewed my bottom lip, trying to find the right words to say. "It just felt good to have him care, I guess. It feels like I can't talk to anyone lately."

"It's not . . ." He trailed off, blinking too fast. His face scrunched up in confusion. "Wait . . . What do you mean?"

"Just that it's been really hard with my dad, the divorce, and now Sawyer is mad at me even though I'm trying my hardest to be the right kind of gay. It's so much damn pressure, and having Mason to talk to helped make it easier, I guess."

The sound of chirping cicadas filled the silence between us. Cohen stared down at his feet. Then he cleared his throat roughly, not looking at me. "You don't have to prove yourself to anyone to be worth something," he whispered finally. "There is no right kind of gay."

"Says the guy who told me I was a bad gay," I pointed out.

"I was wrong." He glanced up at the forest and grimaced as though it pained him to admit. "You lit a fuse in this town, and now everyone is raging in the best possible way."

His throat bobbed again, and the moonlight illuminated the softness in his brown eyes as our gazes met. It was a glimpse into the past. Standing in front of me was the boy who I'd met in the town square—and he saw through my hard-ass disguise.

"You spoke up and did something," he added in a thick voice. "The people in this town are listening. They're rallying behind what you've created. I hope you're proud, Zeke."

CHAPTER 19

Sunshine filtered through the trees, shadows of leaves dancing across the pavement as I steered my dirt bike toward the Fort Wood neighborhood. It reminded me of last night. Each scrap of daylight glinted like the mirror ball, the breeze a reminder of how it'd felt out on the deck. The talk with Cohen had cleared my head. Even though Sawyer was still pissed and Mason had crushed me, I didn't feel the weight of it pressing down on my chest anymore.

When we'd gone back inside, I'd seen firsthand that Cohen hadn't lied. More than a hundred people were dancing, laughing, partying because of me. I'd brought them together, and they were the reason why the Family First ordinance was being met with real opposition. *So what if Sawyer claims I'll make the QSA a target?* I thought, slowing to a stop at the intersection. I was doing what I'd always wanted, instead of boxing myself up. She was just jealous, like she'd been in middle school when I was teacher's favorite.

And now, I was everyone's favorite.

I checked both ways before pulling out, satisfaction manifesting into a smug grin. Right there by the four-way stop was a new sign. White like the mayor's Family First posters, but instead of red ink the words were in pink. VOTE CARMEN BEDOLLA FOR MAYOR! / ¡VOTA CARMEN BEDOLLA PARA ALCALDESA! they read in the same neon as the donkey pictured below them. Beneath that, endorsements included Roaring Mechanics, Beggs Nature Preserve, Jones Hardware . . . the list went on.

Everyone is raging in the best possible way. Cohen's assessment from last night resurfaced as I turned onto Sawyer's street. He might've said that there was no right kind of gay, but I felt like there was—and I was finally *it*.

My phone vibrated yet again in my jacket pocket, and I knew it was the group chat reminding me I was late. More donkey signs flashed by as I twisted the handlebar to speed up. Sawyer had called a mandatory QSA meeting, and the quicker I got there, the quicker we could get this over with. After the success of last night's speakeasy, I fully expected her to apologize. To tell me she was wrong.

Sunlight winked off a silver Camry as I pulled into the driveway. At least Cohen was here. He was on my side now and understood without me having to explain myself. I laughed, the irony of that thought not lost on me. The engine's warble cut off, and I checked my phone to see what fresh hell was waiting for me.

The notification screen twisted my stomach. Right above a text from Mom reminding me about my birthday dinner tomorrow, there was a new DM from bedmas_22. From the preview I could tell he was carrying on our conversation. Like offering me a list of his favorite queer movies somehow made up for him wanting to hook up and nothing more.

I shoved the phone away without replying and angrily kicked the dirt bike's stand. I threw my leg over the seat to dismount, ripped my helmet off. Whatever game he was playing was confusing. It made me regret all the times I'd done the same thing to guys. I'd never been on this side before, and I didn't know how to react. How to be calm and cool like it didn't bother me. How to be the Zeke he wanted me to be.

Maybe it's for the best, I decided, stomping down the basement steps. *I wouldn't know how to be a boyfriend to him anyway.* Ignoring the sadness, I opened the bachelorette pad's door. A gust of AC rolled over me, followed by tense silence. It took a moment for my eyes to adjust to the dim lighting, and when they did, I nearly turned back around.

Sawyer and Kennedy were wearing matching scowls. However, Cohen's welcoming smile gave me the encouragement I needed to come inside. I shut the door quietly behind me and took a deep breath. "Hey," I said as casually as I could, leaning up against the wall. "Sorry I'm late."

"It's all good," Cohen said, but Sawyer narrowed her eyes.

Yep, she's still pissed, and she wants me to know it, I realized. Her less-than-apologetic attitude only angered me more. "Really, I was putting away the decorations and lost track of time."

Cohen cut his eyes between us, picking up on the tension. "Thanks for, uh, coming up with the membership drive for the QSA," he said evenly. "We've had seven sign-ups since last night."

"Really?" I asked, relief cutting through my resentment. He nodded, and my gaze shifted back to Sawyer and Kennedy. "That's great, right?"

"Just means we have to deal with jockstrap bros because of you," Sawyer said.

Before I could ask, Kennedy chimed in. "Some of the guys on the varsity baseball team," she explained. "Damian Jones signed them up."

"Wow." I was surprised by that. It made me wish I'd given the team a chance instead of writing everyone off. "At least that brings us up to eleven members now, including us."

"Us?" Sawyer asked, and Cohen inhaled roughly. Almost as though he was expecting this. "You're gonna stay in the QSA then?"

I shot her a WTF expression, because why would I quit after everything I'd done? "Obviously."

"I wasn't sure you cared—"

"Saw, really?" I cut her off, crossing my arms. Her nonchalant shrug imploded all restraints I had on my temper. "Of fucking course I do. Look at what the speakeasies have done for Beggs, and Carmen's election is stronger because of what I—"

"You?" she asked with a dry laugh. "That's the problem. You're always only thinking about yourself."

"What does that even mean?"

"Your main-character energy is through the roof," she said, shaking her head. "Ever since we came back from winter break, it's been the *Zeke* show. We get it. You don't want to be called Anthony and you changed your entire personality—"

"What she means," Kennedy amended, side-eyeing her as though it wasn't what they'd rehearsed, "is that it feels like you're making Pride Month about *you*, and we're worried that it's getting too out of hand. Something bad could happen."

"Something bad *has* happened," I pointed out. "The Family First ordinance! Which only came about *because* of the QSA, if you want to point fingers."

The tense energy was escalating, and Cohen raised his hands to mediate. "Let's just calm down," he said. "Zeke does have a point. None of this would've happened if we hadn't petitioned for Pride. And Sawyer also has every right to be worried."

"We shouldn't have fought for Pride Day, then?" She turned on Cohen, and I hated the snippy tone of her voice. Hated how she was acting, how she was making me react. "What were we supposed to do? Keep quiet and not fight—"

"That's not what he meant," I said in his defense. "This is a good thing, Sawyer. Everything that's happened *is* good." What he'd told me outside on the deck came pouring out. "The speakeasies have helped other people fight with us. They want us here in Beggs, and it's more important now with the governor and . . . What?"

"When did you turn into such an advocate?" she questioned, cocking her head. "Last time I checked, I had to *beg* you to even join the club."

"Sawyer," Cohen warned. He knew about some of the hell I'd gone through. "Regardless of why he joined, I'm glad he did. The speakeasies have helped the work we're doing for Carmen."

"Now you're a fan?" Kennedy asked. "You're the one who blew us off to work on her campaign because you got scared—"

"Fear doesn't have anything to do with this," I interrupted.

Cohen glared at her. The situation was going zero to a hundred too quickly. "Why are we even fighting? We're celebrating Pride in Beggs like we wanted, and now the homophobic asshole mayor might not win reelection because of the support we've rallied. We *should* be celebrating."

A beat of silence passed as we all stared at one another. I took a deep breath and digested what Sawyer had said about it being *the Zeke show*. She wasn't wrong, but she wasn't right either. I'd been second to her for so long while she called the shots. The only thing that had changed was the fact that I now refused to stay silent.

"At least there is only one weekend left," Sawyer finally said. "Let's just keep it simple, and then we can go back to normal."

Normal? I didn't think I could ever go back to how things were. "It has to be big," I countered. That's what people wanted, for me to live up to the expectations they'd crowned me with. "A huge party to end Pride Month."

Sawyer twisted at her hair, too focused on whatever was happening in her head to talk. It was Kennedy who spoke first. "Zeke, having a membership drive was good. I'll give you that," she admitted. "It's too dangerous, tho—"

"Dangerous?" I narrowed my eyes at her, then Sawyer. "*How* would either of you know? Y'all bailed last night."

"Because if you haven't noticed, Mayor Buchanan is on the warpath since you painted that statue," Sawyer finally said. "He's looking for any excuse to improve his image. We aren't gonna risk getting caught by doing something stupid like throwing a rager."

The expression on Sawyer's face took me back to middle

school. It was the same pinch to her brow, firm set to her mouth that she'd worn in PE. Like I should feel weak and let her push me around. Let her pummel me with the dodgeball and sit out on the bleachers until the next game. That was how our friendship had always been. Until now.

"They're not stupid," I said. "Last time I checked, I was in charge of them, and if I want to throw a giant party then I will."

"You're acting so reckless." She shared a glance with Kennedy that let me know they agreed. Cohen shook his head, but she ignored him. "There's a lot at stake, and if you're not gonna take this seriously . . . then maybe you shouldn't be in the QSA."

She locked eyes with me, the amber honey of hers trapping me in their sticky stare. Then suddenly it was only us. Cohen and Kennedy faded away as every moment in Sawyer-and-Zeke's list of traditions boiled down to one common thread: she was the one who made the decisions.

"I've tried telling you," I said, voice wavering. "Honestly, I'm sick of trying to make you listen. If you're just gonna bully me to quit because you're jealous—"

"That's a low blow." Her words were clipped, her face growing red.

I knew I couldn't take it back, but now she knew how I felt. Deep down, it was me who was the jealous one, though. Sawyer had always been so sure of herself, unlike me. My father disapproved of her, and that made me want to be like her. But it was clear she thought I'd never be as good as her.

"You know what? I don't need your permission to throw my own speakeasy." My breath had grown ragged, and I turned on my heels. "I'll just handle everything by myself," I called over my shoulder. "Again."

The basement door slammed behind me as tears rolled down my cheeks. I knew I should stay and work things out. But if I went back inside, it would be like going back into that shoebox—hiding a part of myself so someone else could have their way.

And I was done suffocating.

CHAPTER 20

BEDMAS_22
Hey, you okay?

Mason's fifth consecutive message taunted me as I sat in the far-right corner at The Cove. I still hadn't answered him. Or the text Cohen sent in the group chat asking the same question. I almost told both of them that I was fine, that I had already planned another great speakeasy on my own. However, that would've been a lie.

Ever since I could remember, I'd always had to ask for permission, whether it was asking my father to join the QSA or Mom if I could go to a concert with Sawyer. I didn't know what I felt without someone telling me how to feel. If Mason was acting like *something* had happened between us, then I'd have some clue how to react. If Sawyer had made an effort to stop me from leaving last night, I would've known I was more than her shadow.

All I could do was stay under a car today, take apart an engine, and put it back together, until Mom flipped the closed sign for Roaring Mechanics. She'd lingered in the doorway, giving me a parting smile before going upstairs to get ready— one full of admiration, like when she'd said she was proud of me. And *I* felt proud too, despite what'd happened. I'd stood up for myself and put myself out there.

I don't need anyone's permission, I decided, glancing back at The Cove's host stand. Sawyer hadn't even bothered to speak to me when we arrived. Not even a second glance as she motioned us toward the dining room, like she forgot it was my birthday. I guess there weren't any celebratory wishes or sneaky traditions this year. Just me stuck at a table with the last person I wanted to see.

"You're being rude, Anthony," my father said, snapping my attention back to the conversation.

"Huh?" I asked. He cleared his throat and nodded toward my phone. Leaving Mason's message on read, I shoved my phone in the pocket of my chinos.

"Your father was discussing the future, as always," Mom replied, setting down her glass of sweet tea. The raised set of her shoulders told me she was holding back her anger. "Please go on, James."

The JACass smiled his fake smile. "I sent the athletics director at UA some videos of your pitching. He thinks you have a good shot at getting admitted based on your skill," he said with far too much gusto. "Your coach is more than willing to let you rejoin the team."

He sat back and waited for me to reply. Judging by the width of his toothy grin, he thought I was finally going to succumb to his demands. The collar of my shirt was threatening to strangle me. I unbuttoned a few buttons and tried to block out the hundred different conversations buzzing in the restaurant.

"It's a lot to think about," he said before I could speak, reaching into his sports coat. A small white envelope appeared on the table in front of me. "How about you open your present first before you decide?"

"What's this?" I asked, taking it from him. His eagerness only exacerbated my skepticism. I ripped open the seal. A slip of paper fell on the tablecloth, and I picked it up. *Huh?* He'd gifted me a check for $1,000 made out to the Beggs High School QSA. "I don't understand."

"Chapman Law is now sponsoring the QSA," he explained.

"Why?" I asked, sharing a look with Mom, who seemed equally confused.

He forced a chuckle like I'd just told a bad joke. "Because you're my son, and I want you to know I support you."

Support me? I read the check again. A thousand dollars to make up for how he'd treated me ever since I came out. *Something isn't right.*

"What are you doing, James?" Mom asked cautiously. "First you throw your support behind Family First, and now this?"

"Katherine," he began, his shoulders rising to match hers, "that was just business, nothing personal."

"Nothing personal," I repeated. "Is that what *this* is, business?"

"Son, I'm trying to meet you halfway, here." He deflated with a rough exhale through his nose. "I accept you, and it would be great if you could accept me."

"What does that even mean?" Mom asked for me.

"That our son doesn't appreciate what I've done for him."
He locked eyes with her, and his jaw flexed. "I let him live with
you in that dump apartment and how does he thank me? By
nearly ruining the life I helped him build, and I refuse to let
him continue to do so."

"James—"

Mom stopped herself and spared a smile as Cohen appeared in his waiter uniform. I could feel the rage boiling in
my chest while he refilled her glass of sweet tea. *He refused to
let me? Like he can still control me? Fuck him. I'm eighteen years old
now.*

"How are we doing this evening?" Cohen asked. "Have you
decided on your entrées yet?"

"We'll still need a few minutes, thanks," my father replied
curtly.

"Are you sure?" Cohen pressed, cutting his gaze toward me.

The thoughtful tilt of his head let me know he'd heard the
entire conversation. Heat seared my cheeks as I nodded once,
hoping he hadn't seen the check. Because I couldn't accept it.
Wouldn't accept a bribe.

"Thanks, Cohen," I said under my breath, and he patted my
shoulder once before moving to his next table.

We sat there for a moment in silence. It was as though all
the air had been sucked out of The Cove. The feeling that I was
suffocating was back, the shoebox lid threatening to seal me
inside. I couldn't take it anymore and tossed the check on the
table.

"Why would I thank you?" I asked, my words daggers.

He leaned forward with a lowered voice. "Anthony, do you
know the town square has video surveillance?" he asked, and

my eyes went wide. *The donkey statue.* "Mayor Buchanan turned over the footage to the law firm for me to go through. The city was prepared to press charges against the culprit, but fortunately for you there was no footage to be found of that night."

My heart dropped into my stomach as Mom swiveled toward me. "You vandalized that statue?" she asked in disbelief.

I dry swallowed and gave her a nod. *Shit, shit, shit.* I was in so much trouble. She would ground me, and then there went the speakeasies—

"Good," Mom said, surprising both my father and me. "Because Mayor Buchanan *is* a jackass, and I'm glad there's a chance he'll get voted out of office."

"Katherine," Dad warned. "Keep your voice down. There is no way in hell he'll lose. A vote for Bedolla won't amount to anything, and it looks bad for Chapman Law if you're—"

"I don't give two shits about Chapman Law." She cut him off. "And I'll be damned if I let you tell me what to do." He opened his mouth, and she pointed a finger at him tersely. "Don't you dare interrupt me while I'm talking. You've been so focused on Family First that you forgot to put *your* family first. You can't play both sides now to get what you want."

"I'm doing what's best for our son," he retorted.

"What's best for Zeke," she began with an eerie calm in her voice, "is making his own decisions about the future. You *will* respect that."

They both locked eyes in a stare down, and the fake politeness slipped from his face. "And what do you want to do, *Zeke*?" he sneered, glaring at me.

It was the first time he'd ever asked me that. I'd been thinking about the answer to that question since that first day I worked in Roaring Mechanics. How it felt to hold a tool in my hand while Zelda Fitzgerald watched over me. To take charge and be proud, live my life and not give a shit about what other people thought was best for me.

My glare met his as I began ripping up his check. Because I knew what I didn't want, and that was to meet him halfway. I wouldn't accept his conditions.

. . .

My birthday officially sucked.

Mom and I stormed out of The Cove before my father could object. She'd tried to make up for it by taking me out for burgers and ice cream in West Point. The entire time I kept wishing I could tell Mason about the JACass's audacity. So, in a moment of weakness, I'd messaged him back. No response had come by the time we arrived home. I'd been so gutted that all I could do was crawl into bed and pull up my favorite *Doctor Who* episodes.

Not even the terrifying Weeping Angels storyline could distract me, though. I was too hollowed out from too much thinking, too much regret for messaging Mason despite myself. With a sigh, I exited the streaming app and closed my laptop.

I knew the speakeasy needed planning, but I wasn't feeling it. Not with the doubt pulling at me or the anticipation that kept me checking my phone. Mason still hadn't replied to the too-honest message. *For real, though, who would blame him?* I thought, unlocking my phone to reread what I'd sent.

ZEKECHAPMAN

sorry a lot has been going on

ZEKECHAPMAN

no I'm not okay bc some stuff went down with my father and my friends and my birthday sucks majorly and yeah

9:02 PM

ZEKECHAPMAN

sorry I don't mean to bother you but just needed someone to tell hope you have a good night

My thumb hovered over the last message to unsend it, but he'd already seen it. And he still hadn't replied. *Could this night get any worse?* I groaned, sitting up. *The only guy who I could be myself around, and I ruined—* The screen lit up with a reply.

11:43 PM

BEDMAS_22

Zeke, I'm sorry. Fuck your dad for ruining it. He's an asshole. That sucks, and I wish I could make it better. You never bother me, just so you know. My night gets better when you message me. Please don't stop. I'm here for you if you want to talk.

BEDMAS_22

Also HAPPY BIRTHDAY! I wish I would've gotten you something. Maybe it would have made the day not suck so much.

A bad idea was beginning to take shape. It would be so easy to sneak over to his house, into his room, into a false reality where we could be together for a few hours. But I stopped myself from typing something thirsty and played it cool.

ZEKECHAPMAN

it's okay or it will be I guess

ZEKECHAPMAN

thank you for saying that

ZEKECHAPMAN

I came home and have been watching my favorite episodes of Doctor Who to cheer myself up

BEDMAS_22

What episode is next? I'll watch it with you.

I felt the beginning of a smile as I glanced around my room. The green dirt bike helmet Mom had got me sat on the dresser with the bow still on it. It would be smarter to blow him off and go riding. Keep myself from getting closer to him after how he'd treated me last weekend. Although, he was the only person I could talk to . . .

ZEKECHAPMAN

the 2023 Christmas special

ZEKECHAPMAN

and thank you for wanting
to be my friend Mason 😊

I leaned back against the pillows and reopened my laptop. Despite the late hour, he was willing to stay up and watch Ncuti Gatwa's first episode as the Fifteenth Doctor. It filled me with bittersweetness, because he'd said he didn't date, and I really wanted to date him. *Regret is a problem for tomorrow me,* I decided, navigating to the episode. Then I went to DM that I was ready and saw his back-to-back messages. It felt like someone had sucker punched me in the nuts.

BEDMAS_22

I really want to be your friend, but I can't if
I'm lying to you.

BEDMAS_22

I'm not Mason.

CHAPTER 21

Who is bedmas_22?

The question haunted me, lurking between all my thoughts. It kept me awake for the last few nights with its eerie presence. The glow of my phone would cut through the dark while I creeped on Instagram for any clues. Anything to reveal his true identity. The only thing I found was a nauseating implication.

I'd been spilling my secrets to a stranger.

Embarrassment pulsed through me as I read his messages again and again—before getting ready for work, eating a bowl of cereal, between oil changes. Every time I tried to reply, my thumb froze over the touchscreen before I could hit send. I wanted to yell at him for betraying my trust. He'd made me feel like a stupid ass, a fool for asking the real Mason out.

I slowly backspaced my "who the hell are you?" as I made my guesses. *Jonathan with the tattoo?* Not likely, given how much he'd cried when I ended things. Delete. *Bailey the skateboarder?*

He'd kicked me out of his car and told me to fuck all the way off. Delete. *Zach from West Point baseball?* Just a one-time thing. Delete. *Damian Jones?* He was straight as far as I knew, but something about that night in the hardware store . . . A new message came through while I tried to think of who else it could be.

12:23 PM

BEDMAS_22

Your silence must mean you're mad.

"Ugh," I growled, tossing my phone onto the lobby sofa. My head hurt from trying to think it through. Somehow my life kept getting messier no matter how much I tried to keep it from falling apart. Sawyer threatening to kick me out of the QSA, my father's performative stunt at The Cove, everything I told the fake Mason. All of it was too much to deal with.

I stretched out on the cushions and tried to tune out the TV's midday news report. The governor's newest hate-fueled bill was only making the ache in my head worse. From my relaxed position, I could see the back wall of the garage. The painting of Zelda peered at me, like she had been all morning. *Did you ever feel free?* I silently pleaded with her for guidance.

"Having a staring contest with her again?"

I leaned my head back and found an upside-down Mom. She had just come inside with our lunch in one hand and the other behind her back. "She's impossible to beat," I said, righting myself on the sofa. *Impossible to live up to.*

"Mmm-hmm," she said, moving sideways to keep whatever it was she was hiding out of my sight.

"Why are you being sketchy?" I asked, trying to peer around her.

"Because," she said with a grin, "it's a surprise."

"Surprise?" There had been way too many surprises lately. "Is it salt to rub in my wounds?"

"Morbid." She tsked and rolled her eyes.

"I can't help that I'm in my sad-boy era." I'd filled her in on everything about Mason and how I'd asked him out. Almost everything. I couldn't bring myself to divulge how incredibly stupid I felt for falling for Fake Mason's lies.

"Maybe a belated birthday present will cheer you up?" She revealed the hidden gift box with a flourish. "It was delayed getting here, but—"

"But nothing." I cut her off with grabby hands.

She laughed, tossing it to me. The sounds of ripping paper drowned out the news update as I opened it. A lump of thick vibrant-green material fell into my lap. I'd helped Mom out enough growing up to know what it was.

"You got me a mechanic shirt?" I asked, holding it up.

"That's not the gift," she said. "Look at the front."

I turned it around and saw why she was excited, why this had been wrapped as a surprise. Above the pocket of the button-up was a patch. Roaring Mechanics spelled out in the same font as the emerald sign out front, and there was cursive beneath it. "Zeke Chapman," I read, feeling the embroidered words. "Assistant Mechanic."

"Do you like it?" Mom was beaming as she waited expectantly. "I thought it was appropriate since you've been such a huge help this summer."

"I love it . . ." Seeing my name printed like that made

something click in my brain, the sum of all the conversations I'd had recently about the future. *What do you want to do, Zeke?* my father had asked. "Do you think I could do this, like, for real?"

"What do you mean?" She gave me a puzzled look.

I cleared my throat. "I mean if I wanted to go to school for automotive technology, like you?"

"Like me, huh?" She took a seat on the sofa arm, taken aback by the question. "You wanna know if I think you can do this?" I nodded. "Hun, you're *already* doing it, and you're good at it too."

"You're not just saying that because you're my mom?" I teased.

"I probably *shouldn't* be saying that, because I'm also the boss," she replied in kind. "You'll put me out of a job one day."

"Never." I absently rubbed my hand over the embroidered letters of my name. If I could go to school like she had, then I could work here once I graduated and maybe even expand to a new location.

A cool finger reached out and smoothed the wrinkles on my brow. "Stop thinking too much. You don't have to know what you want to do, and don't give me that stubborn glare. If you spend too long worried about the future, then you'll forget to live in the now."

"I guess." All my life had been spent preparing for what was next, not examining what was happening right now. Not what was in the news about the issues facing people like me. They didn't teach us that in school; my father didn't sit me down and tell me how to fight back—just that I should go along with things and accept defeat.

"You're really set on not going to law school, then?" she asked, opening the takeout bag from the deli down the street.

I looked back down at the shirt and knew without a doubt. "I don't wanna be anything like *him*," I said, more to myself than her.

"You have nothing to worry about," she said, handing me my usual muffuletta. "You're the complete opposite of your father. Just look at what you've done with the QSA."

Dread filled my stomach, chasing away my appetite. I still hadn't planned for this weekend. And I knew what Sawyer would say if she found out: *You're acting so reckless.* I groaned and set my lunch to the side.

"Everything okay with your membership drive?" she asked through a mouthful.

"It will be," I muttered. Another messy component of my life to worry about. This weekend had to be huge, bigger and better than before. If only I could ignore all the other noise in my head long enough to figure it out. "After I nail down the details for this weekend for . . . um, another one. I just haven't had time to think about it yet."

She swallowed her bite and studied me. "Why isn't Sawyer helping you?" she asked.

"Because she's mad at me for taking charge." I shot her a sheepish grin. "But someone had to do it."

"She's jealous."

I narrowed my eyes and tilted my head to the side. "Why do you say that?"

"I was once a young woman, ages ago," she said, wiping grease off her fingers with a napkin, "and it's not easy to hold your own in a small town."

"You're not *that* old, Mom," I pointed out. "You're like . . . a millennial."

"So much has changed since I was your age," she said with a sigh, "but the struggle is still the same. Having to prove yourself is never easy. Sawyer probably had herself all figured out, and then you stepped into the QSA this year. Started trying to fix things, because that's who you are. Probably even ran your mouth without considering where she might be coming from."

"Wow. I thought this was gonna be a pep talk, but you're totally burning me."

"What do the youth say? I'm 'speaking my truth'?" she asked, ruffling my hair. I gave her a pointed look. "Like when you got that black eye or when you painted that donkey or when . . . Well, the list goes on and on."

"Ha. Ha."

I got what she was saying, but she didn't know the full story. How Sawyer had expected me to defer to her because it had always been like that. No matter how much I'd tried to prove myself, she wouldn't let me. Why should I care how much she was struggling with her own stuff if she didn't care to let me explain mine?

"Speaking of this weekend," Mom added with a note of bashfulness, "I decided to go on the cabin retreat with the book club on Saturday."

"Really?" I asked, pulling out of my thoughts.

"You were right. I need to do something for myself," she said, as though to reassure herself. "Get back to my old girlfriends."

"I'm proud of you, Mom." I wasn't the only one reworking

the past, figuring out which pieces of our old life fit into this new one. "You deserve to have fun."

"Thank you for that." She spared me an appreciative smile, and then her eyes narrowed. "I'll be gone overnight," she began, pointing a finger at me, "and I can't stop you from having a boy over, so if you do—"

"Mooooom," I groaned, throwing my head back on the sofa. "That most definitely won't be happening. Not after . . ." *After embarrassing myself with the real Mason, even more so with the fake one.*

She reached out and patted me on the knee. "I'm sorry it didn't work out like you wanted with Mason."

"It's whatever," I mumbled, even though it wasn't. "I'm fine."

"It's okay if you aren't."

But it wasn't okay. And I didn't know how to make it okay. Mason wasn't the problem to solve; it was the stranger who'd let me think they were him.

Sensing I didn't want to talk about it, she stood. "Well, I have an appointment due in a few," she said, heading toward the shop. "If you have more staring contests with Zelda back there, don't get any wild ideas to party like her while I'm gone this weekend."

I scoffed at her as she disappeared into the garage, then my eyes darted to the painting in her wake. *Got any wild ideas for a speakeasy?* I silently asked, half joking. But then I sat upright as Mom's words resonated in my mind.

She would be gone on Saturday, meaning I'd be home alone. With a very large garage that had plenty of room when cars weren't being serviced. I looked around the lobby, recalling how it'd been transformed into Zelda's Music Emporium for the opening-night speakeasy . . .

Here, I decided. *Right here would be perfect for Saturday.* I could still remember where we'd hung the decorations and moved the tools to make space. Roaring Mechanics would be the perfect place for Pride Month to go out with a bang. I could decorate when she left Saturday and clean up before she got back on Sunday.

Excited and relieved, I grabbed my phone. The selfie I'd taken awhile back for Mason, *Fake* Mason, would be perfect for Insta, with the tools spread out around me and grease smudged on my cheek. *"Gettin' dirty this weekend"* would be a great caption . . . My thoughts stopped short when I saw the message thread still pulled up. He'd sent another DM thirteen minutes ago.

BEDMAS_22

I know you're not talking to me, but I wanted to give you a heads-up. Mayor Buchanan knows about the underground Pride speakeasies.

CHAPTER 22

ZEKECHAPMAN

who are you?

He dodged my question. His reply was that it didn't matter, only that he was warning me. For a split second, his message had me worrying over everything Sawyer had said. *Dangerous* and *reckless* and *if you get caught* . . . But then the comments on the selfie I'd posted—excited RSVPs and pride flag emojis and praise—reinforced how I'd felt last weekend. The people in Beggs were listening, rallying behind what I'd created.

I wasn't scared of Mayor Buchanan, of Family First, or of getting caught.

Screw the warning. The mayor was shaken because of the upcoming election. Because I'd painted that donkey statue and called him a jackass. Him knowing about the Pride events only strengthened my resolve. I'd make this last weekend huge in spite of him, my father, Fake Mason, the QSA. Everyone else was expecting me to be their King of Pride, and I *would* finish this month with a bang.

I reread my DM thread with bedmas_22 for what felt like the millionth time and shoved my phone into the pocket of my khakis. Shoved his warning out of my head as I took the steps up to the rec center. He might've been trying to help, but he was also a stranger who'd tricked me into telling him things I'd never told anyone else. I was so unbelievably ashamed over it, because I'd actually started to like whoever this person was. And I was sick of being betrayed by everyone I let in.

The lobby's doors slid open, and I crossed over to the elevator to press the call button. I welcomed a deep inhale of the AC-chilled air after the stifling heat. Summer break was nearing the halfway mark, and it felt like it was only getting hotter. My reflection in the shiny metal panels glared back at me in a disheveled state. My polo was damp and wrinkled underneath my unseasonable leather jacket, my hair slick with sweat from the dirt bike helmet. I adjusted the shirt and ran my hands through my blond waves while I waited.

The elevator arrived with a ding, and Cohen rushed out as soon as the panels slid open. He collided with me and knocked both of us off-balance. We tangled together, his bookbag spilling. "Sorry," he mumbled in a thick voice, scrounging to shove everything back inside the bag. Then I noticed his bloodshot eyes, his wet cheeks.

"Are you okay?" I asked, picking up a wadded pride flag.

"No, Zeke," he choked out while snatching it from me. "I'm *obviously* not okay."

His snide remark felt too much like how things used to be

between us. "Seriously," I began, putting a hand on his shoulder, "what's up?"

He shook me off with a heavy breath. I almost cussed him out, but the retort died on my tongue. His eyes met mine beneath his glower. I knew that expression, knew how the lurking sadness looked on my own face. "Hey," I tried again, my voice low. "What happened?"

"It's over," he said with a sniffle, gripping at the rainbow material. "They even tore down the flag."

"What is?"

A beat passed before his facade cracked, and then he was hugging me. The smell of rosemary and tea tree shampoo filled my nose as he put his head on my shoulder. I patted him on the back, unsure of what else to do. "The mayor defunded the mentor program," he said hoarsely. "They fired Jess and told the volunteers to go home."

"What the actual fuck?" I asked, pulling away to look at him.

"One of the parents didn't, didn't . . ." He sniffled, wiping his nose on a shirtsleeve. "They said we were teaching their kids to be queer. There was a complaint filed, and now . . . That damn ordinance has ruined everything."

I immediately thought of my father, how he'd told me just to keep my head down and I wouldn't be affected. But Family First wasn't just about me, and it was affecting more and more people in Beggs—this was proof. "That's *such* bullshit," I said. "What can we do?"

"Nothing, Zeke," he replied despondently. "It's hopeless."

Hopeless. I was tired of feeling that way. "Surely there's something. We could do it ourselves—"

"We can't!" He cut me off with a shake of his head. "I've spent the last hour trying to think of something, but I doubt parents are gonna risk singling out their kids now. This meant so much to me and . . . Sorry, I don't mean to be a dick."

"You have every right to be a dick," I offered. "It's okay."

"It's not." He let out a sigh and leaned against the lobby wall. "I'm so pissed off right now. I keep thinking about how much I'd needed something like this when I was younger. How I'd been confused and felt out of place."

That was surprising, and I gawked at him in disbelief. Cohen had always been so sure of himself, going back to when he'd told me about the town founder's statue. That was one of the things that'd made my brain glitch out over him.

"I wish I'd had it too," I heard myself admit. "All I had was a shoebox."

"What?" he asked.

It's nothing, I almost said. Then I thought of how I'd confided in Fake Mason, how it had felt to let some of the panic out. "My father didn't allow me to talk about gay stuff," I rushed to say before I chickened out. "I had to hide everything from him in a shoebox . . . including the QSA forms Sawyer kept giving me."

"That's the reason why you suddenly joined the club this year," he surmised. "Because of your parents' divorce."

I nodded, and he opened his mouth. "Don't say you're sorry." I cut him off. "Nothing you could have done about it."

"But I *am* sorry for you," he said. "Sorry for all the kids in the program who need it. Sorry for so many things . . ."

"I am too," I said, leaning back beside him. "I wish I could do something about it."

"But you already are, Zeke, and I've been sitting on the sidelines playing by the rules." He balled his hands into fists. "What do you do when the rules weren't made with you in mind?"

"You don't follow them then," I said, biting my lip. "You break them."

He looked at me, steely-eyed, and slowly nodded. "Then I'm helping you with the last speakeasy. There's nothing else we can do, not unless the mayor gets voted out of office."

"You'll help?" I asked.

He gave me another nod, jaw clenched and brow furrowed. "We won't let him intimidate us. So, fuck Family First. Fuck the mayor. Fuck his reelection campaign rally in the town square."

"Wait, when is his rally?"

He checked the time on his phone and said, "Right now," with a dejected shake of his head.

I could still remember how I'd felt on Pride Day. The way the mayor had stepped up onto the pavilion just to crush our dreams. The way my father had held his hand up to force me to be silent. The way I regretted not yelling at both of them in that moment, so they'd know how wrong they were. I refused to be afraid anymore. *I won't stand back and let it happen again,* I decided.

"I have to go," I said, shoving off the wall. "And I'll need that pride flag."

"Zeke, it's not safe—"

"I'm not afraid of Mayor Buchanan." I grabbed the wadded-up rainbow from his grip. "He won't get away with this. Someone has to make him listen."

...

If I didn't know any better, I would've thought it was the first weekend of June. A crowd had gathered around the square's pavilion like they had a few weeks ago. There was a charge in the evening air, rumbles of excited conversation mixing with music softly playing through speakers. Signs held up with rainbows on them that gave me the illusion of safety.

But I knew better.

These were the people behind the Beggs Facebook Group, the ones who had protested over Pride Day. Their signs had Xs over the pride flag, the same bold red as the Family First posters on the lampposts. Their loud opinions swarmed me as I parked my dirt bike, small-minded battle cries overlapping as the engine cut off.

Up on the pavilion, the mayor was waving and smiling with a sick kind of glee. A deep inhale, an exhale as I planned to march up there and steal the microphone. Show him, show everyone in this rallying crowd, they couldn't keep us from—

"Gays aren't welcome in Beggs!"

The protest cry broke from the dull roar, and my attention snapped to the woman in front of me. Her giant sign waved back and forth as she yelled it again with vigor. My stomach bottomed out as I scanned the crowd, my shaking hands clutching the flag to my chest. More signs, more cries, more people showing their ass.

Nausea twisted my stomach when I saw the bright-blue truck with a Wildcats Baseball decal. It was parked close to the pavilion, and I knew the JACass was here supporting the reelection campaign. *It's just business, nothing personal,* he reminded me as static crackled from the speakers. But the signs and yells and outright hatred felt *extremely* personal.

A round of applause sounded as the mayor grabbed the microphone. Time was running out. I had to push through the hate and stop him. My legs wouldn't move, though. A ripple of fear kept me still. There was no way I could make it to the front. My pulse quickened as I considered bailing, that maybe this wasn't the smartest idea after all.

I can't be quiet about how wrong this is, not again, I thought, searching for another way around. Then I saw the Chapman Law billboard on top of Jones Hardware. The access ladder had been easy to climb that first day of summer. I'd be able to see everyone up there, and most importantly, they'd see me waving the pride flag.

Thinking fast, I hurried around the edge of the square. My legs wobbled, but I tried to shake it off. All I had to do was get up there and yell at the mayor. Get his attention, my father's. Then I'd make both of them understand how this was personal for so many people in Beggs.

"Good evening, ladies and gentlemen!" Mayor Buchanan's voice boomed from the pavilion. I hit the alley in a run and reached the ladder as his smooth twang resounded. "This town is a mess, and do you know who's to blame?"

Shouts echoed around me as I climbed fast, rainbow material draped around my neck like a boa. Vulgar slurs and curses stabbed at me as I ascended higher and higher. I gulped and risked a glance down at the sidewalk. My fear of heights made me dizzy with apprehension, but I had to keep going.

I couldn't let anyone see me be afraid.

Another rung, and then another. The billboard's metal

catwalk scraped my knees as I crawled it with panting breaths. No time to think. I forced myself to stand up and stretched the flag out over my head and . . . the entire square loomed down below.

Too high up.

I dropped back to my knees and gripped the edge. The metal support beam dug into my palms as I watched the mayor on the pavilion. Same short and neat hairstyle, same obnoxious grin in place as he lifted the microphone like he had a few weeks ago. As my father stood off to the side and applauded him along with the crowd.

"That's right," Buchanan said. "Immoral agendas that are threatening our families!" Cheers erupted as his grin spread wider. "Just today I found out the rec center was conducting a mentorship program, shoving their perverse lifestyles in our children's faces. I've immediately ordered it be shut down and defunded. At least as long as I'm in office by the grace of my voters."

"You have my vote!" someone bellowed.

"Make Beggs safe for families again!" another yelled.

"Don't worry, folks!" He held his hand up, bringing it to his chest. "I'm well aware of the rumors pertaining to certain illegal events happening right under our noses. With the support of Chapman Law, my Family First ordinance is just the beginning. I'm thrilled to announce my One Lifestyle ordinance. Come this fall, if you reelect me as your mayor, all inappropriate books will be banned from the library!" Roars of appreciation rang out as he paused. "Lessons not authorized as in accordance with our values will be banned in school, and our kids will be raised how they ought to be!" More shouts that made his smarmy grin wider, knowing he had them in the palm of his hand. "Together, we can take back *our* town!"

My anger spiked as my father continued to cheer. He was still playing both sides. He only cared about putting himself first. This wasn't acceptance, not meeting me halfway like he'd said on my birthday. Everything he'd claimed to do for my benefit was just another lie.

I glanced over my shoulder at the billboard, at who I used to be. Nerves collided in my stomach, and vomit hit the back of my throat. Because if I hadn't denounced that version of myself, if my parents hadn't divorced, if I was still letting him manipulate me . . . then I would have been forced up on that stage with him. Just like how he had paraded me around the lodge for the firm's anniversary dinner. A united front. He would've found a way to manipulate me into doing it despite it being against everything I was.

The part that hurt the most was that I knew I would've believed him, knew all the people in Beggs I would have hurt. "I'm sorry," I whispered aloud, locking eyes with the picture of myself. "I'm sorry we had to keep ourselves hidden."

My gaze shifted to the giant picture of the JACass beside me. His beaming face was threatening me, choking me, suffocating me. My hand gripped the flag, harder and harder until my fingers ached. Everything I'd had to deal with this year coursed through me: the divorce, being told I wasn't good enough, the canceled Pride Day, the future and college and all the mounting pressure.

The mayor's bullshit speech continued while my breathing went ragged. "I won't stop until we remind folks what kind of town Beggs is," Buchanan said, and I hated it. Hated being told what to do and how to live and who to be. I closed my eyes and saw my father standing there like he had before, holding his hand up to stop me. *Be quiet.*

"No." My voice came out in a tremor, and then I squared my shoulders. "I refuse to be scared."

Slowly, I stood and took a deep breath. Turned to face the square and do what I came here to do. However, as I looked below, I couldn't speak. My voice caught in my throat as I saw how many people were at the rally. How many people were shouting hateful things and waving signs and— Panic recoiled in my stomach. I gagged, and my dinner splashed across the catwalk.

I tried to take a calming breath to ease the panic swelling in my chest. But in between the shouts of "They don't belong here!" and "Bedolla isn't right for our town!" I could hear my father. *A vote for Bedolla won't amount to anything,* he'd said at dinner. It made my hands shake, vision pinprick. I tried to steady myself, but dizziness brought me to my knees as the rally raged.

Is he right?

My chest threatened to explode with each pump of my heart. It was one thing to see this kind of hate on the news, in cities far away. Places where I thought it couldn't touch me. It was too real seeing it here in our small town. I'd thought I wasn't afraid, that I could face the mayor and his supporters and remind them how they were wrong—but *I* was wrong.

I was terrified.

CHAPTER 23

All eyes are watching you when you're on the pitcher's mound. The other team is waiting to see if you screw up, and your team is waiting on you to secure the win. Being caught in the middle of everyone's expectations always made me feel alone. Forced me to steady my stance and roll my shoulders. Breathe through the doubt. Hope for the best while preparing for the worst.

That's what Pride felt like now.

My grip tightened on the grease rag as I shifted my weight from foot to foot. Between the rattling bass of my old pregame playlist and each thumping heartbeat, I could feel the looming loss of control. Buchanan's rally had shaken everyone up. It was all anyone could talk about on the Beggs Facebook Group. His supporters fired off cringe comments about Carmen, reinforcing what my father had said. I'd gotten texts from Sawyer and Kennedy claiming it was too risky to host another speakeasy, but I didn't reply. Whoever the hell bedmas_22 was sent another DM that I couldn't bring myself to open. None of them understood how suffocating it had been to witness that rally. How terrified I'd been or how much I needed to win the game we'd been forced to play.

I wound my arm back, lifting my leg up, and eyed the shop's garbage can. Then I let go of the doubt and followed through. The rag shot out of my grip and thudded into the trash. *Strike!* In my head, the crowd cheered over the chants from last night. The mirror ball's green light danced above me as I held my arms up in triumph. Nothing could screw up tonight—

The music cut off abruptly, a new-message notification echoing through Roaring Mechanics. I found my phone on top of the toolbox. Another alert dinged. *What now?* I groaned, opening three new messages from Sawyer.

TODAY AT 7:23 PM

SAWYER

I know you left me on read

SAWYER

I'm serious Z it's too dangerous tonight

SAWYER

If you're gonna ignore me then fine but at least hear what I'm saying

I almost typed back. Almost made a snide remark that at least Cohen, of all people, was showing up to help. But I forced myself to exit the thread and power off my phone. It wasn't that I was ignoring her per se. More like she wouldn't understand why tonight still had to happen. So what if I was out of the QSA? The main part of the QSA was the *A* for "alliance." It didn't feel much like that anymore, not in Beggs or in my own life. It was just me standing alone at that rally, too afraid to use my voice.

And the speakeasy was an escape from that.

She could wait until tomorrow for a reply. I threw my phone in the toolbox, taking one last look at the decorations. The garage of Roaring Mechanics was the same as it had been for the grand opening. Streamers and lights hung from the ceiling beams, the rolled-out green carpet ready to welcome guests through the inflated archway . . . But I'd added even more. I had emptied out every box of decorations that Mom had stored. Pride Month would go out with a bang.

My last stint as the King of Pride would be remembered.

All that was left to do was change out the shop's music to the playlist I'd made and get ready. For a brief moment, I wondered what I should wear to impress Mason. Then I shook the thought from my mind as I took the flight of stairs up to the apartment. It didn't matter, he didn't matter, whoever bedmas_22 was didn't matter tonight.

The landline was ringing when I opened the apartment door. I hesitated, worried it was my father again. Worried that he'd somehow witnessed my panicked exit from the rally. *That doesn't matter tonight either.* I eased down the hallway and peered into the dinette/office. The old-timey bells went silent, but they rang again as I reached my room.

I took a deep breath to ready myself and turned around. He didn't get to make me second-guess myself. Not when he was the one being two-faced. Nothing he could say would ruin my night, but maybe I could guilt-trip him.

"What do you want?" I answered quickly. "Because I don't want to—"

"Zeke?" Mom's voice cut me off. "Hun, is everything okay?"

My grasp on the landline's receiver slackened, and my head dropped back in relief. "Yeah?" I said, my tone lilting. "Why do you ask?"

The line crackled once, and then she said, "Tried calling your cell but it went straight to voicemail."

"Sorry, uh, I . . ."

Turned my phone off so people would stop bothering me? I couldn't tell her that, because then she'd ask why. She didn't know that I'd gone to the rally or how much the hate in this town was starting to affect me. I didn't feel like talking about either, just wanted to forget. At least for tonight.

"I was downstairs," I finally replied, then bit my lip. "Uh, cleaning."

"You were?" she asked.

"Thought I'd, uh, surprise you." I'd have to clean again tomorrow before she got home anyway.

"That's sweet of you, but you don't have—"

"How're things at the retreat?" I asked to distract her.

"Good . . . we . . . hike . . ." Her voice cut in and out, and then she said, "Sorry, bad service. We went on a hike to get in the spirit, and now we're about to have charcuterie and wine to discuss."

"That sounds fun," I said absently, my mind focused on other things.

There was a moment of silence, static crackling as someone called for her in the background. "Be right there, Eileen," she called back, and then to me, "We're about to get started, but I wanted to check in to see if you were okay."

"Yeah . . . Why?"

"I saw the Beggs Facebook Group."

"Oh *that*," I said with a laugh, but she didn't think it was funny.

"Mayor Buchanan's angry because of some, what were they called? Underground events?" she asked with a note of skepticism. "Do you know anything about them?"

"That's what he's claiming." My words were measured, emotionless. Not lies but misdirected truths. "And he's got his asshairs in a knot."

"Please promise you'll be careful with the QSA tonight—"

"Yeah, I know." I cut her off. "Be safe and—"

"Well, that too," she inserted, her mouth close to the speaker, "but if anything happens while you're doing the membership drive, don't get sucked in. Just walk away."

"I promise."

A beat passed as she cleared her throat. "I'm holding you to that," she threatened. I could practically see her facial expression, eyes narrowed and chin jutted.

"Yes, ma'am."

"I'll text you when I'm heading home tomorrow. Have a good night, and I love you, hun."

"Have fun tonight. Love you too."

We ended the call, and I strolled out of the dinette with a skip in my step. *Tonight will be better than good,* I assured myself. *It'll be great, incredible even.* I needed to remember how it felt to be free, not terrified like I'd been at the rally.

· · ·

Music thumped in the garage, the bass shaking the mirror ball. The spinning green reflections danced around the mass of bodies that'd packed inside. There were too many people to count, all of them bouncing in waves as Lady Gaga blasted from the speakers. But Cohen had bailed instead of showing up.

What a dick, I thought, shoving my anger back. *Just like Sawyer and Kennedy. I don't need his help anyway.*

Sweat drenched my "Exterminate Hate" shirt, my hair dripping as I threw my head back. I'd spent the last two hours dancing nonstop. *This* was exactly what I needed—to not think of the mob of hate in the town square and the election. There weren't any vulgar looks or expectations here. So I screamed along to the track as someone draped an arm around my shoulder.

Damian Jones leaned on me. He was laughing and swaying to the beat of the music. Our eyes met, both of us smiling. *Could he be bedmas_22?* I wondered, eyeing his sweaty shirt stuck to his broad chest. *Maybe he isn't straight—*

"You're killing it, Fastball!" he yelled over the music, leaning in close.

"Thanks for coming," I tried to say, but my voice was lost in the crowd. He wagged his brows at me and then bent down, his arm sliding down to wrap around my waist. The next thing I knew, he was hoisting me up on his shoulder as the crowd raged. A laugh escaped me as he paraded me around. It was just like when we'd won a baseball game, him chanting my name and me unable to stop grinning.

Because tonight really felt like a win.

I could see the entirety of Roaring Mechanics from this vantage point. From the businesses tabling in the back to the mob gathering under the mirror ball, the party was in full swing. It felt like we were all in a bubble of lightheartedness. Never had I ever felt so sure of myself either. That was one thing I'd learned from these speakeasies. That first night Mason had told me no one would be here if it weren't for me, and looking around only reminded me of that. To see people I knew in real life—including my new friends Owen, Jess, and Bronwen—all together felt like the song's bass rattling through me. Every part of my body was alive from the music and high fives and cheers as Damian twirled me around.

My vision got lost in a blur of twinkling lights before focusing on someone pushing through the crowd. *Cohen?* His face was splotchy, eyes wild as he made his way to me. I tapped Damian's *very* muscular shoulder to set me down.

"You didn't dick out on me!" I yelled at Cohen as he neared.

His mouth moved, gaze shooting back to the entrance, but I only caught every other word. "Tried to text . . . called . . . even Instagram . . . your phone . . ."

"Sorry, I turned it off," I shouted as the last notes of the song faded. "Sawyer was blowing it up, but I'm glad you actually came!"

"Shut up and listen, Zeke," Cohen said, pulling me closer to him. "Mayor Buchanan *knows.*"

"Yeah, he mentioned it at the rally—"

"No!" Cohen shook his head and placed his hands on both of my shoulders. "He knows the speakeasy is *here* tonight."

It took a moment for his emphasis to register, and I blinked as my brain caught up. "What do you mean?" I asked, the levity draining from my system. All around us the crowd continued dancing as a new song came on. We stayed still, both of us locked in a stare. "How do you know?"

He brought his mouth right up to my ear, his breath hot. "Someone tipped off Carmen at the campaign meeting, and I tried warning you." He leaned back to look me in the eyes. "Zeke, you have to listen. He's coming to break this up tonight. He's gonna use it to his advantage to rally voters ahead of the election."

My heart thudded as I glanced around the garage, the harsh reality setting in. Breaking up an illegal Pride event would only strengthen what he'd said about the rec center. The speakeasy would give him the perfect ammunition to continue his hate-filled campaign.

"Cohen!" I yelled in terror. "I have to shut this down immediately!"

"No shit, that's why I'm here." He spared a soft smile and then motioned around us. "We have to go. Now."

I nodded once and spun on my heels. He followed closely as I pushed through the crowd, elbowing my way to the back wall. My laptop was connected to the sound system, just under the painting of Zelda. She smiled down at me mischievously as I franticly typed in my password. It was as though she knew what was happening, the rush of being raided by cops like the actual speakeasies of the 1920s.

The music stopped, and the wave of dancing bodies slowed to a standstill. Heads began turning in search of what had happened. Then I heard it: the sound of sirens in the distance— getting closer. "Fuck, fuck, fuck," I sputtered, waving my arms.

"YOU HAVE TO LEAVE! NOW! THE MAYOR IS COMING TO SHUT US DOWN!"

It took a second for my words to sink in before everyone started shoving toward the exit. Owen the ranger shepherded people through the lobby, but they wouldn't all make it.

I rushed through the crowd with Cohen on my heels, pushing to the garage doors, and keyed in the code to open them. Metallic creaks sounded as they began rolling up. A mass of bodies began to flee into the night. Then I saw the flashing red and blue lights, and my heart seized with dread.

"This little Pride party is over!" A familiar twang reverberated, and I peeked around the corner to see Mayor Buchanan holding a megaphone. He was grinning wildly as people scattered around the cop cars, his eyes clocking every face that ran by.

Shit.

The panic from witnessing the rally rippled through me again, and I backed farther inside the garage. Cohen shook his head and tried to stop me. "Where are you going?" he asked. "We have to go."

"There's a back exit!" I yelled, grabbing his hand. "Come on."

He didn't hesitate, locking his fingers with mine and matching my pace. My dirt bike was parked out back. All we had to do was get the hell out before the mayor saw me. Before he had proof that I was behind Pride.

CHAPTER 24

Warm night air blew through my sweat-damp hair as we darted along the back roads. Cohen wore my helmet, his arms tightly wrapped around my waist. My heart was racing along with the dirt bike's warbling engine. There had been no time to think, only seconds to jump on the seat and get as far away as possible. I needed to pull over and get my shit together. But I could still hear the mayor's voice, still hear the shouts of the rally.

Panicked adrenaline kept me driving. My body tensed with pressure as I gave it some gas, and I startled when Cohen let go of my waist. The comfort of his touch fell away, and it was like I was alone all over again. "There," he called, pointing toward the Beggs Nature Preserve entrance. He held on again, and I leaned back into his warmth as I turned off the road.

I slowed to a stop in a patch of moonlight and took a deep breath, killing the engine. Silence thrummed between the cicadas as I strained to hear if anyone had followed us. At least it was secluded enough here to buy time until I could figure out what to do next.

"I think we're safe," I said, voice unsteady as I released the kickstand.

"That was terrifying as fuck," Cohen said with a huff. He released his grip to slide off the back, and I missed it again. Missed how safe I felt being hugged closely. By him. "Think I'm gonna be sick."

"Me too," I said absently, standing from the seat with wobbly legs. "We almost got caught." He took the helmet off, shaking his head at me. "What?"

"I meant your driving," he said with a snort, bending over to catch his breath. "God, I don't know what was worse, having to save your ass or endure that ride from hell."

"It wasn't that bad," I mumbled, and he gave me a look that begged to differ. "Okay, I might've taken a few turns too fast—"

"All the turns," he said, letting the helmet drop to the ground.

I nodded once, crossing my hands over my chest. Rapid-fire memories shot through me as I stared up at the moon. Sawyer saying it was dangerous, reckless, that I would get caught. She'd been right, and now . . . I'd handed Mayor Buchanan the election.

"Zeke, are you okay?" Cohen asked, a steady hand on my shoulder. At some point, I'd slumped down onto the gravel and started breathing heavy. "Hey, it's okay."

"No," I managed to say. "You were right."

"About what?" he asked, squatting down beside me. "The mayor shutting down the speakeasy? Because, yes, I was right about that, and I'm so glad I got to you in time."

I wanted to tell him this wasn't funny. That me fucking up wasn't a joke anymore. I couldn't begin to process what had just happened. My frazzled brain was glitching as he peered at me, drenched in moonlight. "I meant when you said I was a bad gay."

"Not this again," he sighed. "I didn't mean—"

"No, you were absolutely right. About me, about all this." I could already hear Buchanan at his next rally, bragging about shutting down Pride once and for all. "I've only given the mayor more ammunition for his campaign, and votes for Carmen won't amount to—"

"Look at me," Cohen ordered. "You're panicking. Take a deep breath. We're okay, and everything you've done has only shined a light on what the people of Beggs really want. Your speakeasies are the reason why Carmen has a chance of winning, so don't beat yourself up over what happened back there."

"But . . ." I felt too many emotions coursing through me, my father's dismissiveness about the election joining the fray. "What's gonna happen? People here . . . some don't want us in Beggs. I saw the rally"—my breaths were uneven, and it felt like my heart would explode—"and it was bad. I'm . . . I'm scared."

"Take a deep breath," he said again.

I nodded, trying to inhale.

"It'll be okay," he continued in a soft voice. "Everyone you brought together, those are the people Carmen is speaking up for. They won't forget what you've done for them."

I shook my head, everything he just said rolling over me. "What if I m-messed it up, though?" I asked, wiping at my nose. "M-maybe my father was right—"

"Don't you ever say that again." He cut me off. "You told me everything I need to know about him in our messages . . . Why are you looking at me like that?"

"Our messages?" I asked, gawking at him.

"Um." He flushed, the moonlight giving away the sudden blush across his cheeks. "On Instagram . . ."

The synapses in my brain were misfiring as I tried to make sense of him. "What the hell are you talking about?"

"It was me, okay?" He gave me an apologetic smile. "I thought you knew the whole time, but then you said I was Mason—"

"*Y-you?*" I sputtered in shock.

He looked away, tongue licking at his bottom lip. "I really wanted to talk to you after I was an asshole at the rec center, so I sent a DM on Insta . . ."

He has been messaging me this whole time.

The artsy photos, the fact that I hadn't followed Cohen since freshman year, how he asked about my father after I'd revealed too much to him at the rec center—it was beginning to add up. And it pissed me off so much that I got to my feet.

"What the *actual* fuck, Cohen?" I hissed, throwing my hands up. "How the hell was I supposed to know 'bedmas' was you?"

"Does it matter?" He scrambled to his feet. "Because I meant everything I said to you."

I didn't know how to begin processing his confession, but I knew one thing for certain: I'd meant everything I said in the DMs too. I'd confided in him and shared secrets I'd told no one, secrets he didn't deserve to know. Now . . .

"Yes, it matters," I answered. My voice came out tight, like all the air had been sucked from my lungs. "You could've, I dunno"—I tried to breathe—"texted me if it was so important."

He nervously ran a hand through his cowlicked hair, ragged breaths matching my own. His eyes were trained on his shoes as he toed the gravel. "I couldn't do that, Zeke. I didn't want to see our old texts." He gulped and cut his gaze up to me. "I didn't want to be reminded of how much of a dick I was to you. I thought if I DM'd you, it'd be like a fresh start."

I never want to talk to you again. His last text still hurt, still burned in my memory. No matter how many times I tried to delete the thread, I couldn't.

"Why . . . why did you want to talk to me?" I asked, blinking away the past.

His laughter was broken, a choked *ha-ha*. "I spent the last three years hating you, and it wasn't fair. When you told me about your dad, I thought maybe we could be friends again. The longer we talked, it felt like maybe we could go back to before. Now that I know everything—"

"You're not supposed to know!" It was a strangled cry echoing into the night. Traitorous tears fell, and I wiped them away. My voice lowered to a rough whisper. "And I can't go back to how it was before." *Who I was before.*

"I'm sorry." He looked at me helplessly, shoulders slumped. "When I found out you thought I was Mason at the last speakeasy, I tried to tell you . . . but I couldn't."

"Why?"

"You said there was so much pressure with your dad and Sawyer"—his throat bobbed as he swallowed—"and having Mason to talk to made it bearable. I just . . . Zeke, I didn't want you to be alone in all that."

He looked up at me through his long eyelashes, and it took me back to all those quiet moments we'd shared. I couldn't separate the implications of the raid and his revelation. It was dividing me into a disagreement of emotions: shock and anger and panic and hurt and embarrassment.

I was so goddamn embarrassed by everything that'd happened tonight.

My hands balled into fists, and the gravel scattered as I kicked at the ground. As I stomped over to the dirt bike and threw the helmet at him without another word. Everything was falling apart, and I didn't know how to fix it.

. . .

My skin crawled, like bugs were burrowing just underneath. I couldn't scratch the feeling away no matter how much I tried. That unnerving squirm started at my feet and moved up my legs to my stomach, wriggling around my neck as I took in the damage.

Roaring Mechanics was a mess. Most of the decorations had been destroyed in the mass exit, cast aside like garbage on the art deco floor. I stood in the middle of the shop watching the morning sun glisten off the green shatters of the mirror ball. Its pieces covered the same spot where we'd been standing when the raid started. When Buchanan and his homophobic cronies had come rushing into the one place that felt safe.

The dread that weighed me down after the raid had followed me back to the shop. Cohen had given me an awkward wave goodbye and left me standing at the entrance, my anger over his deceit drowned out by worry. Unable to go inside, I'd gotten on my dirt bike again and ridden until daybreak.

The back of my neck itched, and I raised an arm to scratch it. The waft of adrenaline from my sweat-caked shirt made me want to go upstairs and shower. Fall into bed and close my eyes and forget. But I couldn't. This felt exactly like being up on the billboard catwalk all over again. Lonely and terrifying. I could hear the yells from the mayor's rally between every deep inhale, see the faces of his supporters when I blinked.

Everything had fallen apart so quickly, and I needed to put it back together.

The number one priority was to clean before Mom got back. *That I can handle,* I assured myself. *Then I can worry about how much trouble I'm in and what will happen . . .* My thoughts spiraled as I forced my feet toward the supply closet in the back. Every step crunched over debris, memories ricocheting through me. Bodies thrashing to leave and shouts echoing off the shop floor, the mayor's twang plucking at my insides and my father's warning to keep my head down.

Panic surged through me.

My lungs burned.

I was suffocating.

The lid of the shoebox closed over me, and my vision went dark. I reached out to steady myself but slumped against the closet door. The pressure in my chest was swelling. I couldn't—

Breathe, I told myself. My heart ached, my chest threatening to explode with each agonizing thud. The shop slid sideways, and I was on the floor. Hurt rattled my brain as I finally inhaled with a gasp, with the jarring realization of what this meant.

If I'd just stayed silent like my father had wanted, if I'd

stopped acting *so gay* . . . then none of this would have happened. I had wanted to prove I was good enough, but all I'd done was screw everything up. I was the reason Mayor Buchanan had rolled out his new One Lifestyle ordinance, and even if the QSA got enough sign-ups, there wasn't a chance in hell he'd allow—

The sound of keys jingling in the lock cut through the noise in my head, and then the door opened. I lay there as my breaths quickened. *How long have I been here?* I wondered in confusion, and then: *Oh my god, Mom.*

I listened to her steps as she crossed toward the staircase up to the apartment. Her pace got slower, and then an intake of breath. "Anthony Zeke Chapman!" she yelled, her voice racing up the stairs. "Get down here right now!"

Fuck.

"Mom," I tried to say, sitting up. My voice was uneven, and I cleared the emotion from it. "I'm sorry."

She spun around with irritation burning in her eyes. "What the . . ." Her words fell short, and then she was striding toward me. "Hun, are you okay?" she asked, the fury receding. "You're crying."

I am? Reaching up, I felt the wetness on my cheeks. "Sorry, Mom," I said. "I'm . . . I'm . . ." More tears came then. Because I wasn't okay. Nothing was okay.

"Zeke," she began with concern, "what happened?"

"I messed . . . everything . . . up," I managed to say through labored breaths. "I'm . . . sorry."

She eased down to her knees, her eyes locking on mine. "Take a breath," she instructed.

I inhaled, wiping at the tears and snot. Exhaled until my

lungs emptied and my chest felt hollow. She rubbed my arm as I repeated myself, patiently waiting for me to explain. There was no getting out of it, out of everything that had gone down. *Not after last night.* I took another deep breath and launched into an explanation. How I'd had the idea to have speakeasies after the mayor canceled Pride Day, and how they'd got out of hand. How it was about more than just us volunteering at the rec center, and how the mayor's rally had proved my father right.

"No, he *wasn't* right," she corrected.

"He warned me," I countered. "Maybe if I'd kept quiet—"

"Staying quiet isn't the answer," she interrupted. "You did the right thing."

"How?" I turned toward her in disbelief, gesturing at the wrecked garage. "*How* is this right?"

"Maybe not this," she said while she eyed the broken mirror ball. "And don't think you're not in *so* much trouble for doing it either, but you did what was right."

"No . . . I'm the reason for the One Lifestyle ordinance." *Reckless* and *dangerous*. Sawyer was right. I just wanted to be helpful, and now I'd ruined everything.

"Don't blame yourself for that, Zeke." She wiped away a tear from my cheek. "I know what's happening in Beggs is awful, just like all the other crap happening in Alabama. This would've happened regardless of you making space for yourself . . . and ruining my mechanic shop in the process."

"Sorry about that," I said quickly. "Really. I wasn't thinking, and . . . why are you smiling?"

"Because you stood up for yourself the only way you knew

how, and it makes sense." She laughed, each chuckle a long exhale. "You're just like me. And I know you'll keep fighting."

I snorted once in a hiccup of emotion. "Does that mean I'm off the hook?"

"Absolutely not," she deadpanned. "There are rules about kids having parties while their parents are away. You're gonna have to clean all this up."

"Okay, fair." I chewed on my lip, looking around the shop. It would take a few hours to fix the mess I'd made here, but I needed to fix another one too. "Is it okay if I go hang out with Sawyer when I get done?"

"Zeke—"

"I need to apologize," I rushed before she could deny me. "For what I did. I need to own up to it."

She studied me for a moment, pushing my hair back from my face. Then, slowly, she nodded once, agreeing to let me go. I smiled at her weakly, unsure of what fixing my mess would mean. What any of it meant after last night.

CHAPTER 25

I'd lost count of how many times I'd said, "I'm sorry."

When I was younger, my father forced me to apologize every time he thought I messed up. When I ruined my new chinos helping Mom work on the family SUV? "I'm sorry." When I stayed up late binge-reading Sawyer's X-Men fanfic and got an A minus on my history test? "I'm sorry." When I blew my allowance on concert tickets instead of saving it like he'd wanted? "I'm sorry."

Those two words were said so often they'd lost their meaning. They would fall out of my mouth without me feeling it. Two stones worn smooth from the steady stream of apologies. Now, I was starting to remember how to *be* sorry. There was a difference between saying it because someone else thought I should and saying it because I was in the wrong.

And this time, I knew.

I knew why Sawyer had gotten mad. I knew that I deserved it after disregarding her concerns. I knew there wasn't a way to go back in time and make it right without the Doctor and a TARDIS. I knew it was too late to change what I'd done.

However, it wasn't too late to do something about it.

With a deep breath, I raised my hand and knocked twice on the basement door. Silence pulsed as I stood there in my sweaty, disgusting clothes. After cleaning the garage, I'd come straight over to Sawyer's. This was too urgent for me to meander upstairs, shower, procrastinate, let fear keep me from making amends. I had to talk to her before something bad could happen again.

I knocked louder, and then the knob finally rattled. The door swung open, revealing Sawyer in her oversized pajamas and gaming headphones. A bemused expression crossed her face as she stared at me. I braced myself to be scathed, for her to continue our argument from the last time I was here. But then she rushed forward and caught me off guard with a tight hug.

"Z," she sighed. "I've been calling, texting— Are you okay?"

"Hey," I said hesitantly, ignoring her question. "Sorry, my phone is . . ." *Where?* I tried to remember. Flashes of bodies rushing to escape, the mayor and his megaphone, the fear, came rushing back. I cleared my throat. "Guess you heard what happened, then?"

"My dad told me." She took a step back and motioned for me to come inside. "It was all over the local news last night. People bragged about Mayor Buchanan shutting down an 'illegal' event, and I *knew* it had to be the speakeasy."

"Oh," I said absently, my eyes adjusting to the dim lighting of the bachelorette pad.

The TV was bright with a *Final Fantasy* game on pause. The

screen's glow washed over her face as she sat back in her nest of blankets. "Are you okay?" she asked again.

"I, um . . ." I shrugged and perched on the arm of the sectional. "Shaken up, I guess."

"Cohen is too," she said, twirling her blue-tipped hair.

Memories of last night flashed through my mind again, on a constant loop ever since it happened. I tried to smile at her, to play it off like I always had, but that panicked fear twisted my mouth into a grimace. "You were right," I began, glancing away from her focused stare. "I get it now, and I'm sorry I ruined everything."

"Z." My nickname was softly spoken. So soft it made me look back up. Her eyes were as glassy as mine felt. "I don't care about—"

"No," I interrupted. "I was being reckless, and now the mayor is targeting us just like you said . . . and with that One Lifestyle ordinance . . . when he gets reelected, there won't be a QSA or anything queer in Beggs."

"It's not a guarantee that he'll win." Her voice was quiet, laced with remorse. "And I'm sorry for how I treated you. It wasn't fair of me to push you—"

"I deserved it."

She shook her head. "No, you didn't. It's my fault. If I'd helped out, maybe things would've been different."

"How is it *your* fault?" I asked, thrown off by her admission. "You didn't ignore the danger. That's all on me."

"But if I hadn't pushed you out, then you wouldn't have had to do everything alone . . . It's supposed to be my responsibility as QSA president to . . . I dunno, make this place safe? That's all I wanted, and I failed."

"No, you didn't," I countered. "You got Beggs its first ever Pride Day, and it would've been incredible if it hadn't been canceled."

"Look where that led, though." She pushed her wire-frame glasses up in her hair, rubbing at her eyes. "The mayor is using it to his advantage, and . . ." Her eyes went distant, unfocused. It was clear she was flipping through her memories just like I'd been.

"I was at his rally . . . and I don't think it would've made a difference if we'd had Pride Day or not. He'll do anything to get reelected."

She leveled her gaze at me. "*Why* did you even go to that rally?" she pressed.

"I went to the rec center for the mentorship program, but the mayor shut it down. I was so mad and wanted to let him know how much of a jackass he is. When I got there . . . Saw, it was terrifying. Seeing all those people, hearing what they were saying about me—about us. I panicked."

"God, Z. I'm sorry."

"Stop apologizing," I said with a forced laugh. "I'm the one who's sorry. I let the speakeasies go to my head because . . ."

"Because why?"

I chewed my bottom lip while everything the JACass had ever said weighed down on me. "My, uh, my father. You know how strict he is?" She nodded. "Well, it was more than that. He wouldn't let me be out."

"He *what*?"

That overwhelming guilt I'd once felt bubbled in my gut as I tried to find the right words to explain it. "He said that if people didn't know who I was, it'd make life easier for me."

I could see her connecting the dots. "And then the divorce. That's why you finally agreed to join the QSA last semester?"

"All I wanted was to be like you."

"Like me?"

"You know, out and proud. Doing something. Not hiding who you are. And my father, all he ever told me was to stop acting so gay all the time."

She scooted down the sofa and reached out to grasp ahold of my hand. "Why didn't you say something?" she asked with a gentle squeeze, and I shrugged. "You didn't have to deal with that alone."

I thought back to all the times he'd made me apologize for being myself, for any time I slipped up and did something too overtly queer for his liking. "Do you remember when we played dodgeball at recess, and you'd beat my ass?"

"Thought we agreed not to talk about my bully days," she said with a weak laugh, crossing her arms over her chest.

"But that's exactly how it felt living with my father. I kept having to dodge him over and over again. Then it was easier to just sit there and let it happen. I was tired of fighting it, even convinced myself that I needed to be quiet to survive. Then you were out there, being loud and not giving a damn."

"I might've given a little bit of a damn," she admitted. "People started treating me differently. The dude bros fetishized me, and the other girls in our class came at me with microaggressions in the locker room."

"It didn't stop you from speaking up," I reminded her. "I wish I didn't just stay quiet and let it happen."

"You *haven't* been quiet this month," she pointed out. "I really meant it when I said I was proud of you for stepping up.

You have nothing to apologize for. The speakeasies brought everyone in Beggs together to celebrate."

"Look where that led," I countered. "It only gave Buchanan even more of an advantage—"

"But it also made Carmen Bedolla want to challenge him." She cut me off. "Having the speakeasies might've done something bad, but that doesn't outweigh the good they brought to this town."

I nodded as her words sank in. My hands ached to grab a tool, to take apart an engine and put it back together. "I just wish, I dunno, that I could fix everything."

"You can't," she said, not unkindly. "None of us can."

Silence filled the basement, the hum of her PS5 droning in the background. I didn't want to believe none of us could make it right. After the shit I'd been through, I thought I was finally in control of my life. But it turned out that I'd been letting my fear influence me. Fear of being like my father, of not being worthy, of disappointing anyone who got to know me.

"I'm glad Cohen swooped in to save your ass," she added, her voice cutting the tension with a small laugh. "It could have been so much worse."

The mirror ball shimmered behind my eyelids with every blink. A flash of its emerald reflection, the bass thumping in my chest, Cohen rushing in. Then its glisten became moonlight. Cohen and me outside the nature preserve and the revelation that he was bedmas_22. The embarrassment jabbed at my rib cage like a dull blade.

"I'm high-key impressed he did it," she continued. I shot her a silent question. She tilted her head to the side, eyes narrowed in thought. "I mean, it's a known fact that he's terrified of getting into trouble. But he agreed to help with the speakeasy and risked being caught in a raid to warn you—" She gasped, her eyes lighting up. "Kennedy and I *knew* he still liked you."

"Uh . . ." I didn't even know how to begin to tell her about bedmas_22.

"And you like him too!" she added with a giddy squeal.

"No, I don't!" My voice spiked with anger, my face growing hot. The annoying heat spread to my chest, then to my back where he'd sat against me with his arms around my waist.

"I beg your most finest pardon, but consensus says that you've liked him since mathletes, Z." She shook her head with a smile. "Oh my god, I love this for you."

"Abso-fuckin-lutely not," I said quickly. "We're not bringing up Extremely Shit-tacular Freshman Fall right now."

"It's obvious there's something between you two."

"There are more pressing things to worry about," I continued, ignoring her smirk. "So much bad shit is happening in Beggs, and now that Pride Month is over, I feel kinda useless. I don't know what to do now."

"Okay . . ." A moment passed while she collected herself. Focus mode was back, Cohen forgotten, while she narrowed her eyes in thought. "What if we had more speakeasies—and were more discreet this time?" she suggested, and I flinched as those same flashes flickered through my mind at warp speed. "What?"

"I c-can't. Not again." My heart rate sped up, taking me back to last night, to the mayor's rally, to all the times I'd felt like a failure.

She reached for her phone with determination. Her fingers tapped the screen rapidly, and then she looked up in triumph.

"I messaged the group chat. We need to have a QSA meeting," she said matter-of-factly. Her phone dinged almost immediately with a new message, and she read it. "Damn that was fast. They're on their way so we can figure it out together."

"We?" I asked, unsure if I should leave. "Does this mean I'm back in the QSA, or . . ."

She grimaced and flashed a tight smile. "I'm sorry I threatened to kick you out."

"I deserved it, to be honest." I ran a hand through my hair, smoothing it back as I let out a deep sigh. "I'm sorry I was a Zasshole and let everything go to my head."

"You're forgiven if you make me two promises."

"What?" I asked cautiously, unsure of where she was going.

"One, that we resume our list of traditions, because I owe you a sneaky birthday breakfast," she began, and I nodded, "and two, that you won't sit back and let people like your dad keep you quiet." She pointed at me then herself. "*We* have to speak up."

I thought back to the first night I'd climbed up above Jones Hardware to paint the billboard. How a halo had hovered over the town square from the streetlamps, pushing darkness to the outskirts of town. That was where they wanted people like me, like Sawyer and the QSA, to stay. We were tired of it, tired of feeling unwelcome in our own town. Something had to be done, and maybe we could figure it out.

"I titty promise," I finally said, bringing a hand to my chest, and she did the same.

CHAPTER 26

When Cohen and I had arrived back at Roaring Mechanics after the raid, I hadn't thought twice about his shifty eyes. The way he'd hesitated for a moment before leaving. How he'd cast one last look at me before driving off. Now it was all I could think about after what Sawyer had claimed.

Cohen likes me?

I was second-guessing both his actions and my reactions—why I cared whether or not I looked presentable, or why I was so upset by the case of mistaken identity on Insta. He had those sus eyes again as we sat on the floor of the bachelorette pad. His gaze kept lingering on me like it had last night, on my mouth every time I ate a handful of yogurt-covered raisins. When I'd catch him, he'd quickly turn away as though he was afraid I'd yell at him again.

I watched him out of the corner of my eye as he spoke. "Carmen's campaign is picking up speed now," he was saying.

His expression was hopeful, beaming with confidence, even though I had doubt.

He wasn't Mason. With bedmas_22, I'd let my guard down only to find out he was Cohen. The same guy who'd been a nightmare to me until this summer. The same guy who was the reason I'd joined mathletes. The same guy I'd crushed on hard. The same guy who risked being caught in a raid and helped me during my freak-out.

"Founder's Day is in a little over two weeks," he added with such tenacity that it made my pulse quicken. "But it's more than just an election."

"What do you mean?" Kennedy asked.

"Ever since that rally Buchanan had," he replied, "it's become more than just a mayoral race." He finally caught my eye and nodded sheepishly. "There's more at stake."

I felt my face redden, and Sawyer prodded me with the same smirk she'd given me earlier. *It's obvious there's something between you two.*

"So," Sawyer began, still watching me skeptically, "how can the QSA help?"

"Y'all wanna help?" he asked. Kennedy and Sawyer nodded, and then he looked to me. "You too?"

"Y-yeah," I stammered, and a faint smile chased away his worry lines. It was as though he and I were the only ones in the basement. "I, uh, I caused such a mess . . . and it would only be fair to salvage what I can."

"But you didn't," he assured me. "Your speakeasies are the reason Carmen actually has a chance at winning."

A vote for Bedolla won't amount to anything. My father's

unwavering certainty made me nervously tug at the collar of my shirt. "All I did was make the mayor look better."

"That's not true, Zeke . . ." He trailed off. We both shared a look that said we weren't going to talk about everything that happened. Not now. "He would have found some way to give himself the upper hand. But by breaking up the speakeasy, he pissed off a lot of people in town. People who could vote for Carmen."

"You think so?" My voice was quiet, the power shift between us like an ocean tide rising and falling.

"People have been quiet for far too long in Beggs, and now they're speaking up."

Before, politics went over my head, but now it was making sense. "Then how can I help?" I asked.

Someone coughed, and the intense stare down between Cohen and me was broken. "What he means," Sawyer started, "is how can *we* help?"

"Yeah," I corrected, my face on fire. "I meant the QSA."

"We did get some new members signed up," Kennedy said. "We could all get together and do something to help Carmen."

"Like make more campaign signs?" Sawyer offered, and Kennedy nodded excitedly.

"That's a great idea," Cohen said. "We need to get them up as soon as possible."

"On it," Sawyer promised.

She grabbed her tablet, and it was like the QSA planning sessions for Pride all over again. Her thumbs flew over the screen as Kennedy scooted closer, pulling out a pen and notebook from her tote. It left me to sit there on my own while they discussed a plan of attack. I didn't know what I could do that'd be useful instead of making everything . . . messier.

"What about me?" I asked, eyes downcast.

"You should throw one more speakeasy," Cohen said without hesitation.

"What?" I balked at him. "I just told Sawyer I won't do that. Not after what happened. I'll just screw it up again."

"No, you won't." He shook his head firmly. "You won't be doing it alone, either, and what if . . . What if we didn't hide it? We could . . . Wait, we could make it a rally for Carmen in the town square!" I shot him a confused look, and he continued on in excitement, more so to himself. "Yeah, that would work, and I still have the QSA parade float in my garage. We could decorate it for the campaign—"

"Are you sure?" I cut in.

"Zeke," he began, smiling in a new way that I almost didn't recognize, "you're a genius, and we got this . . . but only if you feel comfortable."

A genius? I thought. He hadn't called me that since I won us the mathletes competition. Back before everything fell apart. The versions of me were overlapping again, the past mixing with the present. All that was missing was the future.

"I, uh." He kept smiling like he believed in me, and it was the first time in a long time that someone had. "But, uh." I tried again. "How exactly would it work . . . if we did?"

"First, we'd tell Carmen the QSA will organize a rally," he jumped in, confidently taking charge. "We can reserve the town square, make sure the mayor can't fault us for anything." He scratched at his bedhead and licked his bottom lip in thought. I hated to admit it, but I found this side of him attractive. "You can post to your Insta with the time and date like you did with the other speakeasies. We'll get as many people there as possible and make it feel like a big party."

"It can't be a party," I countered, now aware of how much hard work the QSA had done this year. "If we do it, it should mirror the QSA's original plan for Pride Day."

"Zeke, I love that idea," Sawyer inserted, flashing me a grin.

"What if we had a voter registration drive too?" Kennedy suggested. "Most of our senior class will support her because of Buchanan's new One Lifestyle bullshit."

"That's wonderful, Ken." Cohen beamed, and then to me in a softer tone, added, "See, we got this."

The rich brown of his eyes was warm. Too warm, too sultry to look away from. It was setting me on fire, and I could feel Sawyer watching me from behind her tablet. There was an undeniable blush on my face.

Do I like him back? Did I ever stop?

Upstairs, a doorbell sounded, and Kennedy got to her feet. "Pizza's here," she announced, reaching out to help Sawyer up. "We'll go, um, grab it while you two figure out if we're gonna do this or not."

They left quickly, and I knew they'd be gone awhile. That they would find a hidden place upstairs to make out until the pizza turned cold. Their footsteps echoed up the basement steps, and both of us fell into silence as the door shut.

A few moments passed, and I could feel Cohen watching me. Waiting on me to address the big gay elephant in the room now that it was just us. "Uh . . . they're totally gonna suck face," I finally mumbled.

"No doubt," he said.

I cleared my throat to ask about Carmen's campaign again, anything to keep this from getting weirder. He looked up at me through his eyelashes, and I could see his face in the moonlight. Hear him confessing it was him on Instagram. I had been so mad at him last night . . . but now I was angry at myself. I'd just assumed it was Mason messaging me—I hadn't even asked before spilling my guts in his DMs. Despite that, Cohen wasn't Z-stepping. Maybe he really did mean everything he'd said.

Before I could stop myself, I blurted, "Why bedmas_22?"

The question caught me off guard, and by the looks of it, him too. His face was red, his gaze shifty again. "Because," he said quietly, "we won that math competition with B-E-D-M-A-S."

"We . . . oh." I'd suggested to use that formula for the problem. Brackets, exponents, division, multiplication, addition, subtraction, and . . . it'd worked. He and I beat Geometry Derick to the punch. "Guess I didn't put two and two together."

"It was our math joke," he said, a new softness to his voice. "I honestly thought you knew it was me because of my username. I didn't know that you and Mason were a thing—"

"There's nothing between me and Mason," I rushed out. "I mean, I thought there was. But really it was something between you and me." I blanched, backtracking. "Not that I meant there *is* something between you and me. It was us flirting—" *Fuck.* I just put a name on what we'd been doing, and I couldn't take it back.

"It was kinda nice not fighting," he commented carefully.

There was weight to his words. Their implication only thickened the tension in the bachelorette pad. We'd met so many times here in Sawyer's basement, but nothing was the same now. There was no way I could fight with Cohen like before. Because I wasn't the same either. It was as though all the parts of me—Anthony and Zeke and whoever the hell I was now—were trying to coexist in this new reality.

"I don't wanna fight anymore," I said through the rush of thoughts.

"Then let's do something else instead," he said quickly, face reddening. "I mean, work together on another speakeasy . . ."

"I, uh," I tried to say, blinking away memories of my birthday dinner and the mayor's rally and raid. "What if, um, we did it and something bad happens again because of me?"

He reached out, and his hand touched my knee. I watched as his fingers squeezed reassuringly while he said, "It's okay to be afraid, Zeke. I'm afraid too, but knowing that I'm not the only one . . . That makes me feel like I'm not alone."

I glanced up to see him peering at me through his lashes. My eyes began to burn from the intensity of his hopeful expression. The same expression I wore when I stared at the newspaper tacked up on my bedroom wall, at the protester who had been caught mid-scream as he marched in the name of Pride. I'd spent so long keeping my head down and keeping to myself and keeping quiet. But that guy was who I'd always wanted to be. If Cohen thought that I was like him, that one last speakeasy was worth it, then I had to get loud too.

CHAPTER 27

Last night, I slept.

The temptation to ride the streets of Beggs had nearly lured me out of bed. I lay there with heavy eyes, an odd sense of restfulness sinking me into the mattress. The last thing I remember was looking up at the pride flag and then . . . blinking away early-morning light.

Mom wasn't in the dinette when I emerged from my room still groggy. At least the coffee pot was warm. I needed it to wake up, and three cups later I was downstairs in the garage and ready for another day of work.

The hum of the air compressor reverberated off the tiled floors, and I paused on the bottom step. Mom was already at work, with her feet sticking out from under the family SUV. A deep breath filled my lungs, then I exhaled slowly as I took in the shop. The usual grease-permeated smell was replaced by disinfectant and lemons from when I'd cleaned yesterday. It made Roaring Mechanics feel brand-new again. Different, at the very least. Glimpses of dancing, of screams, of stomping footsteps fleeing filled my vision.

I rubbed my eyes, tried to rub away all thoughts of Saturday night, and crossed over to the toolbox. My hands trembled as I opened the drawer. The dread of what could be waiting after the raid had kept me from retrieving my phone, but I shook off the residual nerves. Forced myself to pick it up and turn it on. I held my breath while the screen slowly came to life. For a second, it was as though I hadn't been offline for more than a day. Then the notifications started loading. Texts, voicemails, Instagram alerts—I checked those first, swiping to the app.

There were a dozen tagged photos of me from right here in the garage. Pictures of the speakeasy and me dancing right before it all went to shit. If I thought hard enough, I could still remember how free I'd felt the moment before hell broke loose. Now that control I'd once had was gone. In its place were Insta Reels. Captured videos of me screaming and opening the garage doors, the rush of bodies shoving their way out, the sound of Buchanan's twang threatening us.

I tried to shut off those memories, my hands shaking as I held the phone. My thumb swiped back to exit the video feed and check my messages. There were countless alerts of tagged posts. I scrolled past them, down to the unread messages until I saw the screen name I was looking for. Cohen had sent multiple new DMs the night it all went down.

SAT 10:13 PM

BEDMAS_22

Just heard the mayor is searching for the speakeasy tonight

BEDMAS_22
I tried calling you but your phone went to voicemail

BEDMAS_22
You might want to call it off

BEDMAS_22
I'm on my way

BEDMAS_22
If you see this before I get there run

The messages lined up with his story about trying to warn me. It made me feel weirdly detached from everything that'd happened. If I hadn't turned my phone off like a dipshit, all this could have been avoided. With a deep sigh, I started typing a reply back.

7:03 AM

ZEKECHAPMAN
thanks for trying to warn me

ZEKECHAPMAN
sorry I didn't have my phone on 🥺

The wheels of the dolly creaked, and I sat my phone on top of the toolbox. Mom rolled out from under the SUV with oil smudged across her cheek. She sat up and startled when she saw me lurking nearby.

"You're up early," I commented, my voice scratchy from sleep.

"I was dying to use a power tool," she said, reaching to turn off the air compressor. I knew exactly what she meant; we both had made a habit of tinkering on cars when life got to be too much. "You feeling better, hun?"

"I think so." I shrugged and pushed my hair off my face. "The QSA meeting helped. We're gonna plan a rally for Carmen, and we're gonna meet her campaign team tomorrow. Maybe we can do something good."

What I meant to say was *Maybe I can do something good*, and Mom sensed where I was headed. "Hey," she said, standing up. "You *will* make a difference. You're taking charge, and I'll help with the rally in whatever way I can."

"Thanks, Mom." Her assessment made my hands itch to grab a tool, but the only thing I could control was myself.

She gave me a reassuring smile and started toward the garage doors. I watched her go, trying to blink away the memories from Saturday. Then my gaze landed on the Zelda painting. I wondered how she would've handled getting raided. If she had ever taken charge of her own life.

"Hey, Mom," I began, still staring at the woman I'd been named after, "you told me all about Zelda escaping Alabama and starting a new life in 1920, but what happened to her after that?"

"That's the reason why I admire her," she said. "She became the person people expected her to be until she realized she could shine on her own. It wasn't always easy, but she did it her way."

I considered what that meant, how someone could find their way through all the versions they'd tried to be. Everyone had expected me to be Anthony Chapman, and then Zeke Chapman. But now? I wasn't so sure who *I* expected me to be.

I turned to the toolbox for a wrench—to do the only thing I knew how to—and hesitated. My phone screen was bright with a new notification. *Then there's Cohen and the avalanche of emotions he makes me feel.* Before I could talk myself out of it, I checked for his reply. But it was a text from Sawyer instead.

TODAY AT 7:36 AM

SAWYER

I'm out front with disguises and a list of hotels 😳

. . .

"Oh, boo-bear, I'm so glad we decided to have a night away from the kids."

Sawyer's voice was thick with exaggerated Southern charm. She reached across the table to grasp my hand. Her long auburn wig glinted in the West Point Inn's LED lighting as she lowered her head. We locked eyes over the top of her giant sunglasses, and it took every fiber of my being not to laugh.

"Yes, dear," I managed as the concierge side-eyed us. Nervously, I smoothed my fake handlebar mustache. "Bill . . . and Bob, they're such little bundles of misery—joy, I mean."

We both held our breath while he passed by our table, then relaxed back in our seats. "I think he's still buying our cover story," Sawyer said. When we'd snuck by the front desk, she'd looped her arm through mine and made loud comments about being away from our kids. Then she casually asked the concierge to have fresh towels sent up to room 425 as we slipped into the dining room.

"Exactly how much trouble will we be in if we get caught?" I asked, grabbing a sausage from my overflowing buffet plate. Mom had agreed to let me skip a few hours of work, and the last thing I wanted to do was call her from hotel jail. *Is that even a thing?*

"Technically," she began with a smirk, "it's advertised as 'free breakfast' without any stipulations. Non-technically . . . maybe a little trouble, so I'd suggest we make a run for it."

"I can live with that."

"Same," she agreed through a mouthful of scrambled eggs. "Besides, I owed you for missing your birthday." Then she grimaced. "I really am sorry—"

"You apologized at least ten times in the car," I said with an eye roll. "And I've forgiven you at least ten times too. We were both being stupid."

She gave me a conceding head tilt, pushing her sunglasses up on her nose. "At least we still have the library's outdoor movie night and the Ferris wheel."

Those were the last two things on our list before the end of summer break. Then we'd have to press play and resume our lives. Start senior year and deal with the One Lifestyle ordinance if the mayor won— *No.* I cut my thought spiral off. That was the last thing I wanted to think about.

"So, uh," I ventured, and took a sip of orange juice, "I think you should invite Kennedy to celebrate our traditions."

"Yeah?" she asked. I nodded while shoving a bite of pancake into my mouth. "That'd be great, Z. I really . . . I really like her."

"Consider my flabber fully gasted," I teased with a wink. "It's been a nonstop thirstfest with you two."

She launched a sausage link at me, and it bounced off my forehead and onto the next table. We both froze as the concierge shot daggers at us. "Well, I'll be gosh darned," she said loudly in a drawl. "That there wiener just slipped right off my fork."

"Sugar tits, you're so clumsy," I added as she grabbed it.

"All better now," she offered with a flick of her wig. Then she lowered her voice. "The University of the South is her top college too, and if we both get in . . . If we're still together next year, then maybe we could have a real shot."

She shrugged, her focus clearly on the future. It had always been something I didn't want to think about. She'd go off to study political science, and I'd be left alone to become a JACass lawyer. But now the future wasn't so bad, not as bad as I thought it'd be.

"About college . . ." I trailed off, tapping at my phone screen for the time. It lit up beside my plate, and we still had an hour before I needed to get back. "I decided I want to do automotive technology"—she started to say something, but I held a hand up to stop her—"and I know it's not law school, but it's something I'm good at."

"You don't have to explain yourself," she said bluntly. "If it makes you happy, that's what matters. Fuck the notion of prestigious assholery."

Makes you happy echoed inside me, ran around the baseball diamond in my mind. It was the first decision I'd made for myself. And it felt strange. But empowering.

"Thanks for having my back, Saw," I said, my phone screen lighting up with new notifications.

"That's what besties are for, Z."

I shot her a smile before checking to see if Cohen had replied. There were two Instagram messages waiting for me, and I felt my smile stretch wider as I swiped to read them.

9:02 AM

BEDMAS_22

You have nothing to be sorry for, Zeke.

BEDMAS_22

By the way . . . Hi, my name is Cohen, and I think it's your turn to ask a question. If you want.

"Why are you grinning like that?" Sawyer asked.

"Just thinking about what makes me happy," I said, catching her eye.

A slow grin spread on her face, matching mine. It was the same look we'd shared after watching *Doctor Who* and finding ourselves. It felt great to have her back on my side—but it was more than that. There were no secrets between us. Well, except for . . .

"And . . . I think I like Cohen," I added.

"No shit," she quipped.

"But I'm also kinda mad at him too."

She pushed her sunglasses up in her wig and waited expectantly. I took a deep breath and launched into the whole case of mistaken Instagram identity. The real reason for the rivalry between Cohen and me. The way I'd ended things abruptly because of my father. The way I missed who I was with him.

"Z," she started once I was done, "I never knew that was the reason why you two, like, hated each other."

"If I had a TARDIS, I'd go back and tell you," I said, twirling my fake mustache. "Maybe then you could've talked some sense into me."

"But we're here now . . ." She beamed at me sweetly, then she narrowed her eyes. "And I'll beat some sense into you now if I have to. It's not like he deliberately catfished you. Granted, he should've come clean immediately. But he was probably just as scared as you were. He did tell you things too."

Oh.

I hadn't thought of it that way. We'd both shared things about ourselves, but he'd known it was me. He was still as bold as he'd been freshman year.

"Obviously there's still something between you two," she continued, "but what are you gonna do about it?"

My hands fidgeted with my phone, waking the screen. I'd once told him we were better as friends, but that'd been an excuse. The message thread between us was still pulled up, glowing expectantly. Before I could stop myself, I typed out a question.

ZEKECHAPMAN

do you still listen to Bleachers?

"Ehem," a gruff voice interrupted. "I'm gonna need to see your room key to verify you're both guests."

We both swiveled to look up at the hotel concierge. His face was pinched as he held his hand out impatiently. Sneaky birthday breakfast had officially been compromised. Sawyer and I exchanged a brief wide-eyed stare before she grabbed my hand.

"Run!" we both yelled at the same time.

We shoved our chairs back and took off through the dining room. Heavy footsteps sounded in our wake. We rounded the corner into the lobby, and her wig came off. It went flying past me in a blur of red. I couldn't contain my laughter as I sprinted after her. And it felt good to let it out.

CHAPTER 28

I had two distinct memories of Estrella Books: the first was the day Sawyer and I reached for the last copy of the X-Men graphic novel, and the second was freaking out about the first speakeasy. Now here I was again, a distinct third time I knew I'd remember.

The door chimed as another campaign volunteer arrived. Each trill brought more laughter, even more people into the bookstore. Conversations fluttered as we sat in the tiny chairs of the children's section. I gripped the edge of my seat and took a few deep breaths.

"Everything okay?" Sawyer asked, and I turned my attention to where she was perched on Kennedy's lap.

"Uh-huh," I said absently, glancing once more around the store.

But I wasn't really okay. I'd gone riding last night, unable to sleep. Unable to shut off my brain. The news cycle of bills with confusing letters and numbers had played on a constant loop as I drove. Each campaign sign flashed by, but all I could see were the people I'd met this summer. From the speakeasies, the rec center, the rally for Buchanan—everyone blazing in my mind. A month ago, Cohen had asked if I was paying attention.

And now I couldn't stop.

"Nervous about seeing Cohen," Sawyer pressed with a smirk, "because you're ready to give in to his yearning?"

"Wait," Kennedy said before I could reply. She held her hand up to her chest in thought. The shades of her pink nail polish were bright against the white dinosaur shirt that I knew belonged to Sawyer. Then her twist braids swooped over her shoulder as she turned toward me in a rush. "You know Cohen likes you?"

"And they're gonna quench each other's thirst," Sawyer teased.

I gulped as Kennedy's grin widened. "About damn time," she said, glancing across the store. "I *knew* y'all were hate-flirting."

"That's, uh, that's not it," I finally said.

Another deep breath as I followed her line of sight. Cohen was snapping pictures of Carmen posing by the front counter. He was in his element, a set look of determination on his brow. Like he knew what he was doing here, like everyone knew what they were doing. And I was in a perpetual state of confusion.

"What if," I began, lowering my voice, "we do this rally and register voters and she still loses?"

Sawyer's smile fell. "Then she loses," she answered. "But that doesn't mean *we* lost . . . Just look around, Z." She motioned to the crowded bookstore around us. "Do you really think all this will stop after the election?"

I shrugged, unsure how any of this worked.

"You only lose if you stop trying." She shared a look with Kennedy; both of their smiles represented a decision made. "And *if* Buchanan is reelected, all it means is that we'll keep fighting so that they know we're not going anywhere. Just like those Last Boyfriends did at Harper Valley High School to oust their principal and superintendent."

"Even if they ban the QSA, Pride events, whatever other shit they throw our way," Kennedy added, "they can't make us feel like we don't belong, not after everything that's happened this summer."

"The speakeasies made a place for us in Beggs. Brought us together," Sawyer said.

Their words sank in as I looked to the front. So many familiar faces were here for Carmen's campaign, from Owen to Jess to so many others I'd seen show up all summer. Their presence was a promise that we were here together. I was still figuring out politics and what it meant to fight for your rights. But there was one thing that eased the fear thrashing inside me, that eclipsed how it'd felt up on that billboard catwalk.

We're not alone.

As though he heard my thought, Cohen caught my eye. He smiled softly and started toward us. Nerves twisted my stomach tighter with his every step, and I ran a hand through my hair. Did a quick pit sniff test. Adjusted my shirt.

"They're so thirsty that they're parched," Sawyer whispered to Kennedy.

"Stop," I muttered under my breath.

It had been different when I was pretending not to care. Now it was growing increasingly difficult to pretend. Because

Cohen knew me, all the versions of me. And maybe I wanted to know him better too.

"Great turnout tonight," Cohen said as he took a seat in a tiny chair next to mine. Then his eyes focused over my shoulder, and I followed his line of sight to where Mason stood. "Even the asshole is here."

"You really don't like him, huh?" I asked, lowering my voice. "Just so you know, he and I weren't ever anything real. That was me and you . . ."

Our gazes locked, and I felt heat bloom across my cheeks. We'd messaged for hours last night, this time both of us knowing the truth, but never talked about what it meant.

For a moment, I let myself actually see him, giving in to the glitch he caused. His messy bedhead was in need of a cut, the brown tufts starting to curl. The pink "TEAM CARMEN" shirt was stretched tight across his shoulders. I thought of all the things we'd discussed, and he turned into someone new before me. Someone who knew me but still liked me, who wasn't disappointed once he realized who I was.

He gave me a slight tilt of his head as the bookstore went silent. As though he was letting me know he was here like he'd been after the raid. It made me smile. *I like Cohen,* I decided, turning to face the front. *I never stopped.*

Carmen had climbed up onto the counter, tucking one leg under her. She was wearing the same shirt as Cohen, with her salt-and-pepper hair pulled back under a matching hat. Her smile was reminiscent of when I'd helped her at Pride Day, when she'd told me to be proud that I'd shown up. And now I finally understood what she meant.

I was proud to be doing something more.

"Thank you for coming out tonight," Carmen greeted. "I know we're in crunch time with the election coming up, but I want each of you to know that I couldn't do this without your support. Hosting the first Pride speakeasy made me realize how important safe spaces are here in our town. The hate Mayor Buchanan is preaching isn't who we are. We have to remind voters of that. We're here to make Beggs feel like home for everyone."

A round of applause sounded, my own joining in. It was so surreal to think speaking with her on a whim, the idea of the speakeasy, her offering the bookstore . . . how it led to this. All these people were here because of something I'd done to fight back, but I didn't feel important enough to have caused *this*.

"We have some new faces tonight," she went on, pointing back to the children's section. "You all know our very own King of Pride, Zeke Chapman." People were staring at me, and I shrank back in my chair. "And Sawyer Grayson and Kennedy Copeland, all with the Beggs High School QSA. Along with Cohen, they started the fire in town by petitioning for Pride Day, and Zeke started the underground Pride events. He brought together hundreds of citizens who support inclusivity. I think they all deserve some love for uniting us against hate."

I swallowed nervously as everyone clapped again, that guilt I'd once carried reawakening. They didn't know why I'd wanted to do it—

"It's okay," Cohen whispered suddenly, leaning into me. "You deserve recognition, no matter how it started. You're here now." I felt his breath puff out, knew there was a grin on his lips. "And you've never been a 'bad gay.'"

Through a jumble of nerves, I laughed shakily. "Thanks, Coco," I said softly, fighting the urge to hug him.

"Together," Carmen continued, with an excited clap, "the Beggs High School QSA has thought of a brilliant tactic that could give us a last-minute advantage!"

She motioned for us to explain, and I waited for Cohen to begin. He didn't, and neither did Sawyer or Kennedy. They were all waiting on me with expectant smiles. *You're here now,* Cohen had said, and it gave me the courage to speak.

I opened my mouth, then closed it, searching for the words to say, as the door chimed. The speakeasies brought together fighters who would continue their efforts no matter what happened. They were in town all along, and now they were here because of us.

"As most of you know," I began, more sure of myself, "the last speakeasy of Pride Month didn't go as planned. We were raided like the speakeasies of the 1920s, and before you ask, yes, I have a lot of knowledge of them thanks to my mom." A few laughs broke out, cutting through my nerves. "She's the reason why I decided to have speakeasies in the first place."

Someone in the crowd whistled, and I grinned when I saw Mom over by the entrance. I felt even more sure of myself knowing she was here for me. *You never know who's listening,* she had said, *so be proud.*

"I witnessed the mayor's rally and saw firsthand the opposite of what we"—I glanced back at my friends—"wanted to do for Pride Month. There was so much hate, so many small minds with too loud of voices. That's what gave us the idea to throw one more speakeasy, but it'll be a rally for you in the town square with a voter registration. We can make it like Pride Day, and we even have a parade float you can use as a stage."

More clapping sounded, but I never let my eyes stray from

Carmen's. "I cannot thank you enough," she said, salt-and-pepper hair swaying with her enthusiastic head nods. "Anything that can help amplify not only my message but what it means to welcome everyone in our town."

Her smile made me feel like I really was a King of Pride—all of us were. I took a deep breath and scanned the room of supporters as I sat down. They were trying to make a difference, and I was one of them. Even if my father was right about the votes, at least our voices still had a chance of being heard.

"Do we have any updates on polling locations?" she asked, continuing around the room.

"All ballot boxes will be set up at the town square for Founder's Day," someone answered.

"We'll have to make sure constituents know where to go, and we need to get them there if they need a ride," Carmen said. "Any ideas . . . ?"

As she addressed the other volunteers, Cohen twisted in his seat to face Sawyer and Kennedy. "What's the plan for tomorrow?" he asked.

"We're hanging up the new campaign posters," Kennedy explained. "We can split up and cover more ground."

"If you two hit one side of town, we"—he nodded to me—"can do the other."

"Yeah," I added, the excitement rubbing off on me. "What else can I do?"

"Z," Sawyer began, "*you* need to be worried about planning this epic speakeasy rally."

"I'll help you," Cohen said, his knees knocking against mine.

There I was again, brain glitching, but I wasn't fighting it. Not anymore. We were in this together now.

CHAPTER 29

I woke up early to start planning for Carmen's rally, taking my laptop with me downstairs. All day, between working on cars, I typed ideas into a document to get everything down I could remember about Pride Day. The QSA had reached out to local businesses for their support. Check. Reserved the town square. Check. Figured out the sound system and setup for tents. Check and check. Everything was ready. All that was left to do was ready the parade float and actually get people there ...

The thought of anyone gathering in Beggs Town Square turned my stomach.

Buchanan's rally still haunted me. Lingering shouts had rattled like ghosts in my mind. Their echoes followed me under each car, back up to the apartment at the end of the day. I knew there was a strong possibility his supporters would crash our celebration. The news coverage of the governor's race only reinforced my worry, protesters heckling a candidate for speaking on LGBTQIA+ rights. It had only reminded me of what I'd witnessed that night in June.

Gays aren't welcome in Beggs!

My Family First ordinance is just the beginning!

Make Beggs safe for families again!

No matter how hard I scrubbed in the shower as I got ready after work, those memories left greasy fingerprints on me. They grabbed at me and sent my pulse into a frenzy. It had been easy to speak up at Carmen's meeting, but it was something else entirely to be doing it for real.

Sweat from the too-hot water—and worry—beaded on my skin as I rushed to finish in the bathroom and then get dressed before Cohen picked me up. I grabbed the stick of deodorant, swiped it a few extra times for good measure, and pulled on the shirt I'd got at the meeting. It was white with a pink donkey and the matching words "VOTE FOR CARMEN." The soft fabric clung to my damp chest, and I spritzed on cologne. The last thing I wanted was to smell like the baseball locker room, especially since I'd be with him.

Alone with him and whatever it was that was happening between us.

With a sigh, I sat on the edge of my bed. *We're only hanging up posters.* That wasn't anything to be afraid of. Yet my legs kept jittering, unable to maintain the cool persona I'd worked so hard on. The anxiety made me feel like the old me, as though I couldn't get rid of Anthony Chapman no matter how hard I tried.

I glanced at the dresser, where I'd displayed the spark plug and the picture with Mom. Then over to the tacked-up newspaper, to the flag above my bed. *Maybe the best parts of me never left,* I thought. They were just too quiet to be heard, too hidden to be seen. Now I was shouting them to the world—and *that* made me nervous.

Shoving the worries of everything that could go wrong from my mind, I closed my eyes and lay back across the quilt. For a moment, I felt safe like I had that first night in the bookstore's basement. Dancing and feeling alive. Feeling like I was welcome. That was the determining factor, like in mathletes when we advanced to the next round by writing the expression as a product of its factors. Everything that had happened this summer had led me to now.

I opened my eyes and looked back up at the pride flag. For so long, I'd been afraid to be the kind of gay person who found meaning in it. Those colors had intimidated me, each rainbow hue a possible threat if I displayed it. And now . . . I'd come so far from the me who had been my father's son. I was about to lead a rally, fighting for everything that had once scared me.

But I had to do it.

Sitting up, I grabbed my phone. The front-facing camera launched with a swipe. I angled it just right to include the flag in the background and smiled. It would be the perfect photo to post to Insta to announce the final speakeasy, and I needed to get on it. Face my fear of people gathering to rally. However, before I could upload it a knock sounded on my door.

"Hey, Mom," I called, startling when I saw who was standing in my doorway. "C-Cohen?"

"Your mom sent me up," he said, and I suddenly felt self-conscious as he eyed my room. "What are you doing?"

"Oh, uh." I shot off the bed with an entirely new nervous

energy. "I was just taking a picture. For Insta. To tell people about the rally."

"Can I see?"

"Sure," I said, waking my screen. Instagram was still pulled up in editor mode with the shirt's message on full display, the rainbow in the background. Then I began to doubt the wide grin I was wearing in it as I held it up for him. "Is it, uh . . . too cheesy?"

"Nah," he said, blushing. "When you, um, smile like that, it makes your eyes shine . . . The way they crinkle makes you look happy."

"I am."

As soon as I said it, I knew it was true. I was happy with how my life was becoming *mine* and excited for whatever would come next. Excited to fight for the future I wanted.

This new feeling drove me to type the caption with details for the rally. Cohen watched and waited in my room, his DM conversation from over the summer sitting in my inbox. It felt like worlds were colliding as I posted the picture—that's what everything felt like.

. . .

The last time Cohen and I had put up flyers in the square, he'd been in a rush. Irritation had fueled his every stomp. This evening was different, though. He fell in step with me as we traced the sidewalks. I was in charge, holding up the posters while he taped them. It made me feel like I had the first day I met him.

Casting a glance over at the monument, I remembered how

Cohen had told me about David Beggs single-handedly building this town. How it'd made me want to do something important. That's what it felt like as I held another poster up for him to tape.

"Done," Cohen said leisurely.

He followed me without trying to stride away. No hurry to leave or puffs of indignation. I kept waiting for the facade to crack, for him to turn back into a smartass. But he showed no signs, not even once in the last few hours.

"Do you remember," I started, and he looked over at me, "when we first met?"

"Um . . ." He scratched at the faint dark stubble on his chin. "Elementary school?" he guessed.

"It was before that," I said, a small smile at the memory. How he'd been clutching his retro camera to take pictures. "Right here in the square when we were kids. We played tag—"

"That was you?" he interrupted.

"I'm *extremely* hurt you don't remember me, Coco," I teased.

His mouth twitched, a corner quirking up as he glanced at the monument. "I *do* recall you vowing to do something important one day."

My steps slowed to a stop, and I turned toward him. "Really?" I asked. "You remember that?"

"It made me want to do something important too." He full-on grinned then, holding up the posters to say that we were doing it. "I won't forget it, just like that day when you— What does Sawyer call it? Z-stepping?"

"Shit-tacular Freshman Fall." My heart fell at the memory. "I lied that day."

He bumped me with his shoulder. "I know that now, and I don't hold it against you. Even though you totally crushed me."

"I'm sorry just the same." My words were soft, floating up and away into the twilight. I kept my eyes on the sidewalk as we moved along. We were on the precipice of the moment we'd both been dodging. "If anyone, uh, Z-stepped, it was you."

My stride quickened with anxiety, and he sped up. "What does that mean?" he called.

"As soon as we . . . stopped being whatever, you immediately moved on to Geometry Derick."

He reached out to put a hand on my arm, slowing my pace. "About that," he began, going splotchy. "God, I feel like such a dick."

"You should."

"To be honest . . ." A pause as he twisted the posters in his hands. "I was trying to make you jealous."

"Wait . . . *what?*" I gawked at him, seeing the boy who'd crushed me all those years ago. "Why?"

"Because I wanted to hurt you like you hurt me." His face was completely red now, and it was so damn endearing I couldn't be mad. "But you know, it was dumb. I should have respected your decision."

"Hell, I don't even respect my decision. I was too ashamed about my father to tell you the truth."

"Yeah . . ."

I gave him a sidelong glance, and the warmth in his brown eyes was growing distant. "You could've at least picked someone else. Geometry Derick always smelled like deli meat. But I was jealous, just so you know."

He didn't laugh but grimaced instead, adjusting his shirt. "You don't have to be nice to me," he said, an edge to his voice.

"What do you mean?"

"I get that you don't like me. I've been a dick to you, unintentionally led you on with the DMs, and, yeah." He motioned at me, from my stomach up to my shoulders. "You're you, and I'm me."

"I don't understand," I said, unable to read through the thousand expressions flitting across his face.

"I know I'm fat." He blinked several times, looking away from me. "I thought maybe... maybe we were picking up where we left off, but you thought you were flirting with Mason. And it's been so awkward between us, and I know it's because you only see me as a friend. Like how you said we were better as—"

"Hang on—"

"Can we just pretend like the whole Insta thing didn't happen?"

I shook my head, my mind racing to catch up with his jumping conclusions. Cohen was breathing heavy and on the verge of making a break for it. I knew how much it cost him to be honest. I'd paid that price countless times this summer.

"Cohen," I started, grabbing his arm to keep him from running away, "it's only been awkward because ... because I *am* interested, okay? I don't want to pretend, not anymore."

"Zeke—"

"No, listen." I put a hand on each of his shoulders and held his gaze. "You're wrong on so many levels. And stop calling yourself fat like it's a bad thing. What does that even have to do with me liking you?"

He shrugged, shying away. "You . . . you weren't happy that it was me in your DMs."

"I didn't know *how* to react to you. I was embarrassed about what I'd told you." He looked at me through his lashes. "But I meant everything I said. Everything."

He bit his lip, his eyes glassy in the dusky light. I could see all the versions he'd been since we met as kids. How they were wrapping together and overlapping just as mine had. We'd lived so many lives since then. And we still ended up back here.

"Cohen—" I broke off, my voice rough.

Ever so carefully, I slid my hand along his shoulder to his neck. Up to his cheek, cupping his jaw. I tilted his face up to mine and hesitated, to make sure I had permission. Then I bent down and kissed him. It was gentle at first, deepening as he leaned into me. My arms wrapped around him to pull him close. It felt like our first kiss all over again, and I smiled against his lips.

CHAPTER 30

We kissed!

The thought raced through my mind every time my phone buzzed with a new notification. Our QSA chat had been popping off all day, and Cohen's texts sent electric jolts through my body. He had messaged about the rally, about hanging up posters, about everything *except* what had happened last night.

I didn't know where to go from here. All those quiet moments we'd shared were roaring loudly in my head. Too loud to ignore like I had three years ago. They were resounding with second chances, and I didn't want to screw things up between us again.

My hands thrummed under the SUV as I twisted on the dolly. Another notification vibrated against my thigh. And then another. I hurriedly dug my phone from my jeans and swiped to unlock the screen. The group chat was still open to Sawyer and Kennedy's discussion on the orientation for our new members. Cohen's latest reply still didn't show any indication whatsoever of how he felt about us, just excitement for the thirty-seven new members.

The phone's glow was bright in the darkness beneath the engine. I held it above my face, my thumb wavering on how to reply. *Maybe they can help with the last speakeasy.* I backspaced. *Do you really think we can make a difference?* Backspaced again. *What if the voter registration is a waste?* And again.

There was only one conversation I needed to have right now. After swiping out of the group chat, I searched for our old message thread. His last message was still there, but this time was different. This time I typed out a message to see if we could talk about what had happened. It was what I should have done years ago.

Deep breaths pushed through my lungs as I waited. The thought of how this could be a fresh start for us raced between each inhale-exhale. Faster as a new notification flashed across my screen. Relief pooled in my stomach. Cohen wanted to talk tomorrow after the rally prep. Before I could reply, another text flashed, making me do a double take.

BILLY PEAK

I'm sorry, Fastball. After the mayor's bullshit, I get how it wasn't easy for you. I shouldn't have run my mouth

I reread his message in shock. Never had I thought that the same dickhead who had made jokes about "brotein" would be apologizing to me. But here he was extending that proverbial olive branch. A ghost pain radiated from my eye as I considered how to reply, but then another message came through.

BILLY PEAK

I've talked to the guys on the team, and we want you back. We need you

The past and the present and the future were all melding together. I wasn't sure if I should even accept his apology, even less sure if I wanted to play baseball again. I'd once loved it, or thought I had. *There were a lot of things I thought,* I told myself as I began typing. *And I've been wrong before.*

ZEKE

I'll think about it

I quickly shoved my phone back into my pocket, shoved that decision out of my mind. Whatever I chose to do, it wouldn't be for him or the team or my father.

I heard the door close, and the dolly's wheels creaked over the art deco tiles while I scooted out to see if we had a new customer. Blinking away the sudden brightness of overhead lights, I saw Mom leaned up against the toolbox. She was holding a letter and reading with a deep scowl on her face.

"Everything okay?" I asked cautiously, sitting up.

She glanced at me, and I saw the anger in her eyes. "I just grabbed the mail from out front," she said. Her voice was as strained as her knuckles gripping the paper. "The mayor has issued a citation to Roaring Mechanics for participating in prohibited activities."

What? I stood up quickly and wiped my hands on my jeans. "Can I see?"

She exhaled roughly and held the paper out for me to read.

The top line noted it had come from "The Mayor's Office of Beggs, Alabama." Then in a big red font, just like on his ordinance posters, the word "CITATION" screamed. I scanned through the details I already knew—the event date, what happened, what ordinance it broke—until I saw the final line.

"Two hundred bucks?" I asked, looking up at her. "I'll pay it since it was my fault."

"No," she said with a severe shake of her head. "You won't be paying it, and I won't be either."

"But it says right here," I continued, reading the letter, "that future infractions could mean losing your business license."

"Doesn't matter." She rubbed at her temples, determination in the firm set of her mouth. I knew that look, had seen that look when she'd fought in the divorce proceedings against my father. "I am *not* paying for violating his homophobic bullshit."

"But—"

"No buts, hun. It might seem like just a couple hundred bucks, but it's more than that. Paying it means you did something bad. Other than, ya know, lying and sneaking around, you did *nothing* bad. I need you to know that, okay?" I nodded in understanding. "It was technically a party, which was well within my right as a business owner. There also happened to be queer kids there, and by the looks of the place everyone enjoyed themselves . . . Did you?"

I thought back to that night, how it'd felt to just exist in the crowd of people. How I hadn't been afraid. How I'd felt safe before Buchanan destroyed everything. "Yes," I decided. "I did."

"Then we won't be paying it."

"What about your license?"

"Let them try." She wadded up the letter and threw it

toward the trash bin. "He trespassed on my property, and I learned enough from that brutal divorce about how going to court can ruin a man."

"Go off."

She stood up from the toolbox, absently adjusting her mechanic shirt. "This only furthers the need for Carmen to win the election," she said. "All the campaign endorsers are meeting tonight to make a plan B if things don't go the way we want and we don't get enough votes."

The weight of her words pressed down on me, and I nodded in understanding. Nothing had gone the way I'd wanted since coming out. This summer was evidence of that. I'd only wanted to prove myself with the idea to have speakeasies for Pride. Too much had happened since because of me, and doubt made me worry that I'd ruined everything.

"Zeke?" Mom's voice cut through the haze. "If your eyebrows pinch together any tighter, there's only gonna be one of 'em. Everything okay?"

"Just a lot on my mind with Founder's Day and just . . ."

I let out a sigh, chewing my lip. *A vote for Bedolla won't amount to anything* replayed in my mind. Would voting for Carmen in two weeks even matter? It was intimidating to think how a singular vote would even help.

"Can I ask you something about this election?" She nodded. "How is a vote supposed to change anything?"

"Hey." She studied me, the overhead lights reflecting the emerald of her eyes. "It's not just a vote," she explained in a soft voice.

I shook my head, that same confusion from watching the news muddling my mind. "But what my father said at dinner—"

"Don't listen to him," she interrupted with a raised hand. "Each vote will join the others who are fighting back because of you. Who knows what will happen on Founder's Day, but it's just the start."

A month ago, Buchanan had climbed up to the pavilion, and my father had stopped me. He'd told me the mayor's plan wouldn't affect me if I kept my head down and stayed quiet. However, it had affected me, affected all of us. But I didn't know if *I* had a plan B.

"I don't know what I'm supposed to do if Carmen loses, though," I admitted. "If Buchanan enforces more ordinances."

Mom considered me for a moment, my words hanging between us. "That was how I felt when I made the decision to leave your father," she admitted. "The worry of not knowing what would happen next nearly stopped me. I had to focus on what I did know, and that was making your life better. Our life. Then it became the easiest decision I've ever made."

"I don't know what to focus on, though . . ." If she had wanted to make my life better, then who was I doing this for? I hadn't known who would show up at the speakeasies or what they'd cause in town. Then everyone played a part in something bigger, something more important that had been set in motion.

"Hun," she began, "what you should do is focus on who you are *despite* the election. No matter what happens, you'll still be you. And you have been working hard with the QSA, for people like you in Beggs. Don't let that citation fool you, because nothing you did was wrong. You've certainly lived up to your namesake this summer."

"How so?" I asked, resting back against the SUV.

"Obviously, attention-seeking—"

"Ha."

"—being fearless, daring, and, most importantly, you knew what you wanted and spoke up. I'm so proud of you and your friends for this community you brought together. I know that no matter what happens, it won't stop you from being you."

Silence fell between us as the baseball game of thoughts played in my mind. I didn't know who I was anymore. If I was the same guy Billy wanted back on the team or the person I'd tried to become. My gaze drifted to the portrait of Zelda with her coy smile. All I knew was that Mom had named me after her favorite woman in history. As though I was destined to be just as loud and rebellious as her. As my mom.

"Just promise me you'll continue to speak up regardless of what happens here in Beggs," she added, pulling me into a hug.

What she'd said about plan B reverberated in my head as she held me tightly. It made me feel like a child again, like we were in the garage at our old house. However, I now knew I couldn't stay quiet the way my father had taught me back then. I'd spent so long comparing myself to him, when really it was Mom and me who were the same. It wasn't because we were capable of fixing everything—we were capable of changing out what was broken. After I'd spent all those years learning from her, she was still teaching me something new. Something just as meaningful.

"I will," I finally promised as she stepped back.

"That's my boy." Her voice was sure, her smile assuring as she checked her smartwatch. "I'm gonna start closing down, and then we can grab takeout for dinner."

"Hey," I began, nodding toward the SUV's hood, "do you think you could help me change the spark plugs before we call it a day?"

CHAPTER 31

I'd grown up in Beggs, Alabama, thinking there were only two sides. Either you blended in with the small-town charm or you were an outcast if you couldn't fit everyone else's definition of perfect. But I'd been wrong. There was another side of this town. I'd just never seen it hiding in plain sight until now.

It was the people who'd helped us pull off the speakeasies. Their support was evidence of allies in town. They were like the twinkling stars I'd seen in the sky while riding last night: always here but not able to be seen until darkness. They were easy to spot if you really looked. Driving through town now, I could see each shining light—the "all are welcome" stickers on storefront windows, pride flags, pink donkey signs—that made up a constellation of safe spaces.

This was the Beggs we had created for ourselves.

I sped past each emblem of support, toward Estrella Books. Today, we were preparing for the last speakeasy. One last chance to make sure Carmen's rally shined on Saturday. I knew

Mom was right and that I would still be me regardless of the outcome. Even though I was still figuring that out, I knew one thing for certain—I was welcomed no matter who I was. The proof was in the bookstore's parking lot.

The QSA parade float took up the middle row of spaces, and campaign volunteers were already decorating it. Flashes of rainbow glinted in the sunlight like armor as they prepared for battle. I turned into the drive, pulled beside Cohen's silver Camry, and killed the dirt bike's engine. At one time I would've felt like an imposter in comparison to all these political advocates. Instead, I kept both my head held high and those feelings of inferiority from causing doubt. *You belong here*, I asserted once more before dismounting.

My hair was already soaked from the helmet, and I ran my hands through the tangled waves. The midday sun bore down with the brutal heat of July. But there was something *more* amid the climbing temperature. A promise of tomorrow in the air, in the sweltering humidity pressing down on Beggs, in the excited buzz of conversation around me.

Wiping sweat from my brow, I made my way over to the crowd. Everyone who had come together for that first speakeasy was here. There were so many faces that had become familiar since that night in the bookstore's basement. Owen climbed down from the float, his beard covered in sawdust. Bronwen and Kennedy spray-painted a Pride mural on the side banner. Jess helped Sawyer hang streamers from the back. Carmen smiled as she addressed new volunteers. And then there was Cohen.

He intently studied a clipboard while my heartbeats sped up. While I fought the urge to run over and grab him by the shirt and kiss him again. As though he could hear my thoughts, he glanced up. A shy smile lifted the corner of his mouth when his eyes found mine. A radio signal from their brown depths promised we'd talk later. The equation of him and me required BEDMAS rules to solve, but I was finally figuring it out.

A sudden thud tore my attention away from his adorable splotchiness. Owen had crossed over to his nature preserve truck and let the tailgate down. The cargo bed was loaded down with a massive podium. It looked newly made, fresh wood stain glistening, and way too heavy for him to unload alone.

"Hey," I called out, crossing over to him. "Need some help?"

"I wouldn't say no," he replied with a gruff laugh.

The detailed craftsmanship was evident as I drew near. Its smooth edges and rounded corners, even a wood-burned inscription of Carmen's name, showed just how much work had gone into its construction. I came to a stop beside Owen, gazing up at it. "Did you make this?" I asked.

"Sure did, with a downed tree from the preserve," he replied with a smile. "A congratulatory gift for our future Madame Mayor."

"Wow . . ." I could appreciate how he'd used his own hands to make something. It was similar to what I'd been doing at the mechanic shop. "But wait," I started, the conversation about a plan B still ringing in my mind, "what if she loses?"

"That doesn't matter," he said simply with a shrug. "It'll still be a podium, still be a gift regardless."

Still be rattled inside my head as we slid it out of the truck. We'd still be here too. *I'll still be here.* But I didn't know what my plan B was yet. The idea of the future caused me to struggle both with what Mom had said about being myself and the weight of the gift.

"This is heavy as fu— heck," I grunted over the echo of his words. My biceps were on fire as we carried it. The muscles I'd had from baseball weren't as strong as they used to be. "Seriously think my arms are gonna turn against me and rip themselves off."

Owen's laugh came out in a rough chuckle. "Not too much farther," he said reassuringly. "You're doing great, Zeke."

"Trying as hard as I can," I mumbled. The rally had to be perfect. I'd messed up too much already, and I didn't want to prove my father right. For everything that had happened this summer to be a waste.

"Did anyone ever tell you that you don't have to try so hard?" I glanced over at him, and he gave me an all-knowing look. "It's like what I tell my child, you just have to try your best."

"Easier said than done."

It came out as another mumble as I glanced around the parking lot. Past the crowd and the bookstore, even farther past the library, I could see the billboard. It was as though younger me was watching the square where Buchanan had said he wasn't welcome in Beggs. The memory sent a ripple of panic through me, and my jaw clenched with doubt. *Will this rally be enough to make a difference—*

"Thank you, by the way," Owen said over my thoughts. He gave me an encouraging smile as we eased the podium onto the float. "Your speakeasies taught me how I can be a more supportive parent. Addi has a rough time at school with their pronouns, and I'm doing everything I can so they don't have to grow up in fear."

The way he said it was so earnest, and I looked away so he wouldn't see my eyes welling up. All the years I'd spent living inside that shoebox made me fear the what-ifs: what if I came out and everyone turned on me, what if I wasn't welcome in town, what if I was targeted and became the moral of someone's story. I'd stayed hidden because of those fears, kept them so long they'd become my truths.

"You don't, um, you don't have to thank me," I managed to say around the rush of emotions.

"Sure I do," he said, wiping his hands off on his Carhartt work pants. "You're trying your best, and it's making a difference."

"I hope . . . so." My voice broke, and I needed to change the subject before I outright cried in front of everyone. "Um, do you need help with anything else?" I asked, then cleared my throat.

"I could use another set of hands to assemble the platform for this monster." He knocked on the podium for emphasis, and I nodded my head in agreement. "See," he said, clapping me on the back. "We're already building a better Beggs."

He climbed onto the float and held out a hand. My mind darted back to the statue in the square as he helped me up. Just like David Beggs and his faithful donkey, we really were building our own community. I guess we just needed the right people—the right parts—to do it.

For so long, I'd been disassembling engines and putting them back together. It made sense in my head, how everything had its place for the vehicle to run. Now I was beginning to understand that wasn't real life. You couldn't keep trying to put your life back together with the same parts. Some didn't belong anymore, and some needed to change. All you could do was build yourself into something new.

And I *had* become something new this summer: bold.

. . .

A lock of my hair danced in the evening breeze. It felt good on my sunburned face as I lay on the new platform. Most of the volunteers had called it a day, and I was exhausted. My hands were the best kind of sore—the tightness of my knuckles a reminder that I'd built something.

"Are you . . ." Sawyer was saying, but I kept zoning out. My mind wandered as I watched the Timmy's Shaved Ice truck. Cohen and Kennedy had gone to get sno-cones while we waited. Every few minutes he'd glance back. Lock eyes with me. Smile. We were on the precipice of *something* again, but this time I knew it was different.

"Spill your guts," Sawyer ordered, snapping me back. She had shifted to face me with an intense stare down. "Right now."

"Huh?" I asked.

The setting sun glinted off her glasses as she leveled her gaze. "Why are you and Cohen acting sus AF?" she demanded with a smirk.

"Uhhh." My uncertainty hung in the air between us. The sticky honey of her eyes was trapping me yet again. I sat there, listening to the rustle of the float streamers, and searched for the right thing to say. She still didn't know what had happened. Not that I was deliberately keeping it from her, but I wasn't sure what everything all meant. "I mean, we aren't—"

She cut me off. "You're cute and all, but he's been intently staring at you like you're a Weeping Angel all day."

"Well . . ." I trailed off, unable to stop my grin.

"I *knew* you liked him!" she gasped. "The tea is scalding, and you better spill it."

"Okay, okay," I said, sitting up. "When we were hanging up posters in the square, he and I . . . we might've kissed."

"It's about damn time," she said too excitedly, too loudly. "Y'all have had this back-and-forth verbal foreplay—"

"It was only kissing!" I hissed. *But was it?*

"Suuure." She scoffed and rushed to ask, "How was it? Tongue? No tongue? Did it give you tingles, or did it give your, you know, *the* tingle?"

"Ohmygod." She made suggestive gestures with her hands, and I glanced over at Cohen again. He tapped his phone to pay for the sno-cones. Any minute now they'd be back, and I had to shut Sawyer up. "It was great, no notes. Tongue. *Both* of the tingles. And before you grill me, he's a good kisser. His lips are soft . . . And okay. Fine. Maybe my crush on him never really went away. Is that what you want to hear?"

"What I want to hear," she started as they began making their way over, "is that you're not gonna Z-step."

Over the last month, I'd let my guard down with bedmas_22— with Cohen. He knew me and didn't run. Knew me and still kissed me back. "I'm not Z-stepping," I said under my breath.

She shot me a look that said she'd hold me to it as they neared. "Then ask him to come with us to the outdoor movie night tomorrow," she suggested.

"I don't know—"

"Got your favorite," Kennedy cut me off, offering Sawyer a bright-red sno-cone, with a disgusted tilt to her lips. "Tiger's blood."

"Don't judge me," Sawyer said, and gave me a wink. "The flavor combo hits different."

"And blue raspberry for you," Cohen added as he held one up to me.

He'd remembered my favorite from back in the day. I couldn't help but smile when I took it from him. "Thanks, Coco," I said, our fingers brushing. Still weird not to be fighting with him, but I could get used to this. Wanted to get used to *whatever* this was.

"Sooo," Sawyer said, jumping off the float. She shot me a mischievous grin and turned toward Kennedy. "Didn't you say you wanted to see if Carmen had that sapphic book you wanted in stock?"

"I did?" Kennedy asked, scrunching her face in confusion. Sawyer widened her eyes and jerked her head to me and Cohen. "Oh. Yes. That book. With the lesbians. That I want to read."

"There's obviously no book," I deadpanned as Cohen climbed up beside me.

"Why are y'all being weird?" he asked, sitting beside me.

"Nooo reeeason," Sawyer singsonged, and steered Kennedy toward the store entrance.

For a brief moment, panic spiked as they held each other's hands. As I glanced around the parking lot in case anyone could see them. But I forced myself to take a deep breath of the humid air and exhale slowly. I wasn't suffocating anymore.

"Y'all are totally gonna make out," Cohen called after them.

Kennedy spun around with an evil grin on her face. "Funny," she retorted, the hazel of her eyes catching what little sunlight remained. "I could say the same to you."

"Not funny," he muttered.

The insinuation meant only one thing. He had told her about our kiss. I waited until they disappeared inside before asking, "So she knows that I, uh, that we—"

"Yeah, that," he finished with bashfulness.

He shoveled a bite of purple shaved ice into his mouth and looked over at me. His brown eyes went wide with nerves as he waited for my reaction. I could see a question in his gaze, the same one I'd been wondering: *What does this mean?* The bubble we'd built around ourselves was back. We were here together, atop the platform, like we'd been in the square and on Instagram. And I didn't want to be anywhere else.

"Don't be sorry," I said with a smile. "I legit just told Sawyer."

His face went as red as the tiger's blood sno-cone. "So, uh." He blinked several times as he tried to form words. "Now they both know. That we did that."

"You can say it, you know." I laughed, nudging him with my elbow. "We kissed, and now . . . I don't know what this is, Coco."

"I don't either," he admitted with a shaky breath.

"I screwed up in freshman year before we had the chance to find out," I began, offering him my hand, "but how about we figure it out now?"

He blinked a few times before slowly reaching out. His palm was warm and sweaty against mine. Our fingers laced together as I held on to him. After taking apart what'd happened between us over and over again for the last three years, it was time to build something new.

"So, um." I licked my lips, suddenly nervous, and paid way too much attention to the wood grain of the platform. "Saw and I have this tradition. We always go to the library's outdoor movie night. They play a book adaptation with a projector, and it's tomorrow. And if you don't have plans and wanna hang . . ."

A beat of silence passed before I forced myself to look up at him. Red splotches had bloomed underneath his sunburn, but he was smiling. "Sure," he finally replied in a soft whisper.

That one word broke the bubble around us. The rest of the world came rushing in with the calliope music of the shaved ice truck. With a gust of wind and rattle of streamers. With a reminder that we were here together.

And it felt right.

CHAPTER 32

The floorboards of my bedroom creaked with unrest, unease. I kept readjusting the shirt I'd pulled on while I paced. The collar was scratchy against my neck, circling my throat like a hand. I checked the time on my phone, letting out a sigh, and tossed it onto the bed. Any minute now, Cohen would pick me up. Then we'd go to the library with Sawyer and Kennedy to hang out, but I didn't know if it was an actual date.

After all these damn years, I admonished, exhaling slowly through the nerves, *why wasn't I more specific when I asked?*

My hands kept fidgeting, and I grabbed the cologne from my dresser to spritz myself. Ran my hands through my hair to try taming it again. It still felt surreal to think of Cohen as someone I was getting ready for, that we would hold hands and kiss until I'd want to other-stuff him . . .

The pride flag on the wall caught my eye, then the crumpled letter I'd taped beside it. I'd fished it out of the trash yesterday, smoothing down the folds from Mom's clenched fist.

Its scolding red ink was a reminder that the mayor thought I'd done something wrong—that trying to make Beggs feel more like home was bad. It only fueled my anger toward him and every hate-sign-carrying asshole from his rally.

And everything I was worried about suddenly felt insignificant.

The weight of reality forced me to sit on the edge of my bed. There was more important shit happening in Beggs. The rally was tomorrow, and I should be brainstorming ways to ensure a vote for Carmen would amount to *something*. Running through our plan. Double-checking the details. Anything other than being self-centered, with main-character energy.

"What the hell am I even *doing* right now?" I asked too loudly.

My outburst echoed through the apartment, and I hung my head. Part of me was glad Mom had gone out to dinner with her new friends from book club. Otherwise, she'd give me a first-date pep talk and only add more stress by mentioning condoms. Then again, another part of me wished she were here to tell me what to do.

Should I even be worrying about this? I groaned, snatching my phone off the quilt.

I swiped to unlock the screen and navigated to my favorite contacts. Sawyer's goofy display photo of smushed cheeks, puckered mouth, stared back at me as I tapped the video call icon. Staccato beats rang three times before a chime sounded. The screen lagged, Chappell Roan blasting through the speakers first, and then she appeared.

"I'm literally about to see you—" Sawyer began, but I cut her off without preamble.

"Helllllp," I whined. "I'm freaking the F out. Gasket fully blown. Lid completely flipped."

She blinked slowly, only one eye done in the little mascara she wore, and stepped out of frame. The music stopped mid-song as she returned. "What's up, Z?" she asked, and then, squinting without her glasses: "Did you do something different with your hair?"

"Does it look bad?" I asked, voice lilting. "I combed it too much, and it got frizzy. So, I used some of my mom's hairspray and . . . Why are you laughing?"

Her giggles echoed into my room, and she pointed the makeup wand at me. "Because you, of all people, are losing your shit."

"What does *that* mean?" I countered.

"You've been with so many guys." She held up her hand and counted. "Jonathan, Bailey, Zach—"

"'D appointments' don't matter," I huffed, glancing back at the citation. "And I don't even know if tonight matters either."

"Oh, Z."

"Don't give me that look," I said as she made a pouty face at the camera.

"It's so precious how you and 'the antagonistic fucker'"— she quoted from all the times I'd shit-talked him—"are sooo enemies-to-lovers coded, and I'm here for it."

My stomach churned at her use of the word *lovers*. "What do I do?" I asked quietly, anxiously smoothing my hair back.

"Seeing as I'm not well-versed in your preferred porn—"

"Not. That." My face was on fire at the thought. "Like, how am I supposed to act tonight with everything that's happening?"

The frame tilted back as she propped the phone up in front

of her bathroom mirror. "Just be yourself," she said, leaning in to finish her other eye.

"I don't even know what that means anymore." My sneakers thudded aggressively as my feet tapped like racing heartbeats. "It feels like I've been waiting forever for this, but now it's here and"—I brought the phone closer for emphasis—"like *how* did you keep your cool with Kennedy?"

She laughed again, leveling her gaze at me. "I didn't," she explained, putting her glasses back on.

"Okay, that actually checks out," I teased, and she stuck her tongue out at me. "So what happened?"

"I tripped in the parking lot of the restaurant, spilled my drink all over my shirt, snorted at one of her jokes that should've been a chuckle at most, and yeah. It got worse from there. But it didn't matter because she likes me. Cohen likes you too, so stop stressing. Let whatever happens tonight . . . just happen."

"I have a track record of messing shit up, Saw."

"That's not necessarily true. Well, on second thought"—she winked at me, holding up her thumb and forefinger—"maybe just a little true. But you're also owning up to your mistakes and fixing them. That's what matters."

"I guess."

"You'll be fine," she assured me. "Nothing is perfect, Z, and that's okay as long as you're trying. Even if tonight doesn't go as planned, Cohen *will* understand. Worst case scenario, you can try again. There's always the theater over in West Point or Founder's Day or . . ."

She continued to ramble off suggestions, but I was stuck on Founder's Day. That implied "after the last speakeasy," a reminder of the upcoming election for the new mayor of Beggs. It made everything about right now feel trivial in comparison to what was to come. "Sorry," I interrupted her. "I know it's stupid to worry about this when I need to focus on tomorrow's rally."

"You've done all you can. We all have," she said, bringing a hand to her chest. "I titty promise, it's not stupid to be an actual person. That's what Mayor Buchanan and the state governor and even the Supreme Court of Dipshits want us to think, that we don't deserve to be people too. So don't give them the satisfaction of dismissing your life."

We've done all we can. I hoped she was right. We had shown up instead of staying quiet, spoken up for our QSA—for everyone in this town. No matter what that citation declared, I knew what we'd done this summer was good. *But is it enough?*

"I'm waiting," Sawyer added, her hand still on her chest.

Mirroring her, I brought my hand up. "I titty promise to not let political fuckwads keep me from living my life," I vowed, hoping it was an oath I could keep. At least for tonight.

· · ·

The running time for the old 2013 movie *The Great Gatsby* was nearly two and a half hours. Every minute was spent wanting to kiss Cohen right there on the blanket. We'd started off holding hands, electricity zapping between our fingers. His head had found a place on my shoulder by the time the famous green light flashed in the closing scene. Sawyer's pep talk had calmed me down, settled my nerves enough to be bold.

Smoothly, I tilted his face up toward mine. He broke the

kiss after a moment, leaning back to say, "I didn't think it was that romantic of a movie."

"I was too distracted to notice," I admitted with a grin. His reactions to the movie had captured my attention. I couldn't stop myself from watching him get lost in the story. Every time he smiled or laughed or widened his eyes in awe kept me here with him, not drifting into worry over tomorrow.

"Ah, yes. I don't blame you," he said through a laugh. "The themes of the American dream and social class, not to mention the irony of the Roaring Twenties and this summer—"

I kissed him again, and our tongues brushed ever so slightly as someone groaned beside us. He smiled against my lips before pulling back. Kennedy and Sawyer were wearing matching unamused expressions from the blanket next to us.

"I stand by my assertion," Kennedy began, digging in her cheer tote. "This is so much worse."

"So. Much. Worse," Sawyer agreed, but she smiled at me like she had on the video chat. "Hurry up with those Takis before I die from this sweetness overload."

"But I'm glad you two *finally* got your shit together," Kennedy added. She set aside cans of leftover spray paint from the rally prep as she kept searching. Finally, much to Sawyer's delight, she pulled out a bag of the Fuego flavored chips like a trophy. "It's about time you went on a date anyway."

Cohen choked, a gurgled cough of embarrassment. "We're not . . . I didn't tell her that, Zeke. Oh my god—"

"It's okay," I interrupted his spiral. "Besides, I'd like that."

"For this to be a date?"

His whispered question was nearly lost in the sounds of people leaving the library's lawn, the car doors slamming, the cicadas chirping. Uncertainty lined his lips in a restrained smile. Almost as though he was afraid if he gave into it, that I'd take it back. That I'd pull a Mason and change my mind because of something inconsequential.

"Yes," I said matter-of-factly.

"Me too," he replied just the same way.

Sawyer snorted around the crunch of chips. "To think all it took for these two to stop fighting was political upheaval," she said, pointing at us with a flaming-red-stained finger.

"What would y'all have done if Pride Day hadn't been canceled?" Kennedy teased, grabbing Cohen's camera from the blanket.

"Stooop," Cohen said as a bright flash went off. Then he giggled as Kennedy snapped another picture of us. I had never heard him laugh like that before. It was soft, sweet even, and made my stomach flutter.

"This is too cute," Kennedy said, looking at the viewfinder. "You have to post it to Insta."

Cohen sat upright but kept leaning against me. "And to answer your question," he directed at Kennedy, "I think Zeke would probably still be himself . . . ya know, a Zasshole."

"Hey," I said, shoving him playfully, and he winked at me.

"What's worse than the word 'worse'?" Sawyer muttered to Kennedy. "Because this is very much *that*."

They laughed, throwing digs at each other, but what he'd said about me being myself made me think of Sawyer's promise. *It's not stupid to be an actual person.* Her words reverberated through me as I glanced over my shoulder. Across the parking lot, two blocks down, I could see the billboard atop Jones Hardware. The memory of being up there and panicking sent a wave of doubt crashing against me again. But it receded as I held on to the fact that I wasn't alone. We were together, being ourselves despite the hate disguised by the haloed glow of Beggs.

"I think we'd still be here even if it hadn't been canceled," I said, tearing my attention away from the billboard. "Still fighting the never-ending bullshit."

It was silent for a moment as they stared at me, and then Sawyer nodded as she understood what I meant. "We'd still have to fight anti–LGBTQ-plus bullshit," she said.

"I'd still be nervous about being fully out in this crap town," Kennedy added.

Cohen licked his bottom lip, catching my eye. "I would still be so preoccupied with planning my future that summer would have passed by without me knowing." He gestured between us. "Without knowing what could be."

I reached out and found his hand, a new habit that I didn't want to break. "And I guess I'd still be fighting my father to be someone else."

"I happen to like who you are," Cohen said with a smirk. "Besides, your 'Rebel's Guide to Pride' is what got us here."

"It can only get us so far, though," I admitted. We'd all done everything we could this summer, and there wasn't a guarantee it was enough. "What's our plan B if . . . if all our work amounts to nothing?"

"That's easy," Sawyer began, the headlights of a passing car glinting off her glasses. "We'll fight for our Pride no matter what."

"We don't call ourselves the QS-SLAY for nothing," Cohen added.

I fell silent as Kennedy brought up new-member orientation, absently staring at the spray paint by her bag. Whatever happened next, we had to find ways to move forward—I had to keep moving forward. When school started back up in a few weeks, I'd try to be a better student. Get my life back on track. Keep working at Roaring Mechanics. Maybe I'd take up Billy Peak's offer to rejoin the baseball team for senior year, or maybe I'd try something entirely new. That was my choice to make now.

My future isn't that billboard, I thought, casting a glance back at the square.

The kid in that ten-foot picture might've once had a life laid out before him, but I got to decide what I did next. My first step toward who I wanted to be had come in the form of a giant graffitied penis. I'd climbed up onto that catwalk to send a message to my father, to let him know he couldn't control me. Now Buchannan and his supporters were trying to control us.

Maybe we should send them a message too . . .

"I just had an idea for the rally tomorrow," I said suddenly, twisting around. My eyes clocked each of their questioning stares before falling to the rainbow cans by Kennedy's bag. "And I'm gonna need help."

CHAPTER 33

Ever since December, I'd been trying fix the past, as though I could travel back to when it all went wrong in eighth grade. My eyes had been opened when Sawyer and I had watched *Doctor Who* for the first time the summer before; however, my father forced me to keep them shut. I'd kept them closed while he made me get dressed up for a matching photo. While he paraded me around Chapman Law's fiftieth anniversary celebration. While he'd unveiled my future in front of strangers while I suffocated.

I'd come face-to-face with that version of me again last night. This time, though, I wasn't alone. My friends had climbed up that rusty ladder to the top of Jones Hardware with me. Together, we tore down that ten-foot picture of my father and me to reveal a blank billboard—a fresh start. It had felt like ripping a hole in the space-time continuum. As though I'd reached into the past and pulled that scared little boy through to the future I'd created for us.

And now, it was time for the sleepy-eyed town of Beggs to wake up.

I stared up at the billboard, squinting against the morning sunshine. The bright beams were a spotlight on the rainbow-colored words **WE'LL FIGHT FOR OUR PRIDE.** Sawyer's words couldn't be truer. That was our plan B, a promise to Buchanan that we wouldn't let him erase us. We were demanding our right to exist. I wouldn't beg for signatures to celebrate Pride, to be me, ever again.

Tightening my grip on the voter registration sign, I started toward the QSA tent. The square felt almost like it had on Pride Day. The parade float, rows of tents set up like before, same flags waving ... But it felt different. *I* was different. Pride had once felt like a war between who I was and who I should be. Now I knew what it meant to me—speaking up and demanding to exist as myself.

I held my head high and marched onward. Community supporters waved as I passed by, each gesture a salute. Their welcoming smiles were co-signatures on the graffiti we'd tagged on the billboard. I returned both in kind, startling when I heard my name yelled. It was an excited yip that sounded like laughter and took me back to the rec center. To that day Cohen had trained me to mentor and told me I was doing something right. *Addi,* I remembered as their afro poofs bounced while they darted from the nature preserve's setup.

"Zeke!" they exclaimed again, grinning as they ran up to me. "I've missed you!"

"Good morning, Addi," I said. "I've missed seeing you at the rec center. You doing okay?"

"Better now with Mayor Butthead leaving office," they said.

"We don't know who will win," a gruff voice added as Owen followed after them, "but we're here to vote for *you*, kid."

Addi rolled their eyes, spinning on their heels. "But maybe the rec center will get the program back if Miss Bedolla wins, though, Daddy," they reminded him. "I felt safe there, more than I did at school."

He and I exchanged a look, both of us recalling what he'd said when we built the platform. No matter what happened in the election, he'd still fight for Addi. I had to keep fighting too.

"You know," I heard myself say, "I've gotten pretty good at doing things the mayor might not like, so I promise to figure out how to do the mentorship program again, okay?"

"Okay!" Addi said, bouncing on their heels. "Where's Momma? I need to go tell her."

He pointed across to the other row of tents. I followed his line of sight to the animal shelter, catching Sawyer's eye as she started our way. He shook his head with a laugh as Addi bounded up to the woman setting up the adoption drive. "I want to thank you, Zeke," he began, turning back to me, "for what you've done to make Beggs a safe space for Addi."

"Yes, sir," I replied. "I think— No, I know I'll keep doing everything I can to make it safe for us."

He held my gaze for a beat before taking off after his child. There was gratitude in his parting smile. A promise that no matter what happened today, he'd be right by my side fighting. I felt myself standing taller as I glanced back up at the billboard.

"Did you really mean that?" Sawyer asked as she came up beside me. "About the mentorship program?"

"If I made the speakeasies happen," I started, watching

Owen and his family, "then why not underground mentorship programs? Or more? Whatever we have to do if Carmen doesn't win. Because I can't go back to hiding in fear." *To living in that shoebox.*

"Z, I really am proud of you."

"Saw," I said, nudging her with my shoulder. "I'm proud of *us.*"

"Don't be humble," she commanded me with a snort. "We both know you were born with main-character energy, so just take the compliment."

I rolled my eyes. "But I wouldn't have been this way if not for you—" She opened her mouth to argue, but I held up a finger. "Please let me finish. You were the first person I came out to, and you helped me be me when I didn't know how. Gave me that epic pride flag, and just . . . Sawyer, I'm so thankful you're my best friend. I don't know what I would've done without you."

Her usual look of focus was back, and she narrowed her eyes. "Don't you dare make me cry," she said, emotions strangling her words. "But . . . I'm so glad we nearly threw hands over X-Men." Then she hugged me, squeezing tight as she lowered her voice. "I never said thank you for speaking up at Pride Day after it was canceled. I'd been so upset, but you had my back. Best friends for life, okay? No matter how far apart we move for college."

I laughed, watching the blue tips of her hair swaying in the wind. So much had happened since we'd celebrated the first day of freedom at the blue hole. Since our last break before senior year began to unravel in the best possible way.

"Titty promise," I said.

I was glad we hadn't stayed in a fight. Some things were more important than arguing over who was right and who was wrong. The proof was all around us. Tiny buttons for Carmen's campaign, rainbow flags, familiar faces that smiled instead of glaring—all stars in our town that shined with more importance than I could've ever imagined.

. . .

"Hey, son."

My hands stilled on the voter registration sign at the sound of my father's voice. I carefully turned around, and the sight of him sent my pulse thrumming. His chinos were pressed, shirt neatly tucked in, not a hair out of place as he took off his sunglasses to study me. His scrutiny made me want to cower as I'd done so many times before, but I squared my shoulders as he approached.

"We need to talk," he said with a note of authority. "Why don't we go to the law firm for some privacy—"

"Kinda busy, if you can't tell," I interrupted him and gestured around the square. "We're getting ready for a rally."

He eyed the Pride tank top I was wearing, and then his gaze shifted to the voter registration sign. "I'm well aware," he said, dropping his voice.

"Are you here to pull our permit?" I asked sharply.

He held up his hands in surrender. "I'm not here to stop you"—he took a step toward me, motioning around the square—"but I do want to warn you about doing this."

From over his shoulder, Cohen locked eyes with me. He was helping Sawyer and Kennedy set up the sound system on the parade float. He tilted his head in question, and I quickly shook mine to let him know I had this. "I'm not gonna sit back and do nothing," I finally said, looking back at my father.

"I'm not here to talk you out of it either."

This close, I could see his—our—blue eyes in the bright sunshine. For so many years, I'd seen him as my only future. We were more alike than I wanted to admit. I wondered if he saw our sharp jawline or the way we both tended to get freckles across our nose in the summer. Or if he saw a failure for a son like I saw him as a father.

"Then what could we possibly have to talk about?" I asked.

"Anthon—" He cut himself off and tried again. "Zeke, you almost got in trouble with the mayor over your illegal party." He pointed up to the top of Jones Hardware. "Not to mention you destroyed my billboard ad again."

"I don't know what you're talking about," I managed calmly.

"Don't." His voice dropped low as he leaned in to whisper, "We both have extremely high IQs, despite your grades suggesting otherwise. I know you're the one who has been throwing illegal events all over town. You're lucky you didn't get arrested, and you're only adding gas to the fire with this rally. This town is in an uproar, and I don't want you to get hurt."

"I don't care." My voice came out sternly, unwavering. "Nothing can hurt me more than staying quiet like I have been."

"You could get in trouble, arrested even, if things get out of hand today. I can't keep protecting—"

"I don't need you to protect me anymore," I said, and knew without a doubt I meant it. He'd tried to keep me safe all these years only to suffocate me instead. "If I get in trouble over standing up for who I am, at least it sure as hell is something I believe in."

I started to turn away from him, already done with this conversation, but then he surprised me. "I'm sorry, Zeke." The coiled muscles of my legs relaxed as his words sank in. "I know you don't believe me, but I am. Sorry, that is. I thought . . ." He trailed off in search for the words to say. "I didn't know how much being gay meant to you."

"You make it sound like a hobby," I pointed out sarcastically.

"We never talked about it."

"That's because you didn't let me." I had to fight to maintain my composure. Fight to stand my ground and not run from this conversation. "You didn't *want* me to talk about it. To be loud. Like Sawyer. Like the people marching on the evening news, in the newspaper. You wanted me to be quiet."

"That's what I thought you wanted," he said, the facade dropping. "You went along with it." The wattage of his smile dimmed into a grimace. "I thought I was doing the right thing. Keeping you safe from all *this*."

I knew he was referencing the state governor, the mayor's ordinances, the hateful people in town who were quick to anger. "That's how you raised me," I said with a waver in my voice. "You wanted me to be the best, so I kept my mouth shut."

"That's not what I want for you." He huffed out, eyeing the pride flag on the QSA tent. "This is what I wanted for you. For you to be safe and welcomed in town."

"Then why are you supporting the mayor's campaign against us?" I asked. "And don't say it's just business."

He wiped the sweat off his forehead with a sigh. "I believed it was the right thing. If I threw my support behind the mayor, then no one would target my son. That's why I said it wouldn't affect you—"

"Well, it did." I stood to my full height, taking in a deep breath. We were nearly eye level now, but his gaze made me feel like a kid again. "It did affect me. I was at Buchanan's rally too and saw firsthand what he stands for. It was terrifying to witness that crowd, to see you up on that stage."

"You shouldn't have been there," he said with a sad note in his voice. "After this election is over, things will calm down."

"Because you still expect Buchanan to win, that voting for Carmen won't amount to anything?" He didn't reply, and I took a step back. "That's what I thought."

"Zeke, wait," he said as I started to storm off. "It's not your job to fight. You're just a kid."

I turned back to him, clenching my fists. "You might've been trying to protect me when I came out to you and Mom," I began slowly, leaning into the anger I'd felt for so long, "but I wasn't happy. Maybe it would be easier to go back to before, keep hiding so nothing would hurt me. I can't do that, though. And if that means I have to fight, then I'm not backing down."

CHAPTER 34

*T*his is how Pride Day was supposed to be.

Sweat dampened my tank top as I took in what we'd created—the last speakeasy. My heart pulsed with too much rage over my father's warning. Too much adrenaline, like we'd been on a roller coaster climbing higher and higher with the temperature. I refused to let what he'd said stop me, and the heat hadn't stopped hundreds of people from showing up.

Our town was revolving around David Beggs and the faithful donkey I'd once painted pink. The sweltering breeze carried with it their excited conversations, shrieks from children playing, a buzz of excitement I couldn't describe—a thrill that took me back. I could still feel the crunch of pea gravel under my shoes. The hydrangea blooms dancing across my face when I came out of my hiding spot. A sense of awe as I gazed up at the town founder . . .

We might be a month late, I thought, *but we are finally doing it.*

"Carmen should be here any minute," Sawyer said, pulling me from the memory, and handed me a stack of campaign flyers. "If you and your *boyfriend* can hand these out, we'll get voter registration started."

Her insinuation was thicker than the humidity. Cohen shot me a look, his face splotchy as he fiddled with the camera strap around his neck. We'd been staying up late to chat and ask each other endless rounds of questions. But I kept going back to the one he'd asked me while we'd been listening to Bleachers. *Will you be my boyfriend?* That same question that I'd let ruin everything between us in freshman year.

Kennedy let out an exaggerated sigh, powering on the tablet. "I think," she began in a stage whisper, "that I liked it better when they were outright fighting. The tension is giving capital H horny."

Sawyer gave a murmur of agreement. "You two need to other-stuff already," she said pointedly.

"Stop," I said, my grin notwithstanding. Even though I would very much like to do that with him, I didn't want to risk messing things up again. It was nice finally getting to know him, letting him do the same.

"Huh?" Cohen asked.

"Don't worry," Sawyer said, making a crude gesture with her hands. "I'm sure you'll understand soon enough."

"Saw," I laughed, but then the chuckle died in my throat when I heard my name.

I turned to see Mason making his way over to us in a slow swagger. It sent me back to the darkened bookstore on the night of the first speakeasy.

Cohen cleared his throat, watching me again. His sweaty palm slipped into mine territorially. Mason might've been a fun idea, but Cohen was real. The future I had never let myself have until now. "You have nothing to worr—" I tried to assure him.

"Hey." Mason cut me off as he approached, deliberately ignoring everyone else. He gave me a slow devilish grin while he checked me out. His eyes lingered on my exposed arms in the tank top, and I knew where his mind had gone. "Need an extra hand?"

"We're good," Cohen snipped before I could reply.

Mason shot him an annoyed look. "I thought Zeke and I could—"

"No."

Cohen had shut him down so fast it only heightened the awkwardness between us. I watched their interaction with my mouth agape. Then the snickers from Kennedy were enough to make me come to my senses. I said, "Meet you in front of the parade float," to Sawyer, and pulled Cohen away before it got even more cringe.

"Sorry," Cohen said after we'd gotten out of earshot.

"What was that about?" I asked, watching too many emotions flash across his face. "You don't have to be jealous."

"But," he said without missing a beat, "it's fucking Mason Bedolla."

"Yeah, you said you didn't like him on multiple occasions," I pointed out, "but what *actually* happened between you two?"

"It's stupid." He shrugged, and I waited with raised eyebrows for him to continue. With a heavy sigh, he added, "We chatted on Insta, and when we finally hung out, he, um, changed his mind."

"I don't understand."

"He only wanted to be friends." He avoided my gaze and kicked at the ground. "He didn't say it, but I could tell by how he acted . . . It's because I'm me and he's perfect. I was so embarrassed that I deleted all the selfies from my grid."

"No, he's not perfect, more like an incredibly stupid asshole." He shrugged again, the muscles in his jaw tense. "And I wouldn't have gone with him just now, if you were wondering. I like that you're you."

The wrinkles on his forehead smoothed, and a shy smile pulled his expression out of the past. Pulled me into the present, where I'd been so afraid of living. We were running full-on at each other, had been since he'd sent me that first DM. Since *that* question all those years ago. It was as though we'd picked back up from where we'd left ourselves in his bedroom listening to our favorite band. But now it was my turn to ask.

"Cohen," I began, tugging him to a stop, "will you be my boyfriend?"

• • •

"Vote Bedolla, a voice for the real people of Beggs!"

The words on the flyers had etched themselves in my mind. Every time I passed one out, I could hear what my mom had told me. It wasn't just a vote. If everyone here joined together, it became a battle cry—a fighting chance.

I glanced up at the billboard we'd graffitied, thinking those words were the final thing I would do to help. But in reality, I knew what it was now. "Hey, Cohen," I said, as we made our way to the parade float. It was nearly time for Carmen's speech and then the drag show. "Can I register to vote?"

"You don't need permission," he said matter-of-factly. "You're eighteen, and it's your right."

"Wow, way to go all textbook propaganda on me," I tried to joke, but it came out as confused as I felt. "I know we're doing the registration, but *how* do I register?"

"It's really easy," he explained, passing out another brightly colored paper. "You just need your driver's license. We're using vote.gov on the tablet, and you just have to fill out the form for our state."

"That doesn't seem so bad . . ."

I trailed off as people started shoving around us. As incoherent shouts rang out. Then I saw a sign, bright-red letters on white. "Gays aren't welcome in Beggs," I read as more of them appeared. Dread sloshed up my throat and rushed into my mouth, the taste of bile making me gag. "Vote Buchanan to keep Beggs safe!" and "Vote for the safety of our kids!" and "Put families first!" and . . .

"N-no," I stammered, unable to tear my eyes away from their hateful messages. "Not again."

"Picketers," Cohen said, and then he was moving.

I followed after him as he wound through the crowd. Each frenzied step took me back to the night of Buchanan's rally. Panic recoiled in my stomach, my vision pinpricking as my heart sped up with dizziness. It had been too real seeing their homophobia from the billboard, but this was different. They could see me, could see how we were terrified, and they still spewed hate at us like we didn't matter.

"We don't want you here!" someone yelled. And then another: "We won't let you corrupt our town."

Cohen looked back over his shoulder, registering my fear,

and grabbed my hand to pull me along. His palm reminded me I wasn't alone, that we were here. I focused on that as he guided me toward Sawyer and Kennedy at the parade float.

"Are y'all okay?" one of them asked when we burst through to them.

I couldn't tell who had said it. Too many shouts were being thrown out, closer than before, and I looked back. The mayor's supporters were storming up the rows of tents. I didn't know what to do, how to help.

"Hey, breathe," Cohen said calmly into my ear. He reached out to touch me but stopped himself. "You're panicking. Just take deep breaths, okay? I know it's scary, but look. They can't get to us here."

I glanced to where he'd pointed and tried to make sense of what I was seeing. People were lining up to block their path. The owners of Ryland Farms were holding their hands out, standing side by side. Owen and the other rangers of the nature preserve. Bronwen the librarian and Jess from the rec center. Even Damian, Billy, and the other guys from the team waving rainbow flags in solidarity. My mom and, most surprisingly, my father.

They were all forming a barricade.

The sound system crackled behind us, and "This isn't our town!" boomed through the speakers with fiery authority. I flinched back and looked up at the float. Carmen stood tall, commanding the platform I'd helped build. Her pink donkey shirt was worn proudly, rainbow paint on her cheek as she lifted the microphone.

"We aren't hate," she addressed the square. "Do you know what I see up here? I see families, friends, loved ones—the support system this town needs. Fighters who ensure our LGBTQIA-plus community and their allies will be welcomed here. This is who we are."

Cries of protest rang out in reply, but then I heard a shout of encouragement. Then another as cheers spread out around us. Their wave of voices rose higher and higher, rushing toward the float in support.

"When I think about Beggs," she began, raising her voice over the crowd, "I'm reminded of when I taught elementary school. When it was story time, I'd gather my students on a giant rug and hold my finger up like this"—she brought an index finger to her lips for emphasis—"for everyone to be quiet and listen. That's what we as citizens have done for far too long, staying seated and silent while my opponent, Mr. Buchanan, tells us a story. But I decided to take a chance the day he announced his first anti-LGBTQIA-plus ordinance. A very brave young individual took a stand to fight back, and it inspired me to speak up."

She paused, searching until her eyes found mine. Her kind smile took me back to Pride Day at the beginning of June. *Need some help?* I'd asked when I'd seen her struggling with boxes, and she'd told me, *What you're doing today is nothing short of beautiful.* A prickle of tears stung, and I tried to blink them away. That one day had changed my summer—the trajectory I was on—because of the grace she'd shown me, and I had no idea I'd done the same for her. That I could be someone that significant.

"When I decided to run for mayor," she pressed on, ignoring the roar of complaints, "it wasn't because I thought I would be a better leader. I *knew* I was a better fighter. And I will fight for the equal rights of my family and this community, for your Pride like that billboard up there says. That's what I set out to do with my campaign. This summer has taught me what it means to be a real person in our town. We're not the ones sitting idly by while someone tells them their story. And, Beggs, story time is over. We're taking action to write our own story, and together we'll tell it our way come Founder's Day."

Her words echoed through the square. More shouts rang out like those at Buchanan's rally, more loud voices yelling more loud opinions at us—this is what my father had wanted to protect me from in this town. The uproar might've started because of the QSA petitioning for Pride, but I knew it had always been here. They wanted us to feel like we *needed* protecting, to be quiet out of fear. We'd been forced to live in the darkness of shoeboxes and underground speakeasies and closets until we forgot who we were.

But I knew who I was now.

From climbing up to the billboard to paint a giant penis to Pride Day to Buchanan's rally, I had faced my fears whether I wanted to or not. But sometimes you had to face your fears because you needed to, and you didn't have to do it alone like so many wanted you to believe.

"We need to get back to the QSA tent," I managed to say, finding my voice. "We have to keep registering people to vote." *I have to register to vote.*

"I don't know," Kennedy said with a shaky voice.

She was as scared as me, Sawyer and Cohen too. However, some fears were worth facing. "These people might've kept us from celebrating Pride Day," I said with a steadying breath. "But they don't get to tell us what to do anymore."

"If any time calls for your melodramatic ass to act up, it's now," Sawyer said, sparing me a wink as she laced her fingers with Kennedy's. "Let's do this together."

"Together," Cohen echoed, and grabbed my hand.

My legs might've been wobbly, but my steps were determined as we edged along the barricade's shield. Each supporter caught my eye in a promise that we were safe. Even though there was no hesitation in the glares being thrown our way, I stood up straighter, like I was walking into a battle.

As we passed by the baseball team, they all held their hands out with one finger pointing down. *Pitch a fastball,* it meant, and that was exactly what we would do. Then I saw my father—my dad, who was finally putting me first. He didn't say anything, just nodded with the same approval I'd sought for years. Then there was Mom in her green mechanic shirt.

"The police are on their way to break this up," she called to me. "I won't let anything happen to you."

"We got this, Mom," I said over the riot.

She gave me a mischievous smile, the same exact one Zelda Fitzgerald wore in the painting at Roaring Mechanics. *She became the person people expected her to be,* Mom had said, *until she realized she could shine on her own.* That was how I felt now—loud and rebellious, but most importantly, capable of fixing things.

I knew my life wouldn't go back to normal after this election was over, though. The mayoral race was more than just a blip on the political radar, more than two sides vying to win. I couldn't fix everything, no matter who won, because those protesters would still be here spewing hate. But I would stop listening to the cautionary story we'd been told as queer kids in this small town.

Our story began today, and we would be the ones to write it.

I'd push my way to the QSA table to register voters. Then I'd wake up tomorrow and keep fighting. Keep discovering myself despite who they wanted me to be. Because to exist in Beggs and Alabama and this country was a fight, and they couldn't blame us for what happened next.

They made us rebels.

ACKNOWLEDGMENTS

Even though it's cliché to admit, this story came to me in a dream. After reading news of proposed drag bans and the threat they could bring to Pride Month, I slept fitfully. My dreams connected this harsh reality to the Roaring Twenties with thoughts of what it meant to live in a time of prohibition and to Zelda Fitzgerald, the rebel from Alabama who became a mystical goddess of chaos back then. When I woke up that morning, I couldn't shake the feeling my dreams had left me with. Pitches for my second novel were due, so I quickly wrote down the premise of this story before emailing my ideas. The rest is history, as they say.

This story wouldn't have left my dreams if it weren't for my literary agent, Katie Shea Boutillier. Like I had with my debut novel, I told her about this idea with one line: "Zeke and friends hold underground queer speakeasies to combat an anti-Pride law." Thank you, Katie, for knowing what this story would mean before I did and believing that I was capable of telling it. As always, I'm grateful to have you championing my stories.

My editor at Delacorte Press, Alison Romig, also knew the

weight of this story amid the chaotic and glittering speak-easies, and she believed I had the wherewithal to deliver the message. Thank you, Ali, not only for your brilliant insight but also for helping me grow. You weren't just editing my words—you helped me become a better writer, person, and advocate for our community.

Everyone at Delacorte Press has provided such care and attention to *The Rebel's Guide to Pride*, and I'm proud to welcome these new characters to the home they've created. Thank you to Publisher Wendy Loggia for both your kindness and being such a bright ray of sunshine. Thank you to Assistant Art Director Casey Moses and artist Jess Vosseteig for bringing my rebels to life with a sparkly book cover that exudes pizzazz. With my deepest gratitude, thank you to Interior Designer Ken Crossland; Production Editor Colleen Fellingham; Managing Editor Tamar Schwartz; Production Manager CJ Han; Marketing Manager Megan Mitchell; and Publicity's Kim Small and Kris Kam.

To my husband, Chris, thank you for always believing in me and being my best friend—and for randomly saying "titty promise" and demanding I put it in my book. I don't know how I'd ever have gotten here today if it weren't for you holding my hand every step of the way. You're the first person to read my stories, and I know if I can make you laugh, then I've succeeded. Out of all the words I'll write, it only takes three to tell the best story I'll ever have: I love you.

To my chosen family, Callie and Chris Perry and Haley Jones, thank you for the community you've given me as well as the inside jokes that found their way into this story. Thank you to K. J. (Kelly) Brower, who cheered me on when this book was just an idea and continued to scream louder for Zeke and his friends as I was writing.

Writing *The Rebel's Guide to Pride* while preparing for the release of my debut novel, *The Last Boyfriends Rules for Revenge*, was a nonstop roller coaster ride. If it weren't for the authors who became my friends, I would have hurled from twists, turns, and sudden drops. Thank you to Becky Albertalli, Jennifer Lynn Alvarez, Charlotte Lillie Balogh, Erik J. Brown, Erin Cotter, Rebekah Faubion, Kathleen Glasgow, Jason June, Brian D. Kennedy, Liz Lawson, Rachael Lippincott, Natalie Lloyd, Trish Lundy, Anthony Nerada, Ellen O'Clover, Steven Salvatore, Adam Sass, Diana Urban, Julian Winters, and Wibbroka (Emily Wibberley and Austin Siegemund-Broka) for the proverbial safety bar with words of wisdom and support.

Unwavering support means the world, and I'm fortunate that my world keeps growing. Thank you to my parents as well as The Book and Cover (Sarah Jackson, Blaes Green, and Emily Lilley), Megan Emery Schadlich, Caleb Finley, Maddie Kertay, Star Lowe, Caroline Mickey, Parnassus Books (Katie Garaby and Rae Ann Parker), Sara Quaranta, Joan Reeves, and Justin Scarelli.

Thank you to Zelda Fitzgerald, who has haunted me in the best way possible, for inspiring this Alabama boy to finally find shine of his own. And thank you to *Doctor Who* for taking me on adventures through time and space . . . and for proclaiming that books are the best weapons in the world.

Last and certainly not least, thank you for reading *The Rebel's Guide to Pride*! To witness the proposed legislation against the LGBTQIA+ community in real time as I wrote this story both hurt my heart and lit a fire in my veins. That rage burned inside me as my characters dismantled small minds and demanded change. However, as I neared the end, my anger turned into something bigger—a sense of determination—right along with Zeke, Sawyer, Cohen, and Kennedy. And I hope this rebel guide will inspire you to find your voice and fight back too.

ABOUT THE AUTHOR

Matthew Hubbard writes the kind of stories he wishes he'd had as a teen in rural Alabama. He grew up on a mountaintop farm and knows more than he is willing to admit about small towns. He studied English, marketing, and psychology in college. When he isn't writing, Matthew can be found on a hike in search of breathtaking views, reading as many books as he can get his hands on, or cheering for his favorite hockey team. He lives in Chattanooga with his husband; their dogs, Layla and Phillip; and Jay Gatsby the cat. He is the author of *The Last Boyfriends Rules for Revenge* and *The Rebel's Guide to Pride*.

matthewhubbardwrites.com

OUT (AND PROUD) NOW!

"A glitter-dusted revolution of a book."
—BECKY ALBERTALLI, #1 *New York Times* bestselling
author of *Simon vs. the Homo Sapiens Agenda*

The LAST BOYFRIENDS *Rules For* REVENGE

MATTHEW HUBBARD